THE INNOCENTS

The Innocents Mystery Series

C.A. Asbrey

The Innocents
Copyright© 2018 C.A. Asbrey
Cover Design Livia Reasoner
Prairie Rose Publications
www.prairierosepublications.com

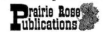

All rights reserved.
ISBN-13: 978-1986737647
ISBN-10: 1986737640

Dedication

To Kit Prate. My adventure simply wouldn't have been the same without her support.

Chapter One

Wyoming 1868

The knife slipped through the skin, twisting and gouging over and over again until the soft flesh was mushy and yielding to the blade. Abigail MacKay's mounting anxiety showed in her clenched fists whitening her knuckles to pearl. She frowned at the hirsute man selling baked potatoes from the charcoal oven on the platform. "My train will leave in a minute. Please, stop chopping at it. I need to get back on board before it leaves."

He rolled his eyes and thrust it in greaseproof paper. "You've plenty of time, missy. I do this every day." He dolloped on butter, stuck in a tiny wooden paddle, and collected a few coins before he moved on to the next in line.

She coddled the warm oval shape in both hands, feeling the heat penetrate her stiff, cold fingers and swung around, straight into a man striding toward the gate. Her stomach sank as she felt the hot buttery mass mush into the stranger's abdomen. A deep mellifluous baritone exclaimed in dismay as she felt strong hands grasp her by the top of her arms.

"Hey, mind where you're going."

Her eyes widened as she connected with a pair of warm chocolate eyes above chiseled cheekbones. The low sun glinted on his golden brown hair, warming the auburn highlights into a glowing halo as his cheeks dimpled into a ready smile. Her discomfort switched to an uncharacteristic speechlessness as his sheer presence robbed her of the ability to articulate. He frowned at her, but she doubted his analysis of her would be more in depth than the one she was already running. Confusion already melded with the fluttering breathlessness which spiraled in her chest. What was wrong with her? She was normally so logical, unemotional, and practical.

"I'm sorry," she spluttered. "I'm in a hurry to catch my train."

She reached out, patting away the greasy mess on the bottom of his waistcoat, but all she was doing was spreading it around. She retracted her hand in horror as she got too vigorous and stroked his groin. "Oh!"

His grin widened. "It's fine. Just leave it."

She looked away, preferring the slimy mess to the penetrating stare and pretended to be struck by his watch fob. It was a lustrous round moonstone, carved to resemble the face of the man on the moon. "That's lovely," she colored from the neck up as he looked down to where her hand had just been. "The little man. The moon," she garbled. She stepped back and pulled herself together. "Well, it would be lovely—without grease all over it."

A whistle blew, cutting through the awkward tension. She shook herself back to reality, smiling at the man and acknowledging his companion. "That's my train. I must go. I'm sorry."

The dishwater-blond in the long coat at his side chuckled and bent to pick up the hat knocked off in the collision. He nudged his companion and handed it to him. "Yeah, we need to get on too. C'mon."

The handsome stranger turned back, following the older man along the platform. "I'm sorry about your food. I hope it's not ruined."

She dropped her head to gaze at the mess in her hands in dismay and walked over to the trashcan. It hit the bottom with a thud as she bustled back to the train, pulling herself together. She wasn't given to schoolgirl fancies, and more importantly, she didn't have time for this. There was work to be done.

♦◇♦

Wisps of smoke and steam drifted past the windows, covering everyone in soot and wrapping the boarding passengers in wraith-like veils of dissipating mist. It was another day and another journey, and she occupied the back row of the railway carriage, half-alert as to who might occupy the empty seats opposite. She was discreet enough not to make eye contact or appear to invite anyone to invade the little space she had carved out for herself.

Abigail's brown eyes rose over the cover of her book, looking around to see who might join her on the next leg of the journey, and was still examining what had set her heart pounding so hard yesterday. She had admonished herself for her behavior. She hadn't so much as thought about another man since Alistair had died. It felt—well —disloyal. Was this how mourning ended? Did someone fill the gaping maws of loneliness in an instant, or did life creep back by inches? Work didn't do it, but for the first time in ages, she suddenly lived in the moment again. It was only for a bright, blinding instant, and it was disturbing. She had accepted her lot; bidding farewell to motherhood, a position in society, and marriage. It had been exchanged for hard work, a degree of derision, and marginalization, but at least she made a difference to the world. Yesterday made her wonder if there were more surprises in store.

She shook herself out of her mood. Maybe she'd just been sitting on trains for too many weeks and was desperate for something to break the impenetrable sameness? Without warning, a small boy barreled onto the empty seat, waving with both arms. "Ma! Over here. I bagged a window seat. Can I sit here? Can I?"

A harassed young woman bustled up, a fair-haired little girl in tow. "Tommy, will you please keep your voice down? And stop jumping on the seat. Sit down proper-like." She turned to Abigail. "Are these seats free?"

"Yes, help yourself."

The boy bounced on his backside. "Can I get the window seat? Can I? Can I?"

"It's your sister's turn. You had the window on the way here."

"Please." Abigail gathered her skirts and shifted over to the aisle seat. "Let them both have one. I'm reading anyway."

Gratitude crossed the flustered woman's face as she dropped into the last seat and settled her excited charges. "Thank you. It's no fun with two young 'uns. Are you traveling alone?"

Abigail nodded.

"I bet you're glad you didn't get some rough cowhand pushing their way in, huh? They'd have been bothering you all the way."

A smile tugged at Abigail's lips. "I suppose so."

"Don't you hate it when someone keeps annoying you and you're not interested?" she asked without a trace of irony. "Is that a Scottish accent?" The woman noted Abigail's nod of agreement. "I thought so. My grandpa was Scottish. He came over here way back, about eighteen-fifteen, as a young 'un. He died last year. Dropped dead in a thunderstorm when his heart gave out, he did. It was like God took him with a bolt from the blue." She giggled. "Grandma always said it should have been the devil opening the ground beneath his feet."

Before Abigail could offer her condolences the woman turned back to her son. "Tommy, get your finger out of there."

The boy slumped back in his seat displaying an impressive pout, leaving Abigail to wonder where it had been inserted.

"Where are you from? Grandpa was from Inver-somewhere and then he went to Glasgow. Are you from Glasgow?"

"No, I'm not. I lived there for a bit before we came to the States though. We sailed from there." Abigail tried to return to her book once more.

"I've never been anywhere. Lived in Wyoming all my life and seen no more'n four towns. I'll probably die here, too," said the young mother with an air of cheerfulness. "My grandpa told me it's always freezing in Scotland. Is it true?"

"Sometimes, not always." Abigail noted the jolt of the train pulling out and tried not to show too much vested interest in her next question. "Are you traveling far?"

"Just to the next stop. My husband is meeting us there. We've been visiting my mother for a couple of days."

"How lovely for you. I expect he'll be glad to have you all home again." Abigail dropped her head to return to her book, trying to hide the tenseness caused by the stream of unwanted small talk. "Only about an hour to go."

Abigail tried to bury herself in Jane Eyre once more, allowing the train to chug and chuff its way through the mountainous terrain to its next destination amid a barrage of questions and gossip from her traveling companion. The book wasn't getting read on this stage of the journey, but it might slow the cross examination. This continued for what seemed to be an interminable time, but in reality, couldn't have been more than half-an-hour. The train slowed, the whistle blasting out until the train creaked and stilled to a complete halt.

"Why are we stoppin', Mommy?"

"I've no idea," the woman peered out of the window. "We're not even halfway there."

The boy kneeled on his seat and peered out of the window, his nose squashed against the glass. "There are men, Mommy, and they've got guns."

Abigail snapped her book closed and headed for the window. "Guns?"

"Oh, my," exclaimed the young mother. "It's a robbery. Get down, Tommy. Get away from the window." She pushed both children to the safety of the floor.

"Hands up, everyone."

Abigail swung around to see a stranger striding into the aisle from the open door at the end of the carriage. He had a gun in his hand and his lower face was covered by a bandana. She pushed the children under the benches and blocked them in with her feet. "Stay there," she hissed.

"My name is Nat Quinn," the stranger said and then indicated the fair man by his side, "and this is Jake Conroy. You're being held up by The Innocents. Everyone get your hands in the air where I can see them."

The two men occupied the aisle, owning the railway carriage in an instant. Quinn stopped a few rows away and glowered at a passenger. "Madam, will you please stop sticking your jewelry into your bosom. We have no interest in robbing the passengers, and it's never a good idea to do anything to encourage criminals to go rooting around in your cleavage."

"You have been held up by a gang called The Innocents," Jake announced. "They gave us that name because we rob only the banks and the railroads. We don't steal from ordinary people, so as long as you all cooperate, we'll open the safe in the baggage car and you can all be on your way."

The announcement met with a ripple of relief. The gang's reputation was obviously well-known and well-received. Abigail frowned, staring at the two men. They were not your average criminals. They were charming and articulate. In smarter clothes, they could pass for intelligent, professional men, and unless you looked very hard, it was easy to miss the shifting devilment in the eyes.

Nat gestured to the grassy bank outside. "Please file out one by one with your hands up, where you'll be allowed to sit outside once we've established you're not armed. You'll be on your way before you know it."

Abigail felt the boy's inquisitive head pop out around her legs and pushed his head back. A male voice drifted over her shoulder.

"I told everyone to get their hands up. That includes you, miss." His blue eyes twinkled in surprise at the rebellious glare she flashed in response. His eyes hardened. "Hands up."

She complied with a show of reluctance and watched the people at the front of the carriage file off the train, men being patted down for weapons, and women having bags searched. The criminals exchanged a look of amusement as little Tommy thrust his arms straight up, striding out into the aisle. "It's alright, ma'am," Nat nodded toward the young mother. "You can put your hands down. You've got two young 'uns and they're hard enough to keep hold of even when you can use your hands."

She gathered her brood about her. "Thank you."

"You're welcome. Get your bag checked at the door. Our men will help you off."

Abigail stepped out into the aisle; the last to leave. Jake frowned at her and stepped in her way. "I thought I told you to get your hands up."

She pointed at Nat. "But he said—" She froze. Her eyes caught the ornate watch fob hanging on Nat Quinn's waistcoat, carved to look like the man in the moon. She had seen it before when she had crashed into its owner on the railway platform. She forced herself not to react and turned back to Jake, hoping Quinn didn't realize she had not only seen him unmasked, but remembered him well.

"He said that to a woman with children. Not you. Hands up, and keep them up until you're told different." The coldness in his tone reached into his eyes. "Please do as you're told and it'll make all our lives easier."

"You expect me to make your life easier? Have you ever met any Scottish women? It's not something we're famous for."

"A feisty one, huh? And she's in no hurry to leave, either." The crinkled lines of his smile etched Nat's brown eyes with roguish charm. He looked her up and down with an admiring stare. "We don't have time for you today. I've got a safe to crack and time waits for no man. Time is obviously both Scottish and female."

She arched a brow, holding his gaze. "May I take my book?"

"Sure," Jake handed it to her. "Now, sit nice and quiet on the grass. It's for your own good."

"Yes. This is all for my good. There's nothing in this for you at all." She held her book high along with the empty hand, strolling over to the henchman by the door. He leaned on the wall picking his nose under his mask. She scowled at him. "Don't you dare touch me with those fingers. I've left my bag at my seat, so there's nothing for you to search. There's no money in it, anyway." She glanced over at the two criminals. "I'm hoping our Robin Hoods over there could put money in."

A couple of men helped her down and she strode to the grass to watch Quinn leave the passenger carriage and climb into the baggage car. Jake oversaw the passengers and the rest of the gang, keeping everyone where they should be and stamping on the slightest challenge. They were a tight team, and worthy of their formidable reputation, but she wasn't here to gawk, she had work to do. She sat on a fallen tree and reached into the spine of her book, pulling out a thin pencil. Abigail turned to the blank endpaper and took notes.

She paused, pulling down her skirts in what looked like an act of propriety, but she had an ulterior motive. It wouldn't do to let anyone see the Derringer in her ankle holster. No, that wouldn't do at all.

The man at the desk raised his head in surprise. She was used to this, as women visiting the Pinkerton Offices were sobbing witnesses or hostile criminals facing capture. A composed, serene, unaccompanied female was unusual. "I'm looking for Mr. Robertson."

"Do you have an appointment?"

"I believe Alan Pinkerton told him to expect me."

"He did?" The man's mutton chops bristled as he opened another book. "Your name?"

"Abigail MacKay."

He frowned, running a finger down the page of a ledger. "Mac—eye?" He imitated her pronunciation. "Nope. He ain't expectin' anyone of that name."

"He must be. Mr. Pinkerton sent a telegram himself."

"How're you spellin' that?"

"M—a—c—k—a—y."

"That spells MacKay. It ends in 'Kay'."

"It's spelled that way, but it's not pronounced that way. It isn't English, so it doesn't follow English rules."

"Then why spell it k—a—y? Spell it the way it sounds."

Abigail rolled her eyes. "Is Mr. Robertson expecting someone with a name ending with k—a—y?"

"Sure, but it ain't you. It's an agent."

"That's me. I'm Abigail MacKay, and I am an agent."

He laughed and turned to the men working at their desks behind him. "I ain't fallin' for this one. Bob, Tubbs, which one of you set this up? A woman? Where'd you get her? The burlesque?"

Her voice hardened. "My name is Abigail MacKay and I want to see Mr. Robertson. Please tell him I am here."

"Don't you go raisin' your voice at me, missy, or you'll end up in a cell. I can take a joke as well as the next man, but this is gettin' stupid."

"Please fetch him—"

The man waved his pen at her. "Enough. A joke's a joke."

Abigail sucked in a breath and filled her lungs, shouting at the top of her voice. "Archibald Robertson. Come out here, now!"

A red-bearded, bear of a man strode out of an office, his Northern Irish brogue cutting through the hubbub. "What's going on here?"

"Sir, there's a woman here who says her name is spelled wrong."

"What?" He darted a dismissive glace at her. "Tell her to go away. We don't deal with rubbish like that. I'm a busy man."

"Mr. Robertson," Abigail stood on her toes to peer over the high desk blocking her view. "Alan Pinkerton sent me to see you and this fool won't let me through."

"Is that right?" Robertson frowned. "Bill?"

"What am I supposed to do? Believe every joker who says they're an agent?"

"I'm Abigail MacKay, and Alan Pinkerton told you to expect me. He sent a telegraph."

"A woman? He said he was sending someone expert at assuming roles." Robertson paused, looking at her before his eyes widened in shock. "Nah, that's not natural. A man should be locked up for looking like that. It's obscene, even if it is a disguise." He looked her up and down. "Mind you, when I was in the British Army there were these men out in India who were real feminine. They lived like women, dressed like them, danced like them and everything. They called them the Hijra. We used to warn the newcomers about them. You're kinda dark. Are you—?"

"Mr. Robertson, I am a *woman* and I am Scottish. I am also very tired of this nonsense. No wonder you can't bring in The Innocents. I've been sent here to help."

"We're working on bringing them in. I have my best men on it." Robertson shook his head. "We don't need typewriters. We teach the men to type their own reports. It's more secure."

"Glad to hear it." She opened the wooden gate and swept over to the glass-fronted office Robertson had vacated. She took a seat across from his desk. "Now, what do you have on this gang so far?"

Robertson's color rose deeply as he followed her in. "Mrs. MacKay—"

"Miss," she corrected, firmly, "Alan Pinkerton does not employ married women."

"Ma'am, I don't care if you're a vestal bloody virgin. You don't work here."

"Mr. Robertson," Abigail stared at him in admonishment, "I simply won't tolerate less respect than you would afford your wife or daughter. Am I clear?"

"My wife wouldn't be seen dead near criminals. She's the type who makes a man want to open doors for her, or offer her a seat. She's a *lady*."

"I mastered both standing and door handles some time ago, so there'll be no need for any special treatment. Simple politeness will be sufficient." She rooted around in her bag and produced a batch of papers; papers which had been kept in a pouch around her waist beneath her skirts until now. "My identification and your orders from Alan Pinkerton."

His face simmered with suspicion. "Orders?"

"Yes, I have been sent here to assume a role to help bring in this gang."

Robertson took a seat, his brow furrowing into folds of pink flesh as he read the missive. "You're from the Woman's Department? I thought that department was disbanded after the war."

Abigail shook her head. "It's a small, but vital, department. I was lucky enough to have training from Kate Warne herself. Mr. Pinkerton holds the female detectives in high esteem. We have been able to infiltrate areas the men could never access, so he sent me to help you. It's not a criticism. It's simply wise to try something else when one tactic doesn't work."

He slid the papers toward her with one stabbing forefinger.

"I've never worked with women in my life. My men have enough to do without mollycoddling you."

Abigail smiled benignly and then pushed them back. "Then it's a good thing you're not my employer. Alan Pinkerton is, and he has stated I have to work in this area. Need I remind you that he is *your* boss, too?"

The thick brows knotted into a frown. "He's gone mad! Putting a woman in somewhere to get the tittle-tattle from the servants is one thing, but sending one to bring in a gang of outlaws? I won't have it. You'll be murdered, or even worse. We'll end up with an even bigger mess to clear."

"Isn't that the risk we all take?"

"These are men are *criminals*. The politeness is just a front to get cooperation."

"I know. Otherwise I wouldn't be here. They'll do twenty years hard labor when caught, which is basically a death sentence, so they'll do what it takes to stay free. The gang were only given the sobriquet 'The Innocents' because they are polite to members of the public. I have no intention of rounding them up single-handed, though. I'm here to collect intelligence and bring you information. That's it."

Robertson sat back in his chair. "This is my problem with it, see. Women have no judgment. They believe the tripe trotted out by the dime novels." He punctuated the air with a thick finger. "There's no such thing as 'handsome, chivalrous criminals.' They're wrong 'uns, pure and simple. Jake Conroy is a cold-hearted gunman who's there to back up Nat Quinn's leadership. Conroy has killed; and d'you think a greasy snakesman like Quinn could keep a band of cutthroats in check without fear? He's a hard man, feared by criminals who've crossed him. He controls his gang with a tight fist, and they all have violent pasts. They won't listen to anyone they aren't scared of."

"Snakesman?" Abigail smiled. "They're boys sent in through

tiny spaces to open the doors for the gang to break in, aren't they? I doubt Quinn has done that in twenty years. He's over six feet tall. I agree that they're criminals. I've done my homework on them. Nat is the brains of the outfit, a brilliant mind and quick learner, by all accounts—an expert with explosives, a safecracker, talented at picking locks, and a wonderful mind for strategy and logistics. He sometimes operates on his own, all over the country if the prize is worth it.

"Jake is both fast and accurate with that gun of his, and he has killed. Witnesses all claimed it was in self-defense, but I'll reserve judgment on that. They work together like a well-oiled machine. They have built that gentlemanly reputation as a tactic to avoid trouble from the public, but it's only a front, and most definitely a strategy. There's an unspoken deal between them and any witnesses; you leave us alone, and we won't steal your money or personal possessions."

"You've read their file. It's hardly ground-breaking information."

She nodded. "I have. It would be unprofessional not to."

"So? Just what do you think you can do?" Robertson demanded.

"Just for the record, I don't buy that 'handsome gentleman robber' rubbish for one minute, but I do believe I can help you to catch them. Nobody expects a woman to be investigating, and that gives us an immediate advantage."

"*If* and only *if* I agree to work with you," Robertson smirked, "what'd be your plan?"

Abigail ignored his contorted face. "I aim to get menial work in a place where nobody notices the help, especially when I make myself as unattractive as possible. Men don't notice women like that. It makes you invisible, and it's where I can overhear a great deal. There are rumors of them having connections to the town of Bannen as children. We can find no actual records of anyone with those names there, but it's

somewhere to start. I plan to work at the brothel—"
Robertson's face turned puce from the neck up so she finished
her sentence to clarify, "*as a maid.* Not in any other capacity.
There's a brothel there which is very high end and they cater to
their clients with excellent food and hospitality as well as the
obvious. They employ maids, cleaners, kitchen workers, you
name it. You have to keep the place looking good for the
money they charge. The prices start at fifty dollars a trick."

"*How much?* That's almost a month's wages for most men!"

"It's as good a place as anywhere to start. There are plenty of
local people working there, too. I can get a general overview of
the town. The customers will either be wealthy or crooked."

"Or both." He tapped his fingers on the desk. "What do you
need from me? I'm in no position to support such a hare-
brained scheme."

"Nothing for the time being; other than making sure you
know what I'm doing and ensuring I have access to the records,
as and when I need them. I'll contact you."

He nodded slowly. "I guess if Pinkerton says you're to adopt
a role, I don't have much say in it, but I'll write to him to
protest in the strongest possible terms as well as having a drive
on The Innocents to bring them in. I'll prove to him we don't
need women out here in Denver." He stood. "In the meantime,
if you want to spend the next few weeks doing futile, dirty
work, it's no concern of mine."

Abigail rose from her chair. "Thank you, Mr. Robertson. I
expected only grudging acceptance. It's what I have come to
expect, but I will bring you results."

"I won't have a woman on my team. You won't make much
of a detective if you don't listen, Miss MacKay. "

"I couldn't agree more, but you appear to be the one who's
not been listening. I won't be under your command. I report to
Alan Pinkerton via the woman's department as he has found
that's the best way to deal with the objections of area

commanders like yourself. He's a man who demands results, and he'll put in a woman if it's the way to achieve them. He won't brook opposition to his plans unless it's to give him a better option." Abigail stood and thrust out a hand. Experience had taught her to maintain her professionalism in the face of prejudice. "Until we meet again?"

He took it, shaking it reluctantly. "My men will have caught them while you're still trying to figure out which hat goes with which dress."

Abigail smiled. "We can only hope so. We are on the same side, after all. At least I'll know if you've arrested the right men. I've seen them."

"How? There are no photographs of them and descriptions are so bland. There are no distinguishing marks or scars."

"By doing my job. I spent weeks traveling on trains carrying payrolls to meet them. I also have a sample of handwriting. Goodbye, Mr. Robertson. You'll hear from me soon. I'll let you know where I end up."

She strolled out of the building, into the cacophony of the Denver streets, ringing with the sounds of horses, wagons, vendors, and street musicians. Abigail never got used to the noise of the modern city. She was a country girl at heart and preferred wide open spaces. A cab pulled up in response to her raised arm. She climbed aboard and waited as her enormous trunk was loaded by the doorman and the driver. "The railway station please."

She settled into her seat and snapped open her reticule, pulling out a five dollar note. She turned it in her hands looking at the inscriptions and the red seal of authenticity. Scrawled across it in pencil were the words, *Take from the rich, give to the poor. N XXX.*

It had been slipped in her bag at Hillside Bend during the robbery. How idiotic of Nat Quinn to give her a sample of his writing. Anything could be used as evidence, and more than one criminal's real identity had been revealed through handwriting; but somehow, it was still very amusing and endearing. He was certainly not your average criminal. What a crying shame he was so dishonest.

She'd had no interest in any man since her Alastair died; not until she crashed into a man so full of devilment and life. She thought part of her had died until his feral challenge sparked her back to life. The fates were obviously playing a sick joke at her expense, but she couldn't help but be intrigued. She sat back and allowed herself to ponder on the brown eyes and the handsome man with the man in the moon watch fob. Thoughts were harmless after all. Weren't they?

Chapter Two

Nat's dark eyes fixed on the woman leaving the railway station and he grabbed his partner's arm, dragging him back into the deepening evening shadows of the sidewalk.

Jake's guard went up, scanning the street for danger. "What?"

"It's her. The woman from the train again."

"What woman?"

"The Scottish one at Hillside Bend. The one who wouldn't put her hands up." His face dimpled into a smile. "The one who sways when she walks and riles when she talks. The one with the potato."

"Remind me to make sure you don't compose any love letters for me." His uncle frowned, staring across the road. "Yeah, it's her. What's she doin' here? We've gotta be well nigh a hundred and fifty miles away from Hillside Bend."

"I suppose she has to be somewhere." The brown eyes slid sideways and gleamed with venal delight. "She was on her own on the train. I wonder who she's here to see."

"It ain't you, Nat. Leave it be."

"She's different. Spunky and kinda fiery."

"So is a stump broke horse. Stay away."

Nat scowled. "I'm not a fool, Jake."

The older man arched his brows. "Neither am I. I know you too well when you see a challenge. We'd best move on and sleep somewhere else tonight. We can't afford to be recognized."

"There's no need for that. We'll be at the saloon. We only need to make sure we keep to places ladies don't go and there's a whole street here where no self-respecting woman would be seen dead." His eyes narrowed. "I need to find out where she's staying so we can avoid it."

"Nat, no. We start avoidin' right now." A muscle firmed in Jake's jaw. "I mean it. We head for Blair Street and we stay there. Women avoid it unless they're workin' girls. If you want female company there's enough there to keep you busy all night."

"I guess." He shrugged. "They're just not very challenging."

A smile tugged at Jake's lips. "You want a challenge? There are women there who'll beat the hell out of you for the right price. I'll even pay for extra whips."

Nat strolled through the respectable side of town keeping to the shadows cast by the covered sidewalk. His dark eyes scanned the hotel on the corner. It was the best in town, and the most likely place a decent woman would stay in this frontier town.

Standing at three stories tall with a brick frontage and a porch decorated with wrought iron work, it was more salubrious than Nat's current accommodation, but way more boring.

It was getting late and two hardy guests gathered on the porch to enjoy the night air before bed, but it was too cold for most people to sit outside for too long. Nat lingered, the brim of his hat pulled low, content in the knowledge she wouldn't recognize him even if she saw him from a window. He no longer wore a business suit and looked like any other cowboy in his brown corduroy trousers and dark shirt, covered in a long duster.

The last person on the hotel porch stood and stubbed out his cigar before he turned and strode inside.

Nat sighed. Why had he come here? Why did he feel drawn to this place on the off-chance of a glance of a woman he would never speak to? What was he going to do even if he saw her? Jake was right; standing here was stupid and pointless. Respectable women wanted to be courted, meet family, and to take their time to work toward a wedding. A decent woman was off-limits.

The metallic click of a gun being cocked behind his head made his blood run cold. A firm hand grabbed his shoulder as a hoarse voice whispered in his ear. "Git your hands up and come with me."

Nat's hands rose along with his hackles. "Why?"

"'Cause I'm robbin' you, you idiot. Why d'ya think?"

Nat heaved a sigh of relief. Robbery was way better than the law. "You're kidding. You're robbing me? This is a joke."

"What's with the questions? I'm robbin' you, now git into that alley where we can work in private."

"We? What's with the idea we're a team? You can't rob me."

"Why?"

"Never mind why. Just go away."

"No, gimme your cash. All of it."

Nat's Irish rose to the fore. "Sod off."

"You ain't listenin', mister. Git over to the alley and hand over your valuables."

"Why?"

"What d'ya mean, 'why'? I want your money."

"Oh, I understand, but why do I have to go in an alley? You can take it right here."

The robber's irritation seeped into the tense voice. "Fine. Give me your money here."

"No. Go away."

Nat felt the hardness of a revolver in the small of his back.

"You realize that if you shoot me now, people will pour out of every building the minute you pull the trigger. You won't get ten feet before you're cut down."

The robber paused. "Get in the alley."

"Now you're repeating yourself. You haven't thought this through. How do you know I've even got any money?"

"Because you're hangin' around the best hotel in town." Nat turned his head but the robber whacked his shoulder. "Stay still."

"You're hanging around the best hotel in town, too. Give me *your* money."

"I ain't got no money. That's why I'm stealin'."

"Well, neither have I. None I'm handing over to you, anyway. Maybe we should split what you've got?"

"What kind of a robbery is this? You're the most annoyin' victim I ever met. I've got a good mind to shoot you for the hell of it."

"A good mind doesn't do stupid things like hold up men in the street without a plan." Nat could detect the growing uncertainty in the man's thin voice. "Am I annoying enough to die for? That's what'll happen."

"I want your money. Hand it over or I'll—"

A dull clang cut the man off mid-sentence, followed by a thump as he tumbled to the floor. Nat swirled around, his eyes lighting with delight at the sight of the woman he was here to see not only wielding a spade, but raising it once more to slice at the robber's right hand as it reached for the gun which had tumbled from his grasp. Nat drew his own weapon and pointed straight at the man's head. "You've lost your gun, friend. Get out of here before you lose a hand, too."

The skinny figure shimmied over the boards of the sidewalk before clambering upright and scampering off as fast as his feet could carry him. Nat grabbed the discarded weapon and thrust it into his waistband, tilting his head to keep his face in the shadow of the brim of his hat. "Thank you, Miss…? Sorry, who do I thank?"

"You're welcome. Don't you want to go to the sheriff?"

"I don't think so," Nat holstered his own gun. "They might want to know why you were taking your shovel for a walk in the dark. It's all a bit funereal isn't it?"

Her laugh tinkled through the chilled night air. "*Funereal?* Now, there's a word I didn't expect to hear in a cowtown," she put the blade on the boardwalk and leaned on the handle. "The spade was over there. And I saw you were in trouble and stepped in. It's none too clean." He found the way her nose crinkled adorable. "I think someone has been clearing horse droppings with it."

He grinned. "So you thought you'd clean up the town? Hang around and they might give you a star to wear."

"A woman in the law? How ridiculous." Her slim brows knotted in curiosity. "Where have we met before?"

He shrugged. "Are you staying at the hotel? Maybe we met there?"

Doubt flickered over her face. "Yes. That must be it. The hotel."

"If you don't mind me saying so, ma'am, you appear unusually calm about an armed robbery."

She nodded. "Unusually? Well, if you've ever taught piano to unwilling boys in Glasgow, this is considered easy. You don't seem too upset, either."

"He was more scared than we were. Let me see you back to safety." He proffered an arm. "You shouldn't be wandering about at night on your own."

"Nor should you," she looked up at him seeing only the white smile flash through the shadows under the brim of his black hat. "Your voice is really familiar. Where do I know you from?" She examined him again in the unlit street but the shadows shrouded everything but shapes in the thin moonlight. "What's your name?"

He glanced around the street seeking inspiration before his gaze came to rest on a shop near the hotel's illuminated windows. "Baker. Thomas Baker. And yours?"

"Abigail—ah we're here." She paused on the bottom step wondering why he didn't come into the bubble of light.

"I'm waiting for my friend." He stepped back into the obscurity. "You go on in."

Her cat-like eyes narrowed and her dark curls melded into the darkness as she tilted her head in question. "If you're sure."

"I am. He's following behind, and he may not have a guardian angel with a spade to protect him." He tipped the brim of his hat. "Goodnight, Abigail. Thanks again for your help."

"You're welcome."

He watched her turn and disappear into the building, unable to suppress the smile she left behind. Jake caught up to him and Nat knew he'd give him a hard time for leaving the poker game.

Somehow, it was worth it.

♦ ◊ ♦

The diminutive man looked at the huge drop from the railway carriage. "Aren't you going to give me a hand? It's got to be at least three feet of a drop."

The outlaw gathered a ball of mucus from the back of his throat. He raised his masking bandana and gobbed a greasy ball of phlegm on a railway sleeper. "So what? You're a man ain't ya?"

"My wife would give you a debate on that, but may I point out I'm a homunculus of the species? The distance is rather more to me than it is to you," the man smiled, "relatively speaking."

"Huh?"

"I'm little. Restricted in height."

"You sure are," the outlaw guffawed. "You could be in a travelin' show. Has your wife got a beard?"

"My wife's beard is irrelevant and I'm not that small," the passenger objected. "I thought The Innocents were supposed to be helpful to people on trains they held up."

"So?"

"Provide some assistance, be accommodating, become benevolent, act in a way which is efficacious," he paused, reading the muddled eyes whirling with doubt and rephrased with emphasis. "Be helpful."

"Aw, right." The criminal frowned. "You sure speak fancy. Where're you from?"

"Boston. You held up a train from Boston. Isn't that a clue?"

"Well, I ain't liftin' you like no lady. It ain't seemly to do that to a man. I'll put my hands together and you use them as a step."

The man nodded his graying head. "I don't want to be lifted like a lady, either. I saw where you put your hands, and there was nothing *innocent* about it."

The outlaw scowled. "D'ya want help or not, mister?"

"Isn't that what I've been saying?" He stepped into the fingers laced together into a fleshy stirrup and grabbed the outlaw's shoulders for support until he was low enough to jump without injury. "Thank you, my man. I shall join my compatriots on the grassy knoll."

"Sheesh," the criminal watched him beetle away in his dapper coat, the white spats flashing in the caustic winter sun. He turned to his fellow gang member. "He says he's married? He's got a face like a frog. I gotta meet me some of them there Eastern women. They've gotta be as smart as bait to get involved with the likes of that. It has to be the easiest place in the country to get your leg over."

"Didn't he say his wife had a beard?"

The first outlaw shrugged. "I don't expect to get a perfect

one. Ya gotta be more realistic, Carl."

The dapper little man grabbed onto his immaculate Derby and scuttled over to the rest of the passengers on his short legs, his instincts for self-preservation sending him right up to the trunk of the large pine tree where he had both a vantage point and a barricade from the unfolding robbery.

"They say they're The Innocents," a lemon-lipped woman spoke to everyone and no one from the depths of a poke bonnet. "I've read about them. They're real polite. These aren't. This gang's gone to the dogs.

Another woman chimed in. "They cuffed my Alfie around the ear, and I don't even want to talk about what they did when they were helpin' Doris from the train."

"You saw that too, ma'am? I most certainly did," the short man called around the tree.

"So did I," a woman with a pointed nose in the poke bonnet asserted. "I was disgusted." She nudged her husband. "Wasn't I disgusted, Robert?"

"Yes, dear."

"Mindless thugs with guns. I wish they'd leave me alone with them for five minutes."

Her husband stared off at the train. "Yes, dear. I wish the same."

She paused, frowning at him. "I beg your pardon, Robert?"

"Just agreeing with you, dear."

"Yes, this ain't the way they operated last time," the second woman said. "I tell ya, they ain't gonna keep gettin' cooperation with the public if they do this. I thought they were better'n this."

"So did I," mused the little man. "Quite brutish, aren't they?"

They stared over to the baggage car where a long metal box lay on the ground and a gaggle of perturbed criminals gathered around in discussion. "Can't we just drag it away behind us?"

"What, and lay out the best trail a posse ever had to find us? Use your brain, Frank."

"How about carryin' it between a couple of horses?"

"It'll slow us too much. Have you felt the weight of that thing? It's 'specially weighted to make stealin' it hard. It took most of us to get the damned thing out here where we could see it."

"Well, I ain't got an answer, Sam. Why don't you come up with an idea instead of shootin' down everyone else's ideas? The last time we blew one open, the lock jammed."

Sam nodded. "I got an idea." The tall, thin man in a black hat, his face masked by a bandana, barked orders at the guard. "Git the security box open! Quit wastin' time."

The railway employee's mouth dropped open. "I don't know how to. I'm just here to guard it. It gets opened at the bank, not before—"

"Then you'd better learn how to open it, and fast." A burly outlaw drew his gun.

"But I don't know how—"

"Frank, the train'll be late by now. They'll send out a posse soon."

The outlaw called Frank tensed. "Git it open."

"I can't. You can shout at me all you want. The bank won't give me the combination for the locks."

"Well, try!"

The railway guard knelt on the ground, his nervous, sweaty hands slipping on the combination and his clumsy fingers fumbling with the delicate mechanism. The burly man's voice rose an octave along with his weapon. "Well?"

"I'm tryin', I'm tryin'."

"Try harder," yelled Sam.

Frank's patience was hanging by a thread. "This is takin' far too long."

"Why don't *you* try it if you think you can do any better?"

The guard stood, his own emotions spiraling. "I thought The Innocents were real good at crackin' locks. You claimed to be them when you took this train."

"Don't talk back!"

The railway worker kicked the box in frustration. "I can't get this thing open!" He stood and advanced on the robber, hands spread in appeal. "I'd like to see you do it better."

Panic flashed over the gunman's eyes and he stepped back. Frank lifted his gun and fired. The guard's chest burst open in a grotesque detonation, and he crashed to the ground. The wound sucked and throbbed as the man's dying, rattling breaths ebbed away. The cries of horror and impotence of the bystanders gave way to the heightened emotions. Angry muttering floated around the outlaws who tensed and drew their guns toward off any revenge attack.

The nervous robbers glanced around, but the passengers had fallen back into shock and they huddled together, herding women and children behind the men; all except the short gray-haired man who peered out from behind the tree. Ragged strains of strangled sobbing cut through the oppressive hush and the aroma of cordite hung in the air.

"What're you lot starin' at?" growled Frank. "He was warned."

"You ain't The Innocents," a shocked conductor hurried over to his colleague who lay bleeding out on the ground. He dropped to his knees crouching over in a daze. "Mike? Can you hear me, Mike?"

"It ain't none of your business who we are. I want the security box opened."

"He was delaying," the conductor sobbed in dismay. "The Innocents can open a lock like that. If we'd known you couldn't do it we'd have done it. We wouldn't risk our lives for nothing! If you'd just told the truth—"

"Well, get it open and fast, unless you want to be next," Sam barked.

"I will, I will." The conductor turned glittering eyes on the gang. "I went to school with him. I went to his wedding."

The passengers watched the box being opened in silence and the contents loaded into saddlebags with a greedy frenzy until the criminals mounted and rode off toward the trees at the feet of the craggy, mountainous horizon.

Groups of people ventured forth bit by bit, the sounds of praying and crying hanging over the scene like a pall. The little man was last to approach, creeping around the edges of the crowd, watching everything and everybody.

"I need men to help me get his body back on the train and to clear the track," the conductor called out. "Who's with me? We need to get moving again."

The prospect of action galvanized the group into action, but the little man from Boston still hung around on the peripheries, observing and listening while he clutched his Derby in his plump, toy fingers.

A weeping woman approached him. "It's shocking isn't it? I think I'll have nightmares for the rest of my life."

He nodded. "No wonder students of the human condition are so depressed all the time. Those of us who recognize the futility of the human condition are so frequently confronted by the most futile examples of humanity."

She eyed him with suspicion, a frown playing over her brow. "Yeah. I guess. Are you some kind of preacher?"

The stranger smiled to himself. "An excellent question, madam. I've often wondered that myself."

Nat scrutinized the newspaper with hungry eyes. "This is bad, Jake. Real bad."

The fair head nodded in agreement. "They killed someone

and put our name all over it. That's a hangin' offense right there." He kicked out at the leg of a chair. "It's the third robbery in the county where a gang claimed to be us."

"Folks cooperate because they know they're treated well by The Innocents. It won't last if they think we'll kill. We need to get these bastards, and soon."

Jake swung into the chair like it was a horse and leaned his chin on the back. "No argument there, but how? My guess is it's an outfit from another territory. No one knows them. I've got nothin'."

"We know someone who people do talk to and in front of all the time." Earnest dark eyes rose to meet his uncle's. "She lives not too far from the robbery, and we're long overdue for a visit. She has a way of getting people's guards down."

"Pearl?" Jake grinned. "When they're at her place they've got everythin' down."

The tainted air swirled with the odor of tobacco and cheap perfume with low salty undertones of human sweat. An excellent pianist turned his opaque blind eyes to the ceiling as his talented fingers flashed over the keys. The blue notes mingled with the heady atmosphere in a room where the drink flowed, flesh rippled, and couples snuck off to curtained-off side rooms for less-than-discreet coupling, and in some cases, tripling. A skeletal man gathered impressive gout of phlegm and fired it at the brass spittoon. He missed the top and watched it slide its greasy way down the side toward the floor. His bony arm reached out and grabbed the wrist of the woman topping up his beer from a jug. "Put it down and c'mere."

She pulled back, but he held fast. "I'm the maid. I'm not here to do anything but serve drinks and clean up." She gestured with her head toward the door. "Pearl throws men out if they break the rules."

"Let 'er go, Sam. Ain't you got enough to keep you busy?" The man with the dark moustache looked her up and down. The stained apron and thick glasses glinting in the light didn't compete with the milky flesh spilling over the tight-laced corset of the nearby woman toying with a cigar in the most suggestive manner. "We paid good money for high class whores. Quit botherin' the help."

The thin man released the maid who melted into the shadows. "Why are you pickin' at cornbread when we got prime steak?" laughed the dark stranger. "These are fifty-dollar whores. The best. We can't usually stretch to more'n two or three dollars." He hunched forward on his chair. "How're you doin' today?"

The dark man with the moustache lowered his voice. "How do you do it, Sam? You ain't never bothered when you kill. I keep seeing his face over and over in my head."

"Pull yourself together, Frank," Sam hissed. "He was warned what would happen if he didn't get the security box open. He delayed on purpose. You saw for yourself the other one got it open fast enough after that. It did the job."

"Yeah, I guess." Frank drained his glass. "He was my first, though. I keep wonderin' what would have happened if he hadn't come at me like that. It don't bother you at all. How many have you killed?"

"That ain't somethin' you ask any man," Sam snapped, the hollows around his eyes gathering deep shadows. "Git yourself a woman and put your mind on somethin' else."

The venal glare pierced the burly man's confidence, causing him to glance away. "Sure, boss." He stood, gesturing with his head toward the coffee-skinned woman reclining in front of the fire. "C'mon, you. You've got fifty dollars to work off."

The door burst open and Pearl Dubois marched in; a yellow-haired pillar of flesh in pinched-in corsetry, her impressive breasts supported by a construction of whale bone and satin. She was flanked by a wall of armed muscle. "You gotta go. All of you." A huge barrel-chested man with a white moustache stepped forward to support her and raised a Spencer Carbine rifle, the thick stock emphasizing the bony knuckle of his missing middle finger. The metallic click of his weapon cocking underscored the echoing repeat of his fellow security men. "You've had some fun, so here's half your money back. Now, git. I heard about today's payroll robbery and you fit the descriptions."

"I thought you said *everyone* was welcome here," growled Sam.

"Everyone from the clergy, thieves, and politicians, I said. Not killers. Never killers." She banged the cash on the bar. "The law was here lookin' for you and I don't need that kinda heat." Her eyes widened to a glare. "I didn't tell 'em a damn thing, but you go."

"Is this a trap?" Frank growled.

"If it was a trap, these men'd be wearing badges." Pearl swept aside in a cloud of powder and cologne to allow the men to do their jobs. "As it is, we want you gone. This is neutral territory and we protect our patrons. We can't do that if the law needs to raid us for a gang of killers."

"Sam!" bawled Frank. "Get the men."

"Are you gonna fold because some uppity madam gives you orders?" A small man emerged from the corner shrouded in nebulous shadows.

"I ain't no fool, Will," Frank retorted. "We git while the goin's good. She's got back up, and I'll bet that she has a man ready to ride out and get the law. You don't get to charge money like this without thinkin' through the details. Get the rest of the gang."

"But I was just in the middle—"

"No buts. Do as you're told!"

The maid edged toward the door, watching men scuttle out from adjoining rooms pulling on their shirts and stumbling into their pants. "Where are you goin'?" growled Pearl. "Get this room cleaned and ready for the next party."

"They're killers?" the maid asked.

"Murderers ain't welcome here, girl. I have standards, but you're safe enough." Pearl nodded toward the huge man toting a rifle by the door. "Make sure they're gone, Bert. And don't be fooled by what the law said. They ain't The Innocents, so you don't need to worry about takin' on Jake Conroy. They're imposters. You can take 'em. Hell, I could take 'em."

The bitter wind whipped Abigail's wet hair across her face, having hidden her mousy wig and glasses under bales of hay in the stables when she grabbed a convenient horse. It wouldn't do to get caught wearing a disguise. She had already taken more risks than she should as it was. Abigail picked her way through the obfuscating darkness as quietly as possible, cursing herself for being so unprepared. The gloom and tree cover meant she had to stick closer to the gang than she wanted to if she were to have any idea where they were headed, and the gusting wind made it hard to listen for the men ahead.

They weren't The Innocents, but they were killers and a more immediate problem. The least she could do was try to establish the location of their hideout and report back to local law enforcement. Thick, inky blackness hung in an almost palpable murk and the thin moon struggled through a tempest of obscuring clouds which scudded over the silver crescent. The poor, thin light did little to help her see her way through the night, but she urged her horse on, searching the ground for their tracks in the damp earth.

Pitted hoofmarks filled with water from the cold rain caused the rich musky essence of pure horse to intensify and steam beneath her. She turned her collar against the weather, rain stinging her face, and rounded the next bend. She heard the explosive blast of gunpowder at the same time she felt burning pain in her left arm. The velocity propelled her backward off her mount and battered her to the stony ground. The horse bolted in panic while she lay dazed. She blinked, moaning in pain at her first movement, before she lay still, testing her limbs one by one for damage. A pair of boots squelched up beside her head and a man crouched beside her.

"Jeasus, Sam. It's a woman."

"A woman?" Another voice drifted from behind. "On her own? What the hell is she doin' all the way out here?"

The gruff reply grated on her already tense nerves. "How should I know, Sam? Why don't you ask her yourself?"

A toe prodded at her wounded arm, causing her to groan out loud. "Who are ya? Why're ya followin' us?"

Her mind ran as best it could through the fog of pain and fear. Perhaps they couldn't interrogate her if they thought she couldn't speak English? She lapsed into Gaelic.

"Tha thu cho duaichnidh ri èarr àirde de a' coisich deas damh."

"Huh? What's she saying?"

The burly one called Frank had a voice she recognized. "Name?" He kicked her again. "I need your name."

"Thalla gu taigh na galla."

"Did she hit her head? She's talkin' gibberish. Is she a native? It ain't Spanish."

A hand grabbed her hair and Frank's voice snarled in her ear. "Name, girl. I want your name."

"Was she followin' us?" Sam asked. "I dunno. Throw her on a horse. We'll question her when we get to the cabin." Frank stood. "Damn it. This is all we need."

"Just put a bullet in her head," Sam growled. "We ain't got time for this."

"Don't be so hasty," another voice drifted over. "We just got flung out of a whore house. A woman might be handy to have around if we've gotta lie low for a while."

"Yeah," another agreed. "And it ain't gonna help us if anyone finds her body. They might start searchin'. Bring her. You can shoot her anywhere, Sam, and we might as well have some fun."

Rough arms dragged her from the ground. The pain shot through her arm and across her shoulders, with no consideration of the best position. She was pushed face-down over a horse as a man mounted behind her. This was bad. Very bad. It was looking like she would have to use one of the most extreme survival techniques taught to the female agents. Would it work?

Chapter Three

She struggled against the pain to stay upright on the wooden seat, but she forced herself to focus and do what she needed to do to survive. Frank glowered at his soaking clothes in dismay, brushing his hand over the wet patch cascading over his shoulder.

He glared at her in disgust. "That filthy bitch has wet herself! I'm covered in piss from carryin' her in."

The little man stepped forward. "She's terrified. She's shakin', poor thing." He crouched and yelled into her face. "We ain't gonna hurt ya! What's yer name?"

She fixed him with glittering eyes, brimming with tears and continued to tremble. At least the act worked on one of them. It was a start, but it was no time to let up. She replied with a deliberate tremor in her voice. *"Beag diabhal."*

"I think she's called Beg or somethin'? What kind of name is that? Aw, she's got real pretty eyes under all that mud. I say we bandage her arm and she could be real good fun tomorrow."

"Why wait? We ain't nursemaids. I don't care if she's hurtin'." Frank leaned in close. "What the hell language is that?"

She bowed her head, a thick curtain of hair sweeping over her face providing just enough cover for her to stick a finger deep into her throat under the guise of raising her hand to her sobbing lips.

This was no time to be cautious. She thrust it deep, setting off her gag reflex, making her guts churn and boil. Her stomach convulsed and the contents fermented and rose until they reached her gullet in a burning acid swirl. She removed her finger and opened her mouth, and vomited straight in Frank's face, keeping her hair in the way.

She needed some of this precious vomit over her too. The words of the woman who trained her rang in her mind. *"Always remember that letting loose your body fluids, no matter how base and disgusting, is a last defense against rape. Men are visual and sensory creatures and are more easily disgusted than the female. It will kill their sexual urges immediately."*

How right she was.

He jumped back in revulsion, his clothes splattered with bile and half-digested gouts of food on top of the already-cooling urine already soaking through his clothes. He pointed mutely at the woman sitting in piss-soaked clothes, draped with matted hair which stuck to her with regurgitated puke. A speechless Frank stood dripping in vomit, but it didn't last long. "Ya dirty whore!"

He pulled back his hand and backhanded her across the face. She tumbled to the wooden floor with a cry. He wiped his soiled hand before it crept to his gun, but the little one grabbed his arm.

"Wait, Frank. Let's stick her in the barn. She'll clean. It's a waste. A couple of buckets of water'll get that off."

"Filthy damned bitch," Frank shook him off and turned away. "Get her outta my sight, Will, or I won't be responsible for my actions."

Will picked her up, holding her at arm's length and walked her over to the door. "She'll clean up real good. You'll see, Frank. No need to rush. We got time."

The barn door closed behind her and she heard the padlock click. She stopped shivering and raised her skirts to remove her wet drawers before she ripped out a huge section of petticoat and bandaged her injured arm as best she could.

She could always put them on again if she heard them

coming. The vomit would have to stay. It might be disgusting, but she needed it as a necessary shield from unwanted attentions. If they were going to kill her anyway, she had no intention in helping them use her first.

She felt her way around the building in the poor light, but try as she might, she could not find a way out. The building was solid. She sighed and dropped into the straw in resignation. She'd have to wait until daylight. It was best to get sleep while she could and take stock in daylight.

Her hands probed the straw and gathered it into a pile before she nestled herself with a huff of pain. It was time to face the practicalities. She'd get further if she rested.

Pearl Dubois sailed through the patrons of her sporting house like a galleon in full sail, her yellow hair a beacon of welcome and her well-upholstered frame a walking hug. There were a select few she didn't mind showing her softer side to.

"Hi'ya, boys," she chortled, her jiggling bosom mirrored in the fat bulging over the back of her ruthlessly-laced corseted bodice. "Long time no see."

She stepped back to admire them, their casual riding clothes showing off their slim hips and long legs as they towered over her. "If you two boys get any handsomer you'll need to give up crime. You sure stand out in a crowd." She smiled at the fair man. "I always find it hard to believe you two are uncle and nephew."

"There are only eight years between us, Pearl," Jake gave her an affectionate squeeze, "but it's a wonder I don't look like Methuselah, lookin' after this'un most of my life."

"With a little help, Jake. You came here when you jumped off the orphan train. Anyone else would've sent you back." She glanced between one to the other with something close to maternal pride. "But look at you now, all growed and twice as spicy as a bubblin' pan of chili."

Nat embraced her, a dimpled smile on his face. "We haven't been in this neck of the woods for a good while. You got somewhere private we can talk?"

She flicked up a penciled-in eyebrow as she gestured with her head toward the backroom with a knowing twinkle. "Sure. I've been half-expectin' you. You boys hungry?"

"Always Pearl. You know that," grinned Jake.

She led the way, a choking cloud of perfume drifting behind her. "It'd be nice if you boys could just make a social call once in a while for old time's sake. I never see you unless you want somethin'." She pulled open the door, a smile of resignation etched through the heavy makeup. "But I guess you always want somethin'. When you turned up here tryin' to keep Nat out of the orphanage, you was no more'n twelve and he were just a little dot of a four year old. It pure broke my heart, it did, but ever since you've been like two baby birds with their mouths open whenever they see the mama bird."

"You're right, Pearl. We're real busy. We should make time to see you," Nat's eyes glittered with innocent regret. "I know we owe you."

"Yeah, you owe me, but somehow that turns into me givin'." A smiling Jake held the velvet-brown gaze of the dusky woman just outside until the door slid closed.

"You're a natural mother, Pearl. That's how. You're family." He turned. "You know we've always got your back. If you ever need us, we'll be here."

She slipped into a chair, her statuesque bosom thrust forward. "Yeah, I do. I guess you're here about the fake Innocents? They were here, you know. I chucked them out. I'll tell you what I can."

Blue eyes glittered in her direction before Jake took a seat. "Thanks."

Nat's long fingers slid a wedge of notes over the polished surface of the table as he held her gaze. "For your time, darlin'. Think of it as a gift."

Her plump fingers reached out and grasped the notes while a note of surprise played in her voice. "Payin' this time? You mean business."

Nat sat back and tilted his hat to the back of his head with his forefinger. "We sure do. Someone'll swing for that death and I need to make sure it's none of ours. We don't kill."

"They looked like trouble from the start, and were flush with money. Too flush. As soon as the law came askin' about a gang who killed a guard I showed them the door. I didn't know who they were when I let them in, boys. Honest, I didn't."

"Got any names?" asked Jake.

"There was a Will. Will Patterson. He was a Texas boy, judgin' from his accent. He was the little one who took a fancy to Monica and was talkative. There was a Sam and a Frank, too, who were in charge. They weren't so friendly. Eight in total. The new girl would have known more, but she ran off with the gang that very same night," her eyes brightened with her recollection. "She asked quite a few questions about you two though, seemed quite fascinated by you."

"New girl?" asked Nat, his interest piqued. "What did she want to know?"

"Yeah, light brown hair, kinda mousey. Irish, sounded like she was right off the boat." She shrugged. "She didn't fit in here but she worked hard. Ran off that night. Some are shocked too easy," she let out a bellowing laugh as the men smiled in unison at her contagious mischief, "but maybe she wasn't as innocent as I thought to run off with them lot."

Nat's brow creased. "What did she ask?"

"If we knew you, did you come around here often, what you look like; anythin' she could find out. We told her nothin'. I guess she had a yearnin' for a bad boy."

She stretched into an unladylike, gaping yawn as she leant back in her seat. "There's one more thing. Word has it men have been askin' questions about you two all over the county. All kinds of men. It made me wonder if these fellas were a ploy to draw you out, so you should be layin' low. Don't do any jobs for a while."

She nodded to the woman opening the door. "The steaks are here for you. I'll get Monica to give you the full rundown on their descriptions while you eat."

Nat flashed a meaningful glance at Jake. "I don't like this. She's been asking questions at the same time as another gang pretended to be us, and then disappears with them. Men asking the same questions all over the county? She's part of this."

Jake nodded. "I'll ask a few questions myself. See what I can find out about her. You can concentrate on how they know the best payroll to hit."

Nat flicked up an eyebrow. "So you question all the women and I head off to the railway office to check their files? You think that's a good deal?"

Jake grinned. "You're the one who's great at breakin' into places. I'm more of a people person."

"Ya think? How do you work that out? I'm great with people."

"Great at bossin' them around. You're the break-in expert, and that information means looking at files in locked rooms. You can't have your cake and eat it too."

"It's cake. What else are you supposed to do with it?"

Jake swung back on his chair a smile tugging at his lips. "You hate it when I'm right, don't you?"

The dark eyes glittered with humor. "Only when you get a better deal than me."

"Trust me." Jake gave his nephew a wry smile. "You're too sneaky for it to happen too often."

"Sneaky? Me?" Devilment twinkled in the dark eyes. "That's the nicest thing you've ever said to me."

♦ ◊ ♦

Abigail came to in the dank, rancid darkness and groaned against her thumping headache. The burning ache in her arm exploded into a sharp pain at her first movement. She swallowed the rising ball of bile in her throat, trying not to vomit, but would it make the surroundings any less revolting? Was there anything in her stomach other than burning acid, anyway?

She propped herself against a stall while trying to support her wounded arm. It was far more agonizing now that the adrenaline had subsided. The bullet had grazed the skin as it whipped past, and she knew she would soon heal, as long as infection didn't set in any further.

Daylight filtered through the cracks in the planks and illuminated the scene in a striped gloaming, lighting a tin plate filled with brown mush a couple of feet away. Someone had been here and she hadn't even noticed. She kicked herself for not being able to stay vigilant.

She collapsed back into the straw devoid of energy, her skin pricking with sweat. One peek behind the torn sleeve to look at the angry wound made her sigh in dismay. The infection polluted her system and her fever made the heat, the pain, and the stench even more unbearable. Her resolve to search around the building to find a way out dissipated with every breath. She closed her eyes and slumped into an uneasy lull.

Soon, she was beyond reason. No one tended to her other than to bring brackish water or leave more repulsive food which remained untouched. She sank further and further into the darkness. At least the deep, silent, velvet-blackness of total oblivion was a relief from the pain.

◆◇◆

"Are you sure this is the place?" Nat whispered.

Oso nodded. "We watched the place for hours. There ain't another cabin with more'n a couple of men in it for twenty miles. There's eight of them, just like you said. It's gotta be them."

"I came back to the meetin' place to get you, Nat," Hank gestured toward his Mexican friend. "Oso stayed and watched while I fetched ya."

Oso peered out from behind the tree. "They ain't left the place other'n to use the outhouse or go to the barn. They's all still there, boss. Did we find the right outfit? Is they the ones that shot the guard?"

"I think so. The Irish girl from Pearl's place took off at the same time as them and the horse she stole was found wandering in this area." Nat stared at the cabin. "There are men in this area searching for The Innocents and they got as far as Bannen. They've now attached a murder to our name. We'll swing if we don't sort this fast. This gang happening at the same time as the area being swamped by men asking questions looks like a dirty conspiracy at a high level. We need to break it."

Jake Conroy crouched low behind the well with his gun drawn, signaling with his free hand for Chuck and Melvin to keep down and stay silent. The door to the cabin opened and a tall, thin man with a shark fin nose strode out carrying a bucket.

"Looks like he's headed toward the well," Melvin hissed through teeth like a broken piano. "Jake's there."

"I can see that," Nat muttered. "Get ready. They'll know we're here as soon as Jake strikes."

"Are you sure this is the right gang?" hissed Chuck. "They could be anyone."

"How many gangs of men are there in these woods who hide at the sight of anyone coming near?" Nat demanded.

"Well, there's us—"

"We're outlaws, you numbskull. It's what we do." Nat rolled his eyes. "Now keep your eyes on the cabin. I'll cover Jake."

The stranger grabbed the well rope and hooked it on the bucket, oblivious to the gunman sneaking up behind him. The sound of a metallic click behind his right ear made him let go and the receptacle dropped into the echoing depths, the handle whipping round and round until the bucket hit the water at the bottom.

"Not one word, friend. Get those hands up."

The man nodded, thrusting his arms in the air and stared straight ahead with his dun-colored eyes. Jake drew the man backward, toward his compatriots hidden in the bushes. "This way. Stay silent."

"Are you the law?"

"I told you to stay silent."

The door to the cabin opened, "Hey, Sam. Can you—" The mustached man blinked in disbelief at his friend being held at gunpoint. "Jees!"

The door slammed and urgent shouts and orders erupted in the cabin. Jake tightened his grasp on the thin man's arm and dragged him over to the rest of the outlaws hiding in the bushes, using him as a human shield all the way. He threw him to Jesse and Hank as soon as he gained cover.

"Tie him up. Gag him." He crouched behind Nat. "What now?"

"We play our hand, I guess," Nat replied. "It's all we've got left." He stood, darting forward to the barn and peering around the edge. "Hey, you. In the house. You're surrounded."

"You ain't takin' us alive."

"Well, that's a pretty dumb move." Nat's rich baritone danced with mocking tones. "Don't you want to find out what you're up against first? Let them have it, boys."

The cabin faced a fusillade of shots, battering into the walls, windows and doors from every direction, splintering the wood and shattering eardrums with a shower of explosive bursts.

"We still ain't comin' out."

Nat called out once more. "We're well-armed and we're ready to blast you out unless you lay down your arms and come out peaceable-like. It's your call."

"Blast us? What kind of posse are you? We ain't comin' out. We're just gonna be hanged, anyway," the voice echoed from the cabin.

"That's where you're wrong," yelled Nat. "We're not the law. We're The Innocents, and we're as mad as hell about you using our name to kill a man. Are you going to face us like men, or do we have to drive you out of there?"

"Ha! And just how do you propose to do that?" a mocking voice demanded.

"What are we famous for?" Nat responded.

"Stealin'." The voice took on a mocking tone. "Oh, and not shootin' folks."

Nat glinted an amused glance at his team over by the bushes. "Yeah, and when we can't break in, how do we get at the money?"

The voice from the building rattled with impatience. "I dunno! What kinda dumb test is this?"

"We blow the thing open," Melvin squeaked with delight.

"That's our explosives man," chortled Nat. "He really enjoys his work," his cheeks dimpled into a smile, "so much so, he's set dynamite under you. I've got to warn you, he never bothers with any of the twenty percent dynamite. Oh, no. He only uses the most powerful sixty percent nitro sticks. That stuff gives the best blast, and he's put it under each corner of that place you're sitting in right now."

He paused, letting this information sink in. "You know what it does, but just to drive your position home we put a few sticks under the outhouse as a demonstration. Watch out of the back window. Let 'er go, Melvin!"

"Sure thing, Nat."

There was a long pause before the lighted fuse fizzed its way toward the little wooden building. The light disappeared under the wooden slats and there was an almighty crashing blast. Planks shattered and flew skyward, revealing the centre of the shed as nothing more than a tower of hungry fire. Shards and splinters scattered all around, causing the outlaws to duck and avoid the smoldering fragments showering on them amid the acrid scent of cordite and the heavy fetid smell of some very organic materials.

Chuck sniffed and crinkled his nose in disgust at the matter plopping around their hiding place. "Couldn't ya have picked a barn, Nat? It's a shit storm. A real one."

"You hear that?" Nat called. "I'll give you to the count of twenty, and then you'll be what's splattered around this place. One!"

"You don't mean it. You're bluffin'."

"Two!" Nat jaw tightened. "I don't take kindly to the likes of you using our name and reputation. You're not dealing with amateurs, here." He paused. "Three."

"The Innocents never shot anyone," the voice sounded less confident. "This ain't your style."

"We don't shoot the public," Nat growled, "but we'll sure as hell deal with anyone else who gets in our way. They say we never shot anyone in a robbery. Nobody says we never killed. But when you think about it, we're not shooting you either, so it's fine. Four!"

"What do you want?"

"Five!" Nat glanced over at Jake, both acknowledging the bargaining had begun. "If we're getting the blame for all those jobs, we want the money. All of it. Then we want you out of our territory and a promise we'll never see you within a hundred miles of Wyoming ever again. Six!"

"All of it?"

"Seven! Yes, all of it. You should've thought about that before you bandied our name about. It's our reputation. So it's our money. Eight."

"You'll blow up the money too."

"Nine. Yeah, well, I thought about that and I'm prepared to take the chance because it gets rid of you. Are you? Ten! That's halfway through."

The voice from the cabin rang with panic. "What'll you do to us?"

"Eleven. We're not unreasonable men, unless you're unreasonable with us. We want the money and we want you gone. Twelve."

"So you'll let us go?"

"Thirteen! Some say that's unlucky," Nat smirked, "but it's getting nearer to a number way more unlucky for you. Fourteen."

"We want your word you won't kill us."

"Fifteen. My word? Sure. I'm not interested in killing you."

"You promise?"

"Sixteen." Nat shrugged. "I promise I won't kill you if you come out, but I can't hold to what'll happen if you don't. Seventeen."

"I need your word you won't kill us," the man was almost screaming now.

"Eighteen. And you have my word. None of The Innocents will kill you."

"Promise. I want you to swear!" There were shouts from within the cabin, signaling spiraling panic in the other gang.

"Nineteen! Yeah. I swear. Nat Quinn gives his solemn word none of The Innocents will kill you. One more, and then the cabin gets blasted to kingdom come."

"Fine. We're throwing out our guns." The door opened a crack and a hand tossed out a pile of weapons, one after the other.

"We're comin' out. Don't shoot." The burly man appeared first, hands straight to the heavens.

"We want you all out here," barked Jake. "There were eight of you. We got one, and you're out here. The other six had better get out here with their hands in the air, and fast."

The men shuffled out, one by one, the smallest at the end of the line with an anxious smile. Nat broke cover, holding his Schofield on them all the while. "Beau, Jesse. Check the cabin. Make sure there's nobody else there. Chuck and Melvin. Tie them up."

"All clear in here, Nat." Jesse's sharp nose appeared around the door. "We found this." Beau dragged out a saddle bags. "They're full of cash."

"Is that all of it?" Nat demanded.

"Nope—" the burly man began.

"Where is it!?" Nat bellowed straight in his face, the fury even catching seasoned gang members by surprise. "Talk."

"We spent it." Frank dropped his head. "We went to a whore house. We spent the rest on whiskey and supplies."

Quinn nodded, holding the man's gaze prisoner all the while. "Which one of you did it?"

"Did what?" the smallest prisoner squeaked.

Nat's face darkened. "Who killed the guard?"

"Frank. Frank did it. Yeah...it was Frank," three voices spoke in unison.

Nat followed the hunted eyes of the men to the large man right in front of him. "Well, I guess you're Frank, huh? A real loyal gang you got there." He stared at the prisoner, his hands tied behind his back, the disgust rising in the outlaw leader's craw. "I should drop you where you stand, you piece of dirt, but I made a promise, and I'm a man of my word."

His fist shot out, catching the murderer right in the solar plexus. The man doubled over and collapsed gasping on the ground.

"Here! That ain't fair, punching a man when he can't hit back," yelled the little man.

Nat flicked a dismissive glance at him. "Yeah, kinda like shooting an unarmed man in the chest, but maybe not quite as low, huh? I ain't no choirboy. What's your name?"

"Patterson. Frank Patterson," the man puffed.

"Your accent. A Texan? You're a long way from home." Nat paced back and forth. "So who put you up to this?" He watched the men shuffle and hang their heads. "Do I need to interrogate you separately?"

"Mister, how did you know we was put up to it?" asked the short man.

"You're not local. It's a long way to come to pretend to be another gang; to make sure you use their names on a robbery. You got trains and banks of your own in Texas." Nat peered at the men in turn. "Who's in charge?"

"Sam and Frank are both in charge," squeaked the little one. "We don't know his name. All we can tell you is he gets called Smitty."

"Will you shit yer yap, Will?" bellowed the burly man.

"And how do you meet this Smitty?" Nat asked.

"He meets Frank and Sam in a bar. Ain't nobody else met Smitty," Will continued, "but I saw him once when I was watchin' the horses. He's a real dude with a shiny stove pipe hat and everythin'."

"Description?" barked the outlaw leader.

"Youngish, real well dressed. It were dark, though, and I never saw his face."

Nat nodded. "Jake, you take Sam and I'll take Frank. I want to know everything about there is to know about this Smitty."

◆ ◇ ◆

Nat walked out of the cabin, pulling his gloves over reddened knuckles, his face grim and humorless. He allowed the gang to drag the bedraggled prisoner behind them, his head sagging and covered in blood from his swollen, cut lip and broken nose. He called over to the fair gunman who stood over the thin man as he lay on the ground.

"What did you get, Jake?"

Jake indicated the skinny man lying in front of them. "Smitty, a young dandy with dark hair and a moustache. He doesn't know anythin' else about him. He paid them a thousand dollars up front to hold up the trains, and they get the haul, too. They were too scared to kill anyone until the third, and it was almost an accident."

"And how does he contact them?"

"All they know is he'll pay them more when he meets them in Denver next month. They're to meet in a saloon there. I got the details."

"Yeah, I got the same." Nat kicked out at a tuft of grass. "Dammit. I need more. There's no point in me walkin' into a bar without knowin' who I'm lookin' for. Denver's full of young swells." He signaled to the gang. "Get them on the wagon, hands and feet tied. I want this garbage out of my sight."

"You said none of The Innocents would hurt any of us," the thin man protested. "Ain't your word worth anythin'?"

The dark eyes fixed on him with withering disdain. "Friend, if you think Nat Quinn is an innocent you're stupider than you look," snorted Nat.

The real Innocents made short work of securing the men in the flat bed of the wagon as Jake approached his nephew. "Are you alright, Nat?"

Nat pulled off his hat and ran his hand through his brown hair. "Sure, yeah. We got them. Why do you ask?"

The blue eyes burned into him, full of knowing calm. "You

said 'ain't'. You only talk like you did when you were a nipper when you've really lost it."

"Do I?" He pulled himself back to normality, his smile filling with a lightness Jake wasn't buying. "Then it's a good job I worked it off, ain't it? I even promised I wouldn't kill them." He paused. "But I never promised any of them the law wouldn't."

The sheriff of Bannen paused at the door of his office, alert to the change of routine signaling something wrong. The door was locked and there was no smell of coffee, in a departure from the long-established routine. It was always open and the late shift always had the pot brewing for those starting in the morning. Someone manned the office day and night, and the deputy should be there bright and alert to handover whatever had happened during the night. Since he wasn't, something must be very wrong.

He pulled out his key and entered the building, calling out as he went. "Dave? Where the devil are you? If you've been sleeping again, I'll—" He stopped short at the sight of the deputy bound and gagged in his chair and the cells full of restrained men. "What in the name of—"

He pulled the gag from the deputy's mouth, watching him work his jaw free from the constriction.

"What's been going on here?"

"They said they were The Innocents, Sheriff. That's the men they say killed the guard in the train robbery. Nat was real mad about another gang claiming to be them, so the real Innocents went right out and brought them in for us."

"They did?" The sheriff turned his keys in the handcuffs, allowing the deputy to rub his wrists. "And these bags. What's in here?" He flipped one open, his eyes widening at the stack of banknotes inside. "Cash?"

"The one who said he was Nat Quinn told me it was almost everything they took. The gang had already spent some when they caught up with them, but he needed the law to see he didn't profit from a killing. He says the rest of the gang are cowards and will give evidence against the one who fired the shot and killed the guard. The big one with the moustache."

"Is that right?" The sheriff lifted the note pinned to the top of the cashbox and smiled over at the men in the cells as he read it aloud. "A gift from Nat Quinn and The Innocents."

"Do you think it was really them?" asked the deputy, pushing himself to his feet.

"Well, the men who held up those three trains didn't act like The Innocents. They don't fit the descriptions neither. I wouldn't blame Nat Quinn if he brought them in. So the rest'll turn on the killer you say?"

"That's what he said. He said he sent a telegram to the press to make sure we stayed honest with the cash too. Someone called Smitty put them up to it to put the blame on The Innocents. Quinn says Smitty paid them a thousand dollars to get them a hangin' charge."

The lawman scowled. "Did you get a good look at them, Dave?"

"No, Sheriff. They wore kerchiefs and got the jump on me real fast."

The lawman nodded, turning over a stack of notes in his hand. "Yeah, but we might not tell the town that bit when we break this news, but you did a good night's work, son. Real good."

"I did?" gulped the young man.

"Sure, you did. Now let's sit and have some coffee. We need to decide what we're gonna tell people happened here last night. We sure as hell can't tell them The Innocents walked away from our cells."

♦ ◊ ♦

Jake pulled the wagon to a halt. "I can't see why we don't just take this thing straight back to Pearl."

"We never had time to search the place properly," Nat dismounted. "There might be more money hidden here. They could have stuff from robberies we knew nothing about. If we're real lucky we might even need a wagon to take it away."

"You're dreamin', Nat. The only hidden treasure around here was splattered all over us when you blew up the necessary."

"Probably," Nat chuckled, "but I want to make sure. Do you want to take the grounds or the cabin?"

"I don't care," shrugged Jake. "You take the house. I'll do out here."

Nat disappeared into the building and Jake explored the grounds. He searched for all kinds of small signs, like disturbances in the soil, flattened grass, or moss growing on the wrong side of stone. He was too experienced to fall for that old wives tale about it only growing on the north side; it depended on the gradient, the moisture, and the surface. When you put it all together, it was easy to spot stones that had been moved to a position where moss shouldn't grow.

His practiced blue eyes scanned the area as he strolled around. What appeared to be a casual wander was anything but. The inspection was systematic, grid-like and efficient, but everything was overgrown and unused. It looked like the use of this place was just opportunistic, but Nat was right; it never hurt to look. He peered into the well, but all he could see was the occasional glint of a watery meniscus in the dank, dark depths of the void. It was too deep for anything to be retrieved with ease, so he dismissed it as a hiding place and moved on. He sighed and turned to the barn Nat hid behind earlier. The ramshackle and dilapidated building settled back into the land from which it was hewn with the help of the invasive vines sending strangling tendrils across the roof and into every nook and cranny. One thing caught his eye almost right away; the padlock. It looked new.

He strode over and gave it a tug. The pristine brass still shone with a patina of recentness which stood out against the peeling, rough wood of the building. His curiosity mounted. Why secure this broken-down old barn? He took out his Colt and stepped to the side and blasted it to smithereens, aiming out into the empty yard beyond.

"What the hell—" Nat appeared gun in hand.

"It was locked." He put his gun back in its holster and stooped to pick up the biggest piece. "A new lock. What could be in there worth lockin' away?"

"That? You didn't have to shoot it, anyone could pick it. Even you."

Jake grinned. "Thanks, but it's quicker to shoot it. Anyone could hit it if they stood near enough. Even you."

Nat smiled and put away his Schofield. "So, what were they protecting?" He pulled back the hasp and opened the door, and both men stepped back, hit by a feculent wall of funk.

"Whoa," Jake frowned. "I don't know what they were breedin' in there, but I don't want one."

Nat stepped inside, his eyes adjusting to the poor light filtering in between the slats. "I don't see any animals. The place is empty."

There was a metallic clatter. "Oh, for cryin' out loud. I trod in somethin'—somethin' sticky. And what's the cloth doin' there? Is that smell piss?"

"Jake—"

"I stood in somethin' now. It's like gruel, or grits, or—sick? Yuck, it's disgustin'. It's all over my boots."

"Jake!" Nat barked. "Is that a body?"

He followed his nephew's stony stare to the dark bundle in the straw before striding over. "It's a woman," he reached out a hand. "She's warm; far too hot." He reached out and lifted her in both arms. "Outta my way."

They needed full daylight to see the full picture. Jake carried her outside and laid her on the grass. Her stiff hair hung over her waxy face, still in the same armor of desiccated vomit which had hardened around her mouth and on her clothes. He lifted the encrusted lace of hair shrouding her mud-covered face with gentle delicacy. "She's burnin' up. How could they leave her like that?"

"The bastards left her here to die." Nat frowned at the disheveled shred of humanity lying in her own waste. "Get her in the wagon. There are blankets in the cabin, I'll get them."

"She's got dark hair. Do you think she's the same one who was askin' about us? Pearl said the Irish girl had light brown hair."

Nat crouched, examining her. "Her face is covered in mud and sick, but she looks pretty familiar through all the mess. I think it's that Scottish woman again. Why's she cropping up all over the place? Let's get her to Pearl's to see if she's been playing the Irish girl, too."

Chapter Four

"Dora?" Jake tapped at the door. He paused, listening hard, sure he heard whispers and rustling inside. A flushed blonde opened it a mere crack. She emerged, closing it behind her as she drew her robe over an enticing porcelain shoulder which emerged from the swathes of fabric.

"Jake," she breathed and pushed a stray lock of hair behind her ear. "I wasn't expecting you."

"Yeah, I'm here with a woman we found out in the woods. Pearl's cleanin' her up with the doctor." He frowned and glanced into the rumpled room behind her. "I wanted to speak to you. Pearl said you weren't with a customer, but it sounds like she was wrong."

"Nope, she's not wrong. I was—tidying," she giggled for no real reason. "What happened to her? Is she alright?"

"Dunno. Pearl said you might know her. She used to work here and helped you dress. It's the Irish girl who ran away. Can we go into your room?"

"It's far too untidy." She slipped a hand into his and led him to the staircase. "Come with me. Does Pearl want me to come and help?"

"No, she wondered if you knew if she has any folks about here." He cast a wary look back at the room and followed her downstairs to the seating area in the main hall.

"Nope. I've no idea. It's been ages since I've seen you."

"We've been busy."

She turned back to him with a meaningful glint as they

descended the staircase. "So I hear."

They reached the bottom and she drew him over to a table, pushing him into a seat with his back to the stairs. She waved to a black woman wiping the counter. "Seraphina, honey. Can we get two coffees?"

"Sure." The woman's wide smile lit the room. "I'll be right back."

"So what did you want, Jake? Long time no see."

He sat back with a warm smile. "Pearl said the new girl was askin' questions, then ran away."

"Annie...Abi...Anna? Oh shoot, what was her name again? That little maid?"

"Abi," Jake flicked a brief nod of thanks at the girl as she set down the coffees. "Pearl said her name was Abi."

"I can't say I had much to do with her. A quiet little thing with glasses? Light brown hair?" She poured cream into her cup before offering to do the same for him. "She asked who comes here. Well, that got a laugh, I can tell you." Dora leaned back and released a delicious giggle. "None of us were gonna tell her about you or anyone else. There's a reason this place is so expensive, and secrecy is part of the service."

"What did she tell you about herself?"

"Nothin' much. She came from Ireland, her folks were dead, and she needed the work. Nothin' unusual in that. I never paid much attention. Sorry, honey. She was kinda insignificant. I don't think she has any folks. She said she had nobody."

"Yeah, it's pretty much what everyone is sayin'." Jake took a sip of his coffee. "So how've you been? How's the boy?"

His eyes drifted to the huge ornate mirror on the wall behind her which reflected the whole upper balustrade. The door to Dora's room opened a crack.

Her eyes lit up. "Great, Jake. I think I've found a way out."

"Out?"

"I ended up here because I had no choice. I have a son to

support."

His eyes softened. "I know."

"It looks like my luck's turned. There's money coming and soon. I'll be leaving here. My David can have a fresh start where his ma isn't called a dirty whore."

"So where's this money comin' from?" Jake hid his observation of the mirror as best he could, but the tapping of a cane signaled a man slipping out as quietly as a blind man could. He felt his way to the top of the staircase. He knew his way around. But he would. He worked here. He was the pianist.

"I can't say," she shook her head. "I've been sworn to secrecy until a lawyer can go through the will, but I'm sure I'll be gone soon." She reached out and curled her fingers around his hand. "I'll miss you. You've been special. One of my favorites." She gave him a playful pat. "Don't look so sad. It's a good thing."

"Who?" Jake frowned. "Men can promise all kinds of things and then drop you when they're bored. He'd better treat you right."

"It's all right. It's family, and a real future," she purred.

"Family?" Jake asked. "You ain't got no family except your son."

A mysterious smile flickered across her face. "It's more complicated than that. My husband had a brother, Michael who died about eight years ago. It's to do with that, but there's some legal stuff to sort out. It's an inheritance from someone who's been dead for a while, but the will hasn't been properly acted on. It's not even sad. Nobody in the world would miss that old sadist. Giving us a future is the only good thing he'll have done in his life."

"Who? You? Is it David? Is your son going to inherit?"

"I was told David can't inherit, but someone who can will look after us. I haven't told anyone yet; not until I'm sure. I didn't want to build up hopes for nothing. I'm bursting with good news but I know I can tell you. "

"Is it male relative? Is anyone putting pressure on you, Dora? I can speak to them for you."

"Thank you, Jake," her perfect skin stretched into a smile without a wrinkle. "No, nobody is pressuring me. I just need to speak to a lawyer when I can get a copy of the will and then I'll be on easy street. It's on its way. I'll be collecting it at a meeting soon. I gotta go." She stood, waving to him as she sashayed into the covey room, the place the prostitutes gathered to be chosen by their clients. "I need to get back to work."

He sat back, deep in thought. Something about the secrecy didn't sit right. Pearl said she wasn't working, yet the blind man had been in her room. The man had hideous scars, his face a mask of distorted flesh with barely a wispy hair on his head. Did she feel sorry for him? Was it love? Friendship? Why did she lie? One thing was sure. He might add an air of class with his soaring symphonies and operatic pieces, but he sure as hell didn't earn enough to pay a fifty-dollar a trick prostitute. And who was this mysterious relative? In all the years he'd known her, she had nobody but the washer woman neighbor who looked after her son while she worked.

Jake shook himself back to the here and now. There were immediate worries to deal with.

The hotel clerk peered at the register. "Mr. R. Daintree?"

The guest nodded his head, the light gleaming off the Makassar oil's slick making his hair appear like patent-leather, exemplifying the height of this praying mantis of a man. "Rigby Daintree, yes."

The clerk reached around and grabbed a key with a gigantic wooden fob. "You're in number twelve. Dinner is served in the dining room right over there at five."

"Five? That's a bit early, isn't it?"

The clerk glanced at the ledger. "You're from Boston, sir? This is Bannen. People here work on the land and rise with the sun. Come five, they're real hungry. We keep serving until nine, so we can still cater for you city folks, too." He clicked his fingers at a lad in an enormous bottle green jacket covered in shabby gold frogging. "Number twelve, Johnny."

The lad bent to pick up the suitcase, but the long sleeve unfurled, getting in the way. "That jacket's a bit big, isn't it?" Daintree chuckled.

"The boss bought it cheap from a circus. I hate it. Ma ain't had time to take it up yet." Johnny lifted the case and tucked the leather bag under his arm. "It used to belong to the chimp and he got a new one. It ain't right when apes get dressed better'n folks."

"No, it's not," Daintree's benign smile twinkled at Johnny's sartorial predicament as he followed him to the staircase.

The boy climbed. "So, you're from the East? What brings you to Bannen, Mr. Daintree?"

"I'm a lawyer. I'm here trying to find some potential heirs."

They turned onto the landing and walked along the corridor. "Oh, who?"

They stopped at a paneled door embossed with the number twelve in Clarendon font. "That's not something I can discuss with anyone except the client, is it?"

Johnny shrugged. "Suit yourself, but I know most everyone around here. I could save you a barrel-load of time." He dropped the bags on the floor and caught a glistening coin before his hands disappeared inside the long sleeves once more. A heavy sigh marked his annoyance. "Just ask for me at the desk."

"You know, Johnny. You might be able to help me, but I need to know I can depend on your silence. Can I rely on you?"

Johnny's face brightened into a cheeky grin. "I keep tellin' folks I can be bought, but you're the first one who offered."

Daintree took out a deck of cards and fanned them out revealing an array of nude and semi-nude women embossed on them. "Let's pretend I'm here to sell novelties like this. It'll mean people'll talk without thinking there's money in it. They're more honest that way. Help from you will mean I can go straight to the right people."

The lad's mouth dropped open. "Wow! Look at her. And that—"

"You want to keep the pictures of naked ladies, Johnny?" Daintree's lips spread into a gap-toothed grin. "What do you know about the Benson family?"

Chapter Five

Abigail awoke to the sun beating in through a window. There had been dreamlike memories of being carried, trees flashing by overhead, and water being dripped over her reluctant lips until her raging throat was quenched, but she knew no more than that. She had no idea where she was, or how long she had been there.

Her whole body was wracked with pain, and she lacked the strength to even speak. A dry rattle rasped from her parched throat toward a concerned pair of blue eyes which hovered into view.

"How you doin'?"

The blurred face came into focus and she started at the realization that the man she knew to be Jake Conroy stood over her, stroking her hair. Was it him? He looked like the man standing behind Nat Quinn on the platform, but she couldn't be sure. She tried to speak, but no sound came out of her ravaged throat.

"Sit up, darlin'. Try to drink some water."

He propped her against his firm chest and put a glass to her lips, encouraging her to drink until the glass was almost drained. Her foggy mind tried to make sense of all this. Jake Conroy was not a member of the gang she had followed. Why was he here? Did he know who she was? No. She must be mistaken. This was a dream.

"You're safe. No one's goin' to hurt you while I'm around."

"What? Where?" She croaked as he laid her back down.

He smiled. It lit up his face with a gentleness she hadn't seen at the train. "You were sick. We found you in the barn. Why'd he put you there?"

"Who?" She shook her head in confusion.

"Frank Patterson."

"Patterson?"

"What's your name?"

Her voice gave out with the exertion as he could see his questioning was getting him nowhere. It would have to wait .He took a damp cloth and mopped her face before continuing to her neck. Cooling waves of refreshment washed over her as she gave in to the weakness and relaxed into the lumpy mattress.

"Go back to sleep. We'll try to get you to eat somethin' when you wake up."

The shrill shriek of birds announced their delight at the new day was her wake-up call as she struggled to open her leaden eyelids. The fever had given her wild vivid dreams, with horrors from her past haunting her, ripping any possible rest from the turbulent sleep. She frowned. She'd even been dreaming about the damned Innocents tending to her. She needed reality, and she needed to wake up. Her eyes flickered open to a pair of kind brown eyes dripping over her like molten chocolate as the man gave her a dimpled smile. "Good mornin'."

No! Not Nat Quinn. What was going on? Abigail took a deep breath as her weak hands fluttered by her sides and her heart thumped, too debilitated by illness and her injured arm to support her leaden weight to sit.

"Let me help you." He placed a hand under each arm and supported her weight while he arranged her pillows in a sitting position. He settled her back. "Better?"

She nodded, confusion still reigning behind her dark eyes.

He answered as though he had read her mind. "You're in a cabin, in a different place. We took you from those men. You're safe now."

He grinned at her bewilderment but made no effort to clarify any further.

"How?"

He shrugged, examining every micro expression. "That doesn't matter. Those men are in jail in Bannen. The law's taking care of them. We're taking care of you."

"Really?" She frowned.

He nodded and lifted a glass of water. "Drink."

He delivered an order, not a request, but she complied and gulped at the contents as he held it to her mouth

"What's your name?"

She considered inventing a new identity before she thought the better of it. It was always better to stick to the story unless there was good reason to do otherwise. She gave the name under which she had entered Pearl's employ. "Abigail. Abigail Ross."

He sat on the bed and faced her, his eyes boring into hers with intensity, making her wonder what more lay behind their dancing lights.

"Well, Miss Ross. Suppose you tell me how a Scottish girl like you ended up in a barn with a bullet graze in her arm? You're a long way from home. That is a Scottish accent isn't it? People don't use fake accents when they're delirious."

She was weak and tired, but her natural cunning kicked in as she detected an undercurrent to the question. He didn't appear to recognize her. "Yes. It only grazed me, but I could see it was getting infected. Am I in Bannen? Are you a doctor?"

His eyes narrowed as he recognized the beginning of a verbal joust. It surprised him considering her weakened state, but he was quick to identify an agile mind behind the brown eyes assessing him so shrewdly. He grinned. "You answer my question, and I'll answer yours."

She gave him a weak smile. "I had a job. I hated it and ran away." Her doe-like eyes widened with feigned innocence. "You've no idea what those women were expected to do. I couldn't stay there. I was scared I'd be forced to stay and be like them. You read stories like that all the time in dime novels. Those men thought I followed them and shot me before they even realized I was a woman. I think that scared them and they didn't know what to do with me."

Nat nodded, not buying it for a second.

She gazed at him through long lashes. "So? I've answered you. What about my question? Why am I here?"

"I'm not a doctor, but he did see you. You weren't fit to travel too far. This was the first safe place to bring you. "

"Did the doctor say I couldn't travel?"

"Sure."

"When was he last here?"

He leaned forward and slammed her with a determined glare. "Enough. You're still weak, but passed the worst. Tell me the truth. Pearl forced nobody to do anything in her life, and you know you're with Nat Quinn and Jake Conroy. You were on the train we robbed at Hillside Bend. You worked at Pearl's with a different accent and a wig the stable boy found hidden in the straw. Stop playing games and tell me why you were with the Pattersons."

She made sure outrage exploded over her face as she processed this information. "You're Nat Quinn and Jake Conroy?"

He arched a brow. "You know who we are. You stick out in a crowd, you know, especially when you stand up to Jake. Not many have the guts to do that, male or female. Why do we keep bumping into you, and why were you asking questions about us at Pearl's?"

Her mind ran like quicksilver, so she dropped her head and

changed the mask. "I had hoped you wouldn't remember me. I was afraid you might not let me go if you knew I could identify you." Her eyes widened with engineered pathos. "It's been a frightening time, to go from one set of outlaws to another. If you thought I didn't know, or care who you were you might just let me go."

"Why the wig?"

"I've been ill. My hair is bad."

"It looks thick enough to me." He snorted, reaching out and running his long fingers through her endless dark ringlets. "Real thick. It was tough to wash all the muck and vomit out of it. You could stuff a couple of mattresses with it and have enough left over for the pillows. What about the accent? They said you were Irish at Pearl's."

"Lots of people don't know the difference. They must have got confused."

He chuckled. "Oh, you're good. This is gonna be fun."

Nat's cheeks dimpled into a grin as he patted her knee and searched her gaze. "It's your call if you don't want to tell me now. You'll talk. There's nothing but time out here, but one thing's for sure, being with Nat Quinn and Jake Conroy doesn't scare you. In fact, I don't think there's much that does."

He stood and towered over her with folded arms. "Hungry?"

She nodded as she dragged her legs out of the bed, pulling the covers back over them as she realized for the first time she wore nothing but a man's shirt. "Who undressed me?"

He twinkled with mischief. "Does it matter? You were a mess. You'd been in there for two days in a fever, you'd been sick, covered in blood, and left lying in your own waste. You've been washed, and the vomit and God only knows what else cleaned from that *thin* hair of yours. Your clothes were burned. It would have been stupid to do anything else with them."

"It matters to me," the words were tempered by her growing weakness as the daunting prospect of these men tending to her overwhelmed her. Her cheeks burned with indignation but her eyes flashed in naked challenge. "Why didn't you send me to town with the outlaws? There would have been women to care for me, unless—" she glowered at him. "They didn't go to town. Perhaps you killed them?"

His smile warmed. "Nope. We didn't kill them, and when you get to town, you'll find out we left them for the law to find with evidence from the killing. It was important for the authorities to see we weren't responsible for the death and that we made no money from it. We'll have no connection to a hanging offence attached to our names. It's good to see there's a real woman in there though, under all that front."

He turned to walk out of the cabin. "I can spot a player at a thousand paces, and you're one as sure as I stand here. Let me break it down for you. You squashed a potato into me at Webberville. On the train at Hillside Bend you were dressed too expensively to end up working as a maid at Pearl's. You turn up in Valleymount, wandering about in the dark with a shovel—"

She cut him off. "That voice! It was you."

"Damn right it was," he grinned. "I saw you, and if it hadn't been about that idiot with a gun you'd never have seen me either." The smile dropped from his eyes. "Then you lie about why you were following the Pattersons, you have a disguise, and put on an accent. You claim to have run away, but you took nothing with you. A woman poor enough to work as a maid in a brothel wouldn't do that. She'd take what little she had, because that little bundle would be all she had in the world. You might not know many people like that, but I spent my life among them," he pulled the door open a crack. "Then, you pretend not to know who we were. You've got an unhealthy interest in outlaws, Abigail, if that is your name. I'll leave you to use the chamber pot, then we'll make breakfast."

His eyes glittered with danger as he paused and then continued. "We got a lot to find out about you, girl, and I'm going to make sure there's nothing else out there ready to bite us on the backside. But one thing's for sure, you're more than an innocent bystander, and you know something about the men asking questions about us. I'm gonna find out what that is before you go anywhere."

She tilted her head in defiance, accepting she'd been rumbled in her moment of weakness. "I don't like being patronized. I'm not a girl. I'm a *woman*, not a child. And don't you forget it."

He looked her up and down before he fixed with the intense certainty. "I'm not likely to, ma'am. Not while you're wearing nothing but my shirt."

♦ ◊ ♦

The rope squeaked on the spindle as Jake turned the handle, watching the dripping bucket rise from the dank, echoing depths of the well. He reached out and grabbed the wooden pail, poured the contents into his own receptacle, and swung the rope back out over the void.

His nephew clattered down the step of the porch and Jake turned to face him, his bright blue eyes alight with questions and concerns. "So she's fully awake. Did you get anythin'?"

Nat shook his head, the thin winter sun warming his brown hair with a bloom of chestnut. "Nope. She's a clever one. Even though she's still weak, she can twist words like a veteran politician." Nat frowned, his brown eyes meeting his uncle's. "We need to find out what she knows. Smitty was prepared to have innocent bystanders killed just to fit us up for a capital charge and she's in this up to her lying neck."

Jake put his bucket on the ground and ran a distracted hand through his tousled, sandy hair. He stared at his nephew, so like him with the square face set with high cheekbones, but where Jake's pale-brown hair ran to the dirty blond, Nat's tended to be darker and streaked with the red of his Conroy mother. The dark brown eyes and dimples were most definitely from Nat's dark father. All the Conroys were known for their piercing blue eyes back in Ireland. At times like this, Jake wished his folks had never left. Disquiet bubbled deep in Jake's guts. "We ain't kidnappers, Nat. She's gotta go."

"As soon as she's told me everything she knows. She knows who we are, so we'll be accused of kidnap whenever we let her go."

"Not if we do it now. Her fever broke. She couldn't travel," Jake's jaw firmed. "We steal money, not people."

"She's not only working with a man who's prepared to kill to bring us down, she knows what we look like. I need to know more about Smitty," Nat's face darkened with a grim scowl. "I can't have someone that ruthless out there who can identify us when we don't have a clue who he is."

"Dammit! Why don't we just lay low for a while? A year, maybe two?"

"And live on what? We make decent money, but we spend it like water. We wouldn't last more than six months before we had to pull another job. We'd have to plan something like that."

Jake sighed and leaned on the well. "We ain't hurtin' a woman. I know I raised you all wrong, but I still taught you better'n that."

His nephew's eye glittered with indignation. "Of course I'm not going to hurt her. What do you think I am?"

"Since you ask—a lyin', cheatin', thievin', genius. You're better than this. You're a decent man with a lick of larceny and mind like a machine. You're like your pa. He could read anythin' and understand it," Jake cast a hand toward the cabin, "but it doesn't do any harm to remind you there's a helpless woman laid in there. She'll be scared. You can be too clever for your own good, and sometimes, it's better to choose your battles. Why not let her go and watch who she contacts?"

"Why? Because she knows us. We'd be spotted in a second.

Our best hope is to get as much as we can before we let her go.

"I don't know about this –"

"Then leave here and let me deal with her, Jake. I'll get the information I want outta her."

Jake shook his head. "No way, she'll have you wrapped around her little finger in days. I saw the way you looked at her when she mushed that potato into your belly. If I'd done that to your good suit you'd have cracked me on the jaw."

"They got the stain out," Nat grinned, "and you don't have eyes like a baby deer."

"No. I've got a nephew who's as stubborn as an ox, though and I'm used to cuttin' through his crap." Jake folded his arms. "I ain't goin' anywhere. You need protectin' from her as much as she does from you."

Indignation burst over Nat's face. "Hey, I've never hurt a woman in my life," an eyebrow arched in response to his uncle's lips parting to respond. "I mean physically. Sure, I broke a few hearts, but that doesn't count. You've got a track record of your own to be ashamed of."

"Leave Jess outta this. She's the mother of my children and she's moved on. That's my fault. If this woman is mixed up with someone ruthless enough to kill to bring us down, she could be clever enough to manipulate you."

Nat's cheeks dimpled. "Manipulate me? Hell'll freeze over first. This questioning will be like a game of chess. She'll have to work hard to keep up."

"Or maybe it'll be more like her throwin' a stick for a dog? I'm stayin' to make sure everythin's above board," Jake lifted the bucket of water and headed over to the horse trough, "for both of you."

◆◇◆

It took a few more days before she was well enough to get out of bed, but her strength and stamina grew daily. She still feigned weakness and sleep though, avoiding questioning as much as she could. It wasn't a great strategy, but she held onto the hope they'd have to move on. It was becoming clear that would not happen anytime soon.

Most of her time was spent staring around the cabin. She occupied the brass bed while the men slept on bedrolls on the floor. There were shelves filled with supplies and dried goods with a brick chimney breast and open fire facing the door. Two rocking chairs sat either side of the fire. It was very modern, given that an iron range sat against the wall, where most similar habitations still used only the hooks and spits still attached to the open fire. The owner had spent some money on this place.

The table and chairs sat between the bed and the range, and a colorful rag rug covered the hearth. It wasn't exactly homey, but it wasn't completely basic, either

It was breakfast time, and Jake helped her over to the table, supporting her against her unsteady gait as she tied a sheet around herself to protect her modesty. "So you use a nickname?"

He turned in surprise. "My name's Jake Conroy. You know that."

She shook her dark head, her wild curly hair cascading to an untamed jumble of corkscrews to her thighs since its release from restraining grips and clasps. "And that's your real name?"

"Yeah. Everyone calls me Jake."

"Is that what your family calls you? Nobody knows where you two grew up."

His glare was a stiletto of ice. "My family ain't your business, lady."

The abrupt chill in his eyes shocked her. "What's wrong? Did I say something?"

He plunked her on a chair. "You say too much. The sooner

we get you out of here, the better."

"What? What did I do?"

"Leave him be. You keep our family out of this and we'll do for the same for you." Nat put a plate of scrambled eggs in front of her with a clatter and fixed her with a meaningful stare. "Trust me. It's a damned good deal."

She glowered at both of them, unsure what she had done to provoke the blond man. She picked up the tin mug. "Urgh! Who made this coffee? It's horrible."

Nat raised a brow. "What's wrong with it?"

"What's in here?"

"Coffee and water. What do you think?"

"No old socks?"

He glared at her while Jake stopped playing with his food and shoveled a forkful into his mouth with a smirk at his nephew. "I told you, Nat. Your coffee is terrible."

Nat forked at his breakfast. "Don't push it, Abigail, or whoever you are…"

She fixed him with a steady stare. "My name is Abigail. Abi to my friends." She pursed her lips. "You can call me Miss Ross."

"Are you sure it isn't Albert Ross?" quipped Nat. "It sure feels like we've got a burden to carry with you," he stared at the uncomprehending eyes of both table companions and felt forced to explain further. "Albert Ross. Albatross – an albatross around your neck. Get it?"

"Oh, I got it," Abigail responded. "It just wasn't very funny."

Nat rolled his eyes and assessed her, looking for tells and clues in her body language. "I'm not sure about the surname, Abi."

She gave an impatient snort. "When are you going to give me some clothes? I can't keep sitting around half naked."

"We ain't got any women's clothes," Jake snapped. "Just

count yourself lucky we found you at all."

She sighed and ate her eggs, dropping her fork about halfway through. Her pensive dark eyes stared off into nowhere. Nat narrowed his eyes. "What's wrong now? Food not good enough, either?"

"It's fine, thanks. I've had enough."

"Got a name yet?" Nat pushed.

She paused. This couldn't go on. "It's Abigail. Abigail MacKay."

Nat darted a glance at Jake. "Why'd you lie?"

She looked from one to the other, her chest heaving with indecision before she spoke again. "It's time to come clean. I'm a Pinkerton Detective."

Jake bellowed with laughter. "Now you're just bein' stupid!"

Her eyes widened with indignation. "I am?"

"You're a woman."

"You noticed?" she barked.

"Sure did. No doubt that saved you from a barrel load of trouble, if not your life," Jake returned to his eggs.

"Look. My name's Abigail MacKay and I'm a Pinkerton Detective. I was following the fake Innocents to find out where they were hiding." She dropped her head in shame. "I got careless. They moved out before I was ready, and I had to get closer than I wanted. You found me. That's about it."

Nat leaned on the table and fixed her with a mean glower. "You were already out here when they started working this area. You were at Pearl's place. We checked. The Pinkertons are based in Chicago. No Eastern detective would have had time to get involved in the hunt for the fake Innocents that fast."

"I was already here." She narrowed her eyes and held his gaze. "I was sent for you."

Nat wasn't so easily put off. "You were in Valleymount at the same time as us before you worked for Pearl. You were following us?"

"No, I wasn't. I had no idea it was you. If I had I'd have pulled a gun on you, not a spade."

Jake snorted with contempt. "Stupid. Just stupid. A woman detective? How are you supposed to bring us in? You expect us to believe this trash?"

"Yes, because it's true. I went after the fake gang because they were killers. You could wait. It was no accident I was on the train at Hillside Bend. I traveled with payrolls for weeks, but I had to prioritize the worst crime when it presented itself."

"And the men asking questions about us all over the county?"

"I can only guess the regional commander flooded the place to make sure a man got you rather than a woman. He was very unhappy Alan Pinkerton sent me in."

The men exchanged a silent conversation in a glance of derision as they stood and cleared the plates. "There are no female Pinkertons," Nat reached over to take hers.

"You mean, there *weren't*." Her mouth firmed into a line. "There have been female Pinkertons since the war. Women even guarded President Lincoln."

"Yeah, well, that figures. He got shot. She could be right." Jake shook his head. "Lord. What is the world comin' to where that could even be considered?"

"If you are a Pinkerton, why are you telling us this now?" Nat demanded.

"I thought I could lie to you but you weren't buying it. You're holding a law officer against their will and you need to know that. You need to take me to a town. There's nothing else for you to understand or do."

She spoke with great authority and maintained a steady tone against the gaze of two of the most notorious outlaws in the West. Whoever she was, she was gutsy, but the men's skeptical faces betrayed their incredulity.

Nat walked over to the door and darted a glance at his

partner. "Whatever we're doing, we aren't holding you against your will. You're free to leave anytime, but you're not well enough to travel yet; not to mention the fact you haven't got a horse, or clothes, or shoes. We'll take you back when we're all good and ready. In the meantime, we've saved your life and we're keeping you safe and well. You'd do well to remember that, Miss MacKay. Now, do you want help to get back to bed or can you walk?"

The last comment drove home her vulnerability at their hands so she stood in a great show of obstinacy and wobbled her way to the bed, despite having been helped to the table in the first place. A Gaelic curse rang around the room as her legs gave way beneath her.

Jake caught her before one arm wound around her waist.

"Seems like you've bitten off more than you can chew, Miss MacKay. Let's hope you can swallow the consequences."

She looked into the burning blue eyes and gulped down a knot of helplessness as her impotence sank in. Whatever they intended to do with her she was not going anywhere soon, but surely she would be fine? They treated people well and behaved honorably toward women, didn't they? A worm of worry niggled at the back of her mind; those rules applied to the public during robberies and were strategic. What did they do to their enemies when nobody else was around?

Chapter Six

"Out of bed?" Nat appeared at the door, the light highlighting his tawny hair. "Looking for something?"

She paused, guilty eyes dropping along with the hand trailing along the shelf. "Yes. Something to read."

"A book?" his eyes scanned the room, checking to see if anything which could be used as a weapon had gone missing. "You should've said."

"All I can find are a few science books. Whose cabin is this? A doctor's?"

"The owner was a prospector. Those books are mine."

Her brows arched in surprise, and she turned and picked one up. "'Carl Friederich Peschel's Textbook of Physics.'" She continued along the spines. "'Ganot's Elementary Treatise on Experimental And Applied Physics', 'Balfour Stewart, An Elementary Treatise On Heat.'"

"So?" Nat's jaw firmed in challenge. "Have you got anything against a man who wants to improve his mind?"

"Physics? You?"

His brow furrowed. "I'm supposed to believe you're a Pinkerton and you can't believe I'm interested in science? I like to learn all kinds of things. Something wrong with that?"

"But you?" She stared at him incredulously. "You're a common criminal."

His brows met. "Really, Miss MacKay? There's nothing common about me. I'm particular about being about as uncommon a criminal as you'll ever meet. I've got a Dickens if you want something simpler, but no women's stuff. I prefer my heaving bosoms to be tangible."

"Really?"

"Of course. Who wants imaginary bosoms?"

She huffed in exasperation. "Can we forget about the bosoms?"

His dark eyes twinkled with devilment. "I wish I could, but men are kinda made that way."

"Science books?" Abigail changed the subject. "Are you trying to give up crime?"

"Nope, just trying to be more efficient at it. I'm a modern man. You have to move with the times, you know." Nat's cheeks dimpled. "But look who I'm talking to. You're a veritable pioneer for females. You know how it is. I bet you've got all kinds of modern detective tricks. I'm looking forward to seeing those. When do they start? Are you doing it now?"

Abigail sighed. "I'm sorry I asked. Never mind. You have a Dickens? Which one?"

"Charles." Nat's eyes warmed as he relented at her exasperated glare. "Sorry, just having a bit of fun, but you're too tired for it. You're getting bored. I understand. I'll dig out the book for you. Oh, and I found you a brush. It's Jake's, but I've cleaned it real well. I even soaked it in carbolic."

Her eyes lit up surprised by his thoughtfulness, only to be quickly dampened by suspicion. "Thank you. My hair is getting knotted."

He walked in, holding it behind his back. "I'll help. You've got an arm injury and your hair's real tangled." His cheeks dimpled and his beguiling eyes danced with charm to ward off the objections about to tumble from her mouth. "Come on. Let me sort that out for you." She paused and the dimple deepened. "You're not fit to travel yet, but there's no need for us to be enemies. Truce?"

She sighed. "Fine. A truce." She sat, gathering her limited clothing about her. "It is a mess. You won't tug at it, will you?"

"I have brushed hair before. I'm not a savage."

She sat. "Women's hair?"

He pulled over a chair to sit behind her, running his long fingers through the mad dark curls. "Do I look like I go around offering to brush *men's* hair? Jees, your hair is thick."

"Yes, it's like my mother's, but hers is red."

She relaxed, enjoying the pleasurable sensation of his hands in her tresses, loosening the strands and identifying knots and tangles before working on them. "You were a mess when we found you." He finished attending to an obstinate knot. "There."

He ran the brush through her hair from root to tip marveling at the length as the ringlets unraveled and stretched. "Beautiful, just beautiful. As long as you are tall."

She sat, luxuriating in the hypnotic strokes and the gentle caress of the brush as it traveled through her hair over and over again, reminding her of her childhood, and how much she missed her late husband's soothing, sensual touch. Her heart broke yet again, just as it had a million times before. She was used to piecing it back together. Nobody touched her anymore. Nobody cherished her. Nobody cared.

Nat worked through the shock of hair with a soothing, reviving pressure. Somehow, his relaxing light-hearted chatter made this abnormal situation seem less stressful. She dropped her guard and allowed herself to unwind, settling into a luscious melting frame of mind, sinking further and further into indolent compliance.

The long fingers swept her neck with a feather-like touch as he gathered her hair and her lips parted at the exhilaration which rushed through her. Did he know the nape was one of her most sensitive areas?

She arched against the deep strokes of the brush and the delicate touch across her neck and shoulders. Stresses and strains melted away, and she lived in the delicious, delectable moment. The growing warmth deep below reminded her of her forgotten primal need for intimacy, growing until she suppressed the growing moan.

"There, that should do it," he murmured in her ear as though under the same yielding spell of surrender. He pulled his chair alongside hers and brushed a few wisps from her face.

"You are exquisite." Crooked fingers pulled her around to face him with a gentle tug. He leaned in, touching her lips with his own, a velvet caress which released an exhilarating rush. The hand slipped into her newly-brushed hair, gathering a handful in a gesture which promised power but delivered tender restraint. His teeth caught on her lip, tasting her, before pushing on into a full hungry kiss.

He pulled back, looking into her eyes. "This is so difficult. I don't even know who you really are. You might have a husband or lover."

"I told you who I am."

"No lovers? No men?"

Her eyes narrowed and she shook herself back to reality. "What was I thinking? This is just another ploy isn't it? You worm your way in and try to seduce information from me when I'm at my weakest?"

"I'd never—"

"No?" she snorted. "You don't want to know about me, just men I'm connected to?" She stood. "Well, I'll tell you once more. I am a Pinkerton Detective, and the only man I'm connected to is Alan Pinkerton. You can question me as much as you want. It's all you're going to get. Sooner or later, you'll have to accept it and let me go."

"I wasn't—"

"Oh, save it. You were dismissive earlier, now this?"

Her eyes widened as they fell on the brush on the table behind him. "Is that a horse brush? You used an animal brush on me."

He fought the smile tugging at his lips. "I washed it."

"A horse brush! You were so desperate to soften me up with this tactic you used a horse brush? You're unbelievable." She scratched at her scalp like a mad thing. "I've probably got fleas."

"Hey! We look after our horses."

"Look after?" Nat ran for the door as she grabbed the brush. "I'll show you *looked after*."

Jake sat on the porch, his eyes lighting with amusement as the door opened. His nephew ran out. Nat turned, pointing a finger and opened his mouth to say something in the face of the tirade of impenetrable gibberish filling the air behind him. He ducked. A missile flew, right where his head had just been, and the brush clattered to the ground.

Nat squared his shoulders, his voice hardening. "That's enough. Put that down—" His eyes widened and he slammed the door, just in time for Jake to hear the metallic clatter of something against the other side.

"So, your seduction technique didn't work, huh?" Jake swung back on his chair. "It's good to know her throwin' arm's good and healthy, though."

"What the hell language is that?"

Jake shrugged. "She's Scottish, so it's probably Gaelic. It ain't quite the same as the Irish my grandpa taught me, but I think she just doubted your parentage."

Nat propped his hands on his hips and scowled. "She insulted my mother?"

Jake's smile stretched into a full grin. "Your ma was my

sister. If anyone had used an animal brush on her hair you'd have heard all about it. I think you got off real light."

"So what now?"

Jake shook his head. "Keep me out of it. You're the criminal genius. I'm only the muscle. You'll just have to try somethin' else."

She slept off and on for the next two days, and her strength continued to rally as her arm healed under a regime of salt and honey, but she still had nothing to wear other than a shirt and a bed sheet. Her anger grew, seeing through their deliberate tactic to keep her off balance and increase her reliance on them. So much for not holding her against her will. How could a woman set off through the wilderness barefoot and half naked?

Nat had questioned her intently on her identity, who she knew in the agency, the information she had on them, and who had sent her; but Abigail refused to tell him anything, confirming only that they could contact the Chicago office to confirm her identity. He was getting as frustrated with her as she was with them. He had tried all kinds of techniques ranging from sympathy, anger, and bribery, until today when he walked in and sat on the side of her bed. His brown hair was neat and brushed and his just-shaven skin looked smooth, pink, and temptingly touchable. He dropped his head, his open-necked shirt providing a glimpse of the strong, thick musculature reaching into his square shoulders.

She averted her eyes, only to find herself staring at his fine hands and delicate, long fingers. Those talented fingers which were so sensitive they could feel every click of a tumbler as he cracked a safe. She sighed and turned away.

He smiled, his face etched with resignation. "This can't go on, Abi."

"I'm glad you've realized that, too."

He paused. "You're a very beautiful woman. This isn't easy for me. I noticed you as soon as you bumped into me at the station. I remembered you."

She raised her guard at the first sign of a compliment. "You noticed a hot potato pressed into your belly."

Pique fluttered in his eyes. "Well, if you hadn't been in such a rush, I'd have had the chance to talk to you, perhaps even get to know you in normal circumstances."

"Normal? You held up a train. You were probably at the station checking out those carrying payrolls."

The puppy-dog eyes feigned even more innocence. "Maybe if I knew someone got a really good look at me I wouldn't have?"

"I'm not an eejit. What makes you think I'd have talked to you anyway?"

He arched a brow. "The way you were looking at me, for a start."

"I look at everyone. It's my job."

He narrowed his eyes gleaming with mischief. "I saw you. You looked away in embarrassment. We had a moment. You know we did."

"And now we've had a week. When does it end, Mr. Quinn?" Her brow furrowed. "Let's just go our separate ways, huh? Your manipulation isn't working. I'm immune."

"Tell me what I want to know and it'll happen right away." He reached out and grasped her hand. "I promise."

She caught her breath at the electric jolt of his touch and pulled her hand away. "I've told you everything I'm going to. Everything I have. There's nothing else to add."

"There's more. We both know it." He leaned forward, his hot breath hitting her face. "Please, we both know there's a man behind this. I just want to know who sent men to kill innocent people so they could give me a death sentence. He needs to be exposed."

"If he exists at all?" Her jaw firmed. "Mr. Quinn, has it occurred to you this gang was just a coincidence and that it popped up independently of a Pinkerton operation to bring you in?"

"I don't believe in coincidences any more than I believe in female Pinkertons," his brow furrowed. "I'm trying to protect you. I need the name of the man who put you up to this. It had to be someone pretty special to have you wear disguises and mix with men like the Pattersons." He grabbed her hand again. "Work with me, Abi." She pulled her hand back, but he held firm this time, staring straight into her eyes. "Come on, talk to me. Please. I can't keep Jake from questioning you forever."

She stiffened. "Jake?"

"Yes. I really am trying to protect you. Just tell me what I want to know and it'll all be over. He deals with anything which affects the security of the gang. If you were a man he'd have dealt with you long before now."

"I work for Alan Pinkerton," she repeated, tugging her hand free. "There's a Denver office, too, but I don't report to them. Send them a telegram. They'll confirm who I am."

His brows gathered. "So he's a Pinkerton? You've got that covered and he'll answer for you? He wouldn't be the first corrupt lawman." He paused deep in thought. "I understand he'll have told you all kinds of things about us, but we aren't savages and we treat people well. These people have been prepared to kill innocent bystanders. We never do that. We've treated you with kindness, haven't we?"

"Until now." She glowered, "Horse brush excepted."

"So help me to help you. The railroads and the banks have put an incredible reward out on us. I'm guessing it's not working fast enough for someone and they set up the

Pattersons to dirty our name. They told me he was called Smitty. Please, Abi. What's his name? Who is he?"

"Alan Pinkerton."

His mouth formed into an irritated line. "Fine. Have it your way. I've tried my best." He stood and strode over to the door. "I'll go tell Jake."

"What do you want me to do? Lie to you with an invented name? I've never heard of Smitty."

"We've had enough false names from you, thank you very much." He closed the door firmly behind him and strode over to his uncle on the porch who raised questioning blue eyes.

Jake swung back on his chair. "Anything?"

"Nope," he shook his head. "She's as obstinate as a temperance spinster at a barn dance."

Jake arched his brows in question. "So? What now?"

"I guess we're gonna have to scare her a bit."

The older man's eyes widened with disapproval. "Nat—"

"I know," Nat rubbed his face with his hands. "I don't like it, either. I kinda like her, you know. She's different. She's smart and dumb all at the same time."

"Yeah. She's just your type. What other woman would be in this mess?"

"She's loyal is all, probably in love with that damned Smitty. We need that name, though. Whoever it is'll set us up again if they're desperate."

Jake nodded. "So who deals with her? Who gets it out of her?"

"I told her you would." Nat's innocent smile only peeved his uncle more. "What? You're the scary one. I'm charming. Everyone knows that. It's in all the dime novels."

"Nat, someday I'm gonna swing for you. We just let her go and walk away. Fast."

"No. We need that name. Someone's framing us for a

hanging." Nat took out a coin. "I'll toss you for it."

Jake dropped the two front legs of the chair back on the floor. "With you? You're as crooked as a snake with colic. You always make sure you win a coin toss by switching it for your double-headed nickel." He ignored Nat's faux innocence. "And *yeah*. I know about that. Fine, I'll do it. You're gettin' nowhere anyway, but I ain't hurtin' her, and we'll leave her to dwell on what might happen first. If it doesn't work, she goes. Got that?"

The impasse needed to be broken and the time had come for her to take control of the situation as the gunman's blue eyes were chilling her to the bone.

His powerful and menacing presence simmered in the background, while their tolerance for her wore thin. It was only a matter of time before they turned over her questioning to him, and that had to be avoided at all costs. There was something frightening and unpredictable about the gunfighter who looked at her as though he hated every fibre of her being.

"I'm gettin' supplies." Jake pulled on his gloves. "Need anything?"

"Clothes. Any kind of clothes." He stared right through her with eyes like a Mediterranean storm. "I'm goin' for *food*. I know nothin' about women's clothes."

"Men's, then; working clothes, trousers, anything. You can't keep me like this."

He darted a glance at Nat, a discreet smile playing around his lips. "You're fine. We can't see a thing improper. The sheet is long and you have a long-sleeved shirt on. You're almost a nun."

She let out an impatient huff. "When are you planning on letting me go? You must see by now I've have got nothing else to tell you."

Dark eyes glittered at her from across the cabin. "When you're fit to travel, Miss MacKay. We don't want to harm you by setting out too soon."

"I'm fine now. Stop this masquerade and take me back, right now. I'll go with him, dressed like this, if I have to."

"You ain't ready." Her stomach lurched at the rawness in the blue eyes. "We agreed I make that call. When I get back, we'll have a chat, just you and me. I'll do whatever it takes to find out what I need to know. Nat's been far too soft on you."

Both men registered the brief flicker of fear before she pulled herself back together. "It'll be no different."

"That's for me to find out, ain't it, Abi? It's up to you to decide if we do it the hard way or the easy way." The gunman strode over to the door. "I'll see you when I get back."

Jake's words still rang in her ears when Nat left the building to tend the animals, so she had to move fast. She rummaged around until she found a pair of navy suit trousers. They were huge, but the gray ones were broader and would have been even worse. She slid them on and fastened them with a rope around the waist, and folded the ends back multiple times.

Shoes were pointless. She would have to go without as there was nothing even close. Why would they burn her shoes? Did they ever intend to let her go?

She stood behind the door with a huge earthenware jug in her hand, her heart pumping so hard she felt sure it could be heard as far as the barn. No way was she going to let a man like Jake Conroy interrogate her.

After what seemed like an eternity, the door creaked open. She raised the jug, the handle feeling warm and slippery in her nervous, sweating palm as the adrenaline pulsed through her system.

She brought it straight down on Nat's head just as he appeared through the door. Her hand slipped, as her injured arm let her down, and it bounced off the door decreasing the impact on her victim, but the cry and the trickle of red confirmed she had made her mark. He dropped to his knees, clutching his head.

She bolted out the door. A quick reconnaissance had her heading toward the barn, where she grabbed a saddle and threw it on the horse which nickered and flicked his ears at her as though he wondered what all the fuss was about.

Without warning, she felt herself grabbed around the waist and lifted off her feet. "Goin' somewhere?"

She twisted around and stared into a pair of angry face of the gunman. "Jake?"

"Thought I'd gone? Thought wrong, huh?"

Her heart sank. There was no point in trying to defend herself against this furious man. One look at his partner would confirm her actions, and he was dragging her back to the cabin to face the consequences. Jake swung her inside, where Nat sat clutching his head with a trickle of blood spreading its way down his pale face as his bleary eyes darted up to greet their entrance.

"Look what I found."

Abigail glanced at the enraged face before she swirled round in surprise at the other voice behind her.

"Howdy, boys. What's the hellion done now? Has she hurt you, Nat?" It was Pearl, and she showed no surprise about her being here.

Nat groaned as he stumbled from inside the cabin to the porch and glared at Abigail. A trail of blood etched its escape from his injured scalp across his temple and his hands formed into fists. The mask of charm slipped and she stared into the cold, hard eyes of one of the most intimidating men she had ever encountered.

He had hidden this side of himself behind the twinkling eyes and dimpled smile full of positivity, but she should have known better. How could anyone control a gang of outlaws without a hard core? She had walked straight into this thinking she had escaped a confrontation with Jake. She would now give anything to face him rather than the cold fury of the man who now glared at her with revenge on his mind. Nat appeared to grow in stature, his whole demeanor changing before her eyes.

"What the hell do you think you're playing at?" Nat growled.

Abigail's stomach turned over and her accent strengthened. She lapsed into the unguarded Gaelic syntax of her mother tongue; a sign of stress not lost on Nat as she stuttered and stammered her reply. "You weren't letting me go—what did you expect at all?"

"What do I expect you to do? I expect you to do as you're told, woman!"

Abigail released the breath she hadn't realized she'd been holding before she shouted back. "For how long? You can't keep me here. I swear. I'll keep trying. Either let me go or kill me."

"Don't tempt me," muttered Jake.

She swung around. "The law coming after you is an occupational hazard, just as fighting back is for me. We all know the deal. This—" she gestured around the cabin to the bed sheets discarded on the floor, "whatever it is; is not the way, and you know it."

Nat ignored her and strolled passed her with a stony face. He strode down the porch steps and stopped at the horse trough, dipping his head in the water before throwing it back, scattering a halo of drips everywhere as he washed the fog from his mind.

"Why'd you come back?" he asked Jake.

"I bumped into Pearl. She needs help. Two girls have gone missing from her place."

"They've been with me years, Nat. Real good girls, rode out and never came back. They'd never do that. They left everything, money, clothes; the lot. The sheriff ain't interested. He says workin' girls go missing all the time. Something's happened to them, and I have to find out what. I have to help them."

He nodded as he rubbed his concerned face. "Where'd they go?"

"Bessie's pa died and she went for a physic reading out at the Schmidt's place. The girl there does them. That's the last anyone saw of them. No sign of the horses, the wagon, nothin'. Two women in summer dresses don't just take off cross country, Nat. They ain't dressed for it."

"Schmidts?" He turned toward Abigail and fixed her with a chilling glare. "Jake, tie her up. I ain't finished with her yet. Pearl, come with me. We need to talk."

The room had an atmosphere of heightened anxiety and Pearl's alabaster skin had touches of pink fighting through the heavy powder, the nearest she ever got to being flushed. Her long-time employees felt a loyalty and indebtedness to her, knowing the alternatives were a big step down.

Both men knew neither of the girls would have run off. There was nowhere for them to go but down, and Jake and Nat had genuine concerned for their welfare.

"Dora and Bessie have gone missing."

Nat flashed a glance at Jake. "Dora? The blonde one? You liked her didn't you, Jake? She's a young widow."

"Sure is. Lost her husband at twenty-three. She's got a young boy to support. She wouldn't just leave him, Nat. He's her whole world."

Nat sat. "Tell me what you know, Pearl. Of course, the sheriff isn't interested in anything other than collecting bribes or rewards. What do you think happened?"

"It's bad, I just know it is. They'd have told me if they were leaving. Bessie's been with me for years, and Dora's a real sweet girl."

"Where is this place?" Jake demanded.

"About ten miles out east, on the way to Twin Rivers."

Nat sat at the table with pensive eyes drinking everything in. "Who are these people? What do they do there? The name sounds similar to one who's been bothering me recently."

"They're German farmers, they've lived around here nigh on fifteen years or so. Ma and Pa hardly speak any English, but they take in boarders, usually people who can't get to town before sundown 'cause it's just too far. The place is pretty basic. Their son, Kurt, is a bit simple but friendly enough, the daughter, Anna, is real sweet. She's early twenties and does séances."

"Do you want me to ride out and search for them?"

"I can't ask you to do that, Jake. It's a long way past town. You wouldn't get there until nightfall."

Jake folded his arms. "I'm going, Pearl. Is there anything else? Has anyone been leanin' on you?"

"No, the mayor leaves me alone. When the boys can't afford the high end of the market, they end up in his places, so he's happy enough. You want any of my boys to ride with you?"

Jake shook his head. "No, Pearl. I'll work alone. I'll leave now."

Nat's eyes filled with regret. "I'm real sorry, Pearl. We'd both go, but we got *her* to look after."

He tilted his head toward the barn where Abigail had been left bound hand and foot by Jake. Pearl wrinkled her brows in query, more questioning than concerned. "What's goin' on, here? I ain't never seen you boys do anythin' like this."

"We ain't never seen anythin' like this either, Pearl," snorted Jake. "She claims to be a Pinkerton. Have you ever heard the like? But we need to know who she's really involved with; the real name of the man settin' us up."

"There are men all over the county contacting people connected to us to ask them questions," Nat added. "Some of them are direct, others more sneaky. There's something going on, and she knows about it. I'll put money on her knowing that Smitty who paid the gang to pose as us."

"Won't talk, huh?"

"Nope. As soon as she does, she's outta here."

A grin spread over her face. "What you gonna do if she don't talk?"

Jake ran a hand through his tousled hair and shook his head. "I don't know, Pearl. Just let her go, after givin' her a fright about gettin' involved with outlaws. I've got a theory it's a lover of hers who's put her up to this. She seems well-educated and almost as smart as Nat, but when it comes to choosin' men she's as dumb as a box of hair."

"What if she's tellin' the truth?"

Nat hooked her with a questioning glint. "You can't believe she's a Pinkerton. A woman?"

"Why not? Some of the most successful spies durin' the war were women. We're gettin' everywhere now—pharmacists, doctors, nurses—especially in the West where the rules are more 'flexible', shall we say? Folks are just grateful to have someone around with a bit of learnin'. She could be tellin' the truth."

The men exchanged a look before they dismissed the idea.

"Nah. She's got a boyfriend, and he's more interested in us than what's healthy," retorted Jake.

"Maybe her boyfriend is a Pinkerton?" Pearl suggested.

"That's more likely," Nat agreed, "and that's the type of information I need to get out of her. She says if we contact the agency they'll confirm who she is, but all it tells me is she has a plant at the other end. A corrupt lawman working with someone who'll let innocent people get murdered to bring us in."

"One question, boys. If she were in on it with the Pattersons, why was she locked away and left to die? It isn't somethin' you do to your own side."

Nat nodded. "I've thought about that. It could be they had her to make sure Smitty paid? There are only two options as far as I can see. She either has deep links to the man who set us up, or she is who she says she is."

Jake strode over to the table and picked up his hat. "I'll get it outta her when I get back. She's scared of me. I can see it in her eyes. She's gutsy, but it's there, and that's how we'll crack her. You saw the state of her when we brought her here, Pearl. You even cleaned her. What a mess. She couldn't travel before now anyway, so we went gentle."

"It seems like she changed the rules. Gentle's over." Nat's feral eyes glittered across the table at Pearl as he held a cold compress to his scalp. "We'll get rid of her soon, but I want to know everything she does first."

Jake rode out into the gathering dusk. He covered the ground right up to the Schmidt's place with no sign of the wagon the girls had ridden out in. His search of the Schmidt's outbuildings was the best he could manage in the bad light. He could find no sign of the women or their transport.

Peeking in through the window, he saw the family sitting round a large table in a meager, unkempt shelter. Ma, Pa, a lad with a deformed mouth, and pretty redhead were gathered around the table deep in conversation, but there was still no sign of the women. It was time to ask some questions.

He hammered on the door, habit ensuring he didn't stand in front of it, but off to the side.

He heard a clamor of unintelligible voices inside before a male voice called out. "Ja?"

"Sir, I've come from Bannen. Two ladies came here today. They didn't come home. Open the door."

He heard scrabbling and more talking before the door opened a crack and a grizzled face appeared.

"Sir, I'm coming in. I need to speak to you about the women."

The door opened, throwing a trapezoid of light on to the ground. "My folks don't speak much English, sir. Can I help you? My name is Anna Schmidt."

Jake examined at the petite girl. She was pretty and well-dressed, but that in itself seemed alien in the disarray and clutter of the squalid cabin. The room was large but was divided into two by a large stained curtain which hung behind the table. Her family gathered behind her, an eclectic mix of incongruous shapes and sizes.

"Ma'am, Pearl Dubois sent me. Two ladies came here for a reading today. Nobody's seen them since."

"Yes. They left hours ago. Mister—?"

"Black. How long ago?"

He paused while Anna explained his questions to her folks in German and listened to the answers.

"About two o'clock I think." Anna paused. "This is terrible. Those poor people. What do you think has happened to them?"

"That's what I'm hoping to find out, ma'am. You folks mind if I have a look around?"

Without waiting for them to agree he walked to the back of

the room and swept back the large sheet acting as a divider. He peeped behind it but could see nothing but a few hammers, saws and other tools leaned against the wall.

"Any other rooms?"

The old man and woman garbled something to the girl. "Yes, upstairs. Mama apologizes for the mess. We weren't expecting anyone."

Jake followed the old man up the rickety wooden stairs and walked through each of the three shabby rooms in turn. He glanced at the girl, wondering where she fitted in the hovel he saw unfolding before him.

"Someone told me you take in boarders. Where do you put them?"

"They have Kurt's room. He'll either sleep in the barn or in front of the stove, if it's winter. Would you like to stay Mr. Black? It's getting late to ride back to town."

He scanned the bleak cabin, thinking most of the hideouts he had used were more homey.

"No, thanks, ma'am. I'll get back to town. I think Miss Dubois will be worried. She'll want to know if I've found anything. If you don't mind, I'll take a look around the barns before I go. Do you have a light I can borrow?"

He stopped about a mile away and left the road, taking his horse behind the trees. Creeping back he lay on the ground near the road and waited. It took about fifteen minutes before Jake could hear the clear rattle of the bridle and the blowing from his stalker's mount. The silvered light from the moon was bright enough for him to see the face of the German boy with the twisted mouth as he passed by on the road to Bannen.

Was he following him, or was it just a coincidence?

Chapter Seven

Abigail twisted around in the straw at the sound of the barn door opening. Nat Quinn stood over her, his stony face betraying his dark mood. She felt the rope around her ankles being sliced through before he leaned over and grabbed her good arm to drag her to her feet.

"What is it with you men locking women in barns?" It was a half-hearted attempt at lightness, but the hostility in his silent glare made her regret it in an instant.

He pulled her out into open air and marched her across to the cabin, as she stumbled and protested all the way. "Slow down. My legs aren't as long as yours. There are stones. I don't have any shoes on." She missed her footing on the porch steps, stubbing a toe. "Ow!"

He yanked her through the door and pushed her into a chair, taking a seat across the table. Abigail's heart pounded in her chest as she twisted her still bound hands behind her back. The mood had turned very dark, indeed.

"I guess things have changed. We're quite clearly keeping you here against your will, now." He leaned back on his chair, swinging on the two back legs as he watched her bite her bottom lip. "We'd all better put our cards on the table if we want you out of here."

"That would be nice." She shrugged her unkempt hair from her face as a corkscrew curl covered in straw kept tumbling in front of her right eye.

"Tell me the truth, and no more games. I'm losing patience

with you. Why were you following the Pattersons? Who do you know and what were you told to find out?"

"I've told you until I'm blue in the face. I was investigating them, just as I was investigating you. I work for Alan Pinkerton."

He stood and walked over to her, holding eye contact all the way before he leaned over and placed his face inches from hers. "Are you still gonna keep that up?"

"It's the truth."

"Who is he?"

She jumped as he yelled straight into her face, his hot breath burning into her cheek.

She garnered her fire and yelled right back. *"Who?"*

"The man behind this. What does he want with us? What did he send you to find out?"

"Alan Pinkerton. He wants you in jail." She turned to face him as she barked her reply, "And so do I."

"Be very careful, Abigail. My whole life hangs in the balance if I'm caught, not to mention my uncle's. I'm not above doing what it takes to avoid that. This is not a game."

"Your uncle?" Her brow crinkled. "Jake Conroy is your uncle? That makes sense, family loyalty, I suppose. Lot of criminal gangs consist of extended families. I could see he was older, but he didn't seem old enough to be your uncle."

"You didn't know?"

She shook her head. "Why would I? I've read your criminal records, Mr. Quinn, and you were not always so loyal. You two split for a few years, didn't you? Why was that?"

"I'll ask the questions here."

"You'll get the same answers you've already been given."

"What's the name of the man who sent you here? Who is Smitty?"

"Alan Pinkerton sent me. I'd never heard of Smitty until you brought him up." She stared straight ahead. "You can ask the

Chicago office and they will confirm I'm employed there. That is all I'm prepared to tell you."

"What's Smitty's real name?"

"I don't know."

He paused, deep in thought. "What if I play your game and accept you're a Pinkerton? What's the name of the man you report to and where is he staying?"

"I work alone. I report to Alan Pinkerton, but Archibald Robertson at the Denver office is aware of where I am."

"You expect me to believe they'll send a woman into Bannen without a man to back her up? Do you think I'm stupid? Who is he?"

"I've told you the truth."

"One last chance, Abigail. I need the names and whereabouts of the men you are giving information to and who's your informer."

She huffed and rolled her eyes.

"So, you want to pretend you're a Pinkerton? *As a female?*" His eyes darkened. "I've questioned one before, although he didn't know who I was. They're trained real well on being both sides of interrogations. You don't want to do this. Not as a woman. He had a real hard time. You'll have it even harder."

She sat staring ahead once more, her face impassive and stony.

"You've nothing to say?"

Her eyes flashed. "Beating the hell out of me won't change anything but my view of you."

Nat reached out and entwined a hard fist in her hair and dragged her backward until the chair balanced on the back legs. He brought his face close to hers, his hot breath burning into her cheek. "Think harder, lady. This isn't a game. Who are you?"

Abigail felt the dragging pain at the back of her head as shards of pain lanced across her scalp. He held her, balanced between his painful grip and a clattering fall to the floor but her stubborn nature wouldn't let her acquiesce.

"Others will come after you, no matter what you do to me." She darted her eyes to meet his, unable to move her pinioned head. "I won't be the last."

"More pretend Pinkertons? As long as they look as good as you I'm fine with that, honey." His eyes dark glittered. "But maybe you've got another motive?"

"Such as what?"

Intense brown eyes seared into hers. "Perhaps you like outlaws. Some women are attracted to dangerous men," he continued, whispering in her ear as he nibbled on her ear lobe. "Is this dangerous enough for you, or do you like pain? I can arrange it, real soon."

She writhed in the chair, unable to turn away. Her breath came in great gulps of panic. "Let me go. Right now!"

He was quick to identify the uncertainty in her voice. This was new, and he was getting to her in a way straight physical intimidation hadn't. "Then talk, sweetheart. Tell me what I want to know, or I'll take you right now on that table and keep using you until you do."

She bucked, trying to kick out at him before he let go of her hair and she rattled to the floor, jarring her elbow on the wooden planks. She shuffled backward, kicking out at him as he strode over her.

"Talk!"

"Go to hell."

He picked her up, holding her by her underarms as she screamed and raged in a language he didn't understand. "Finally, we're getting somewhere. Tell me what I want to know and it'll all stop, Abi."

Her bound hands formed impotent claws behind her back as she jerked herself away, but he was too strong. His free hand roamed across her full mouth, caressing her fragile jaw before settling on her throat in a gesture of complete domination. Their eyes burned into one another as he searched her face for surrender.

"Names, Abi. I want names."

"I have nothing to tell you. I work for Alan Pinkerton. That's it." He felt her angry sob vibrate through the fingers on her throat. "Please. Don't do this. It won't get you anything."

He watched the angry tear run from the eyes, almost ebony in the poor light. She had given up; she had reached the bottom. He had found the weakness he had been searching for and shame kicked him straight in the guts at her final words on the subject.

"You bastard! It'll just prove everyone who ever loved you was wrong."

His eyes softened and a warm, caring smile of reassurance spread over his face. He nodded. "Yes. It would."

He pulled her upright and left her standing, head bowed. The fallen seat was righted, but as he put out a hand to lead her forward she kicked and screamed like a wild animal, recoiling from his touch. Nat put his arms around her in a tight embrace as he felt her tremble against him.

"Hey, hey! It's fine. I'm not gonna do anything to you. I never would. It was a test. It was only to scare the truth out of you." He felt her stiffen in disbelief as he continued to hold her, rocking her from side to side as he whispered in her ear. "I'm not that kind of man. I needed to find your weak spot to get the truth out of you. I did that. I got you to the place where I'd get as much from you as you'd ever give. Nobody is gonna hurt you. It's over."

He pulled back to look into the confused face, refusing to believe his assurances. Doubt and fear crowded her expressive eyes, which widened as he pulled out the knife from his belt.

He sliced through the rope binding her hands, and led her to a seat before backing off, his hands raised in surrender until he stood in front of the range. He dropped his head and folded his arms as he allowed her to collect her rasping breath and shattered nerves. She crouched over and nursed her injured arm, staring off into the corner, the floor, or her feet; staring at anything but him.

A wave of guilt washed over him. He was better than this, but he was fighting for his life. He had to be sure, but now that he was, he would make it up to her. "I'm sorry. I really am. I had to get the truth."

Accusing eyes darted over to him. "By threatening to rape me?"

"By doing what it took to strip away your front." He frowned. "Don't look at me like that. You're a professional, and so am I. We both understand this life risks everything." He raised his hands in appeasement once more. "And it doesn't mean I'll *take* everything. I just had to see what you'd give me when pushed to your limits. I know the answer now. If you were just a random woman, you'd have told me everything far earlier. I believe you. You work for Pinkerton and you're loyal to your colleagues. What you do there remains to be seen."

Her slim brows met in a scowl. "I am a detective, and a damn good one."

"Yes. You probably are. I'm a thief, and a damn good one. I'm sorry, but I had to find out who's searching for us. At least I know they're Pinkertons. That's a lot better than rival criminals. At least, they play by a few rules."

His soft smile made his face look as gentle as a puppy. "How about a drop of bourbon? You look like you need a pick-me-up."

She eyed him with suspicion. "Are you trying to get me drunk?"

He flicked up an eyebrow. "I thought we just established I don't need to." He put down two shot glasses and poured out some amber liquid.

Her stomach fluttered with nerves as she picked up the glass with a trembling hand. "So? What the hell was that all about?"

Nat stood opposite and sipped his drink. "I've never seen a prettier lawman, that's for sure."

She scowled and backhanded away tears. "I'm not a lawman. I'm an agent. If anything, I'm a law woman."

"Yup, and I didn't believe you until I saw how desperate you were. You had nowhere to go. You were scared to death, and I was starting to think I'd never see that." He raised his glass to her. "You're a brave woman, Miss MacKay. More than a bit foolhardy, but gutsy as hell. If you'd been a man, it'd have been easier. We could hardly call you out for a beating. What could we do with you? If it's any consolation, you're more loyal than any man I ever questioned."

She gulped as she felt her thumping heart subside at last. "So? What now? I'm still your prisoner and I have been from the start, no matter how much you want to dress it up as recuperation. Just what do you intend to do with me?"

He stared into her deep brown eyes, his voice tinged with regret. "I'm gonna let you go." He shrugged. "I have to. I'd like to know you better though…you're really quite remarkable. In all my born days I've never met another woman quite like you."

"Jake said he had the final say on that."

"Yeah, he does a good scary stare, but that's as far as it goes with him and the ladies. He's a pushover when it comes to women, so I had to yank something else out of the bag." He pulled out a chair for himself and beamed his most charming smile at her. "You're not in a hurry are you? You wanted to get to know more about us, why not stick around for a bit? I never met a law *woman* before." He arched a mischievous eyebrow. "You could try to reform us?"

She glowered at him. "I'm not ready to be flirted with, not after the little display you just showed me, Mr. Quinn."

Shame chastened Nat's face, the dimple dropping from his

cheek. "I'm sorry. I don't like frightening people, but it was the only way. It was me or Jake, and he'd never do anything like that to a woman. I guess you'd got a bit desperate. It was my last effort," he leaned over the table, "but we both know the dangers." He rubbed his wounded head as he gazed at her, driving home his point, none too subtly.

"I'm sorry I hurt you, but I thought things would get tough. I felt that I had to get away as fast as I could."

"Well, as it's only a matter of time now, how about a truce? Let's get to know one another like equals. One professional to another?"

She flashed a glare at him. "I still intend to bring you in, and I'm very good at what I do." She grimaced at the irony of her own words and rolled her eyes. "Generally, anyway. This has been a complete disaster, though."

"And I intend to do what I can to stop you. We could call this neutral territory." He grinned. "We all have off days, there's no need to be embarrassed. In our line of work when it goes bad it does tend to snowball real fast."

"A truce?" she shrugged. "What does that mean to me?"

"It means we're pleasant to one another and you stop smashing pottery on me. You realize you're useless now as far as we're concerned? We know you. You can't get near us without us knowing why."

Abigail glanced at the floor. "I guess they'll send someone else."

His eyes narrowed, sensing duplicity. "Yeah. I guess that accounts for all the men asking questions about us—I hope."

The men sat at the table the next morning, a tired Jake stretching out after his journey back. "I couldn't find a thing. It's like they disappeared off the face of the earth. I told her to keep her girls in town and use any influence she has to raise a stink. She'll definitely have politicians and business men as clients, so that might help. The sheriff ain't interested."

"'Cause there's no money in it, no reward. I've got no time for dishonest lawmen. At least when we're dishonest, we're honest about it," muttered Nat. "Only the worst have ethics for sale." He shot a glance at Abigail, whose face lit up in anger.

"Neither are mine. Don't look at me like that."

Jake shook his head and nodded toward Abigail. "How sure are you she's tellin' the truth?"

"I'm sure. Absolutely sure."

"Then I guess that's good enough for me, but women in the law? How they goin' to deal with the likes of me? It's loco."

"You don't need physical strength to pull a trigger, Mr. Conroy. Nor does it take muscles to be fast."

"True. Strength helps though. I'm more than just fast and accurate," he turned to Nat. "When are we lettin' her go?"

Nat sat back and smiled as he gazed off at nothing in particular with his hands behind his head. "We need to get her clothes first. I should've gotten you to get some from Pearl. She's not going anywhere with my trousers. It'll ruin the suit."

"They look a lot better on her than they ever did on you," Jake sat back. "What did you do to get her to talk?"

Abigail blushed scarlet as Nat glinted with devilment at her embarrassment. "Let's just say I made advances."

The blue eyes narrowed, reading the subtext. "I guess it was effective." He gave her a lopsided smile and tried to lighten her caustic scowl.

She shrugged. "It's over. We're still on different sides, but at least we all know where we stand."

"Yeah, I guess we do." He glowered at his nephew. "I hope he didn't frighten you too much."

"He did, but I'm not going to dwell on it. It's something we train for, and I don't frighten easily or I wouldn't be doing this job. He did less than the men who trained me. I didn't expect him to stop so suddenly. I thought he was playing emotional games, then I realized he meant it. You have a very confounding nephew, Mr. Conroy."

"Tell me about it," Jake sighed. "I'll ride out tomorrow and get you some clothes. We'll drop you two miles from town to give us time to get away."

"Thank you, Mr. Conroy."

"It's no problem. I want to leave money for Dora's son before we go. He's only eight and his ma's disappeared. It's a terrible thing. The poor boy has nobody."

Abigail gasped. "She had a son?"

"Yup. His pa died three years ago. That's why she had to work at Pearl's. Try to keep Pearl outta this, will ya? She's never hurt a soul in her life. She's just someone we know and we won't see her again after this. It'll lead to nothin'."

She frowned. "Dora's dead; you understand that, don't you? I don't believe she'd leave him, not with no other family."

"We know," Nat muttered, "but the law doesn't care. She's just a prostitute to them."

Abigail's brows met. "That's not true. *I* care."

"Yeah?" snorted Jake. "Just what can you do about it?"

Her dark eyes blazed with determination. "You'd be surprised, Mr. Conroy. I can find out a lot. I'm very good at it, and with a little help, I'm certain I can do more than just get information." She paused. "You wanted to call a truce, Mr. Quinn. How about it? I get the information, and you two back me up? No one else cares enough to do it. What do you say?"

"Why would you care?" demanded Jake.

"Because I know what it's like to lose people. It's why I became a Pinkerton. What hope does that little boy have in getting justice? I could help. Besides, you saved my life. I pay my debts, and this seems like something I can help with." She paused, "And I don't like owing criminals."

The men exchanged a look. "What can you do we can't?"

Nat asked. "Dora's boy needs a fighter. He needs to see she matters, and that someone cares about him and his Ma, or he'll be angry for the rest of his life."

"Angry? That sounds like the voice of experience to me. Your choice, gentlemen. I'm offering you a cease-fire, no questions asked, to find the killer. As far as the agency is concerned, I was never held against my will until I tell them different, and no criminals are helping me. They'll know what I tell them. It's up to you. Do you mean it, or do you just talk a good argument? If not, I'll walk away and put all my energies into you." She tilted her head. "What have you got to lose?"

"Our freedom." Nat leaned forward. "How can we trust you?"

"I messed up and I don't go back with you, but at least I don't go back empty-handed if I find the killer." She fixed Nat with a gimlet eye. "After what went on here yesterday, Mr. Quinn, the question is how can *I* trust *you*? I'm out here on my own—you're not."

Nat stood. "Let me think on it." He gestured to Jake to follow him, walking out to the porch where he leaned on the handrail and stared out into the cool November air.

The gunman closed the door behind him and eyed his nephew in disbelief. "Nat, you ain't considerin' this. Throwin' your lot in with a Pinkerton? We'll be carted off before the end of the week. It's crazy."

"Is it? It might help us to get to the bottom of what happened to Bessie and Dora," Nat mused. "I can't think of a better way to find out how they work, and that can only ever help us. We have a good chance of spotting the other agents that way. We need to recognize them to avoid a trap."

"Or we could be walkin' straight into one," muttered Jake. "We can't trust her."

"Yeah, I know," Nat grinned, "but she sure as hell can't trust *us*, either."

Chapter Eight

"So, she was the law?" Pearl's chins gathered above her well-upholstered bosom. "Well, dingle my dangle, if that ain't the sneakiest, most underhanded, low-down trick I've seen since, well…" she paused, "since I met you two. I'm gonna have to be a lot more careful from now on."

"She's gonna keep you outta this. She promised us. It just means we can't see you again. I guess it was bound to happen eventually." Jake's eyes glistened with regret. "You sure we can still use the cabin until we head off, Pearl?"

"Yeah, sure, Jake. No one's been near it since old man White died. He left it to me. I guess we helped to make his last years more, 'comfortable'. Is that a good idea, though? She knows where it is, and you've let her go. It'll be the first place they head for."

"She's been blindfolded and has no idea where it is. She's now investigatin' what happened to Dora and Bessie."

A cynical frown creased Pearl's brow. "And you believe her, Jake?"

The gunman folded his arms. "Hard to believe, ain't it, Pearl?"

"You're idiots. Dumb as boiled bones. Stupid as glue. Brainless as bolloc—"

"Now, Pearl," Nat chuckled. "We've spent a long time with her. She's idealistic and kinda rigid. I can use that. You forget how good I am with people, especially when I can spot their weaknesses."

She glinted a warning at him. "They call it *manipulatin'* people, Nat. And I never forget that about you. Not ever. You might be underestimatin' her, though. Men usually do, when there's a pretty face around."

"She owes us. We saved her life, and the least she can do is speak to the folks who wouldn't open up to us." Nat tilted his head. "Folks here know us as old friends, the Ryan boys you gave a roof for doin' odd jobs for you when they were little. They don't know we're the famous Nat and Jake from The Innocents, or that we used Ryan as a fake name to keep us together as orphans."

"Well, the Pinkertons know it now, and if they don't, they will very soon," Pearl asserted. "You're gonna have to stop visitin' for a very long time."

"Not until we find out what happened to the women, Pearl." Jake folded his arms. "We blindfolded her until just outside town. She doesn't know where the cabin is. We've got time. It ain't like we're gonna pull any jobs with the Pinkertons lookin' for us."

"So, we're going to need help to search, and some other stuff." Nat sat and twinkled a wide grin at her, preparing her for his next big favor.

"Other stuff? What do you want, Nat?" Pearl demanded. "I can see your brand of usin' comin' miles away."

He smiled the smile of the caught in the act. "Can you see your way clear to takin' Abigail back?"

Pearl's alabaster face turned puce as she blustered at the very idea of entertaining anyone involved in law enforcement in her establishment. "Are you mad?"

Jake grinned at the stately madam's affront as her feathered head dress trembled and danced in tandem with her blustering conniption fit.

"I've often wondered that myself when I end up listenin' to Nat, but in this case, we got good reason," Jake replied. "We need someone in the place to find out about what could have happened to the girls, and she owes us a favor for savin' her skin."

"Nobody will speak to her if they think she's investigatin', but they'll speak to a maid, a fellow employee." Nat added. "She'll be different. She'll lose the disguise and be Scottish again. No glasses or paint to look dowdy. This one'll be pretty. You can invent her past. Make her as pathetic as you want. Get creative with it. Have fun."

"What about her name?"

"It's common enough to have another Abi. Change it to somethin' real ugly," grinned Nat. "How about Gertrude or Ethel?"

"Ah, go on Pearl. She's free help and you don't even need to be nice to her. You can be as mean as you like," chortled Jake. "You'll love it."

"Well, it's a free pair of hands and the thought of gettin' the law to empty all the chamber pots and clean the latrines is real temptin'." She sat back and mused. "No. She'll use everythin' she hears here. I can't do it."

"We'll pay," Nat cut in. "I've got another reason. I need to know everyone she speaks to. I want her watched."

"In a brothel?" Pearl guffawed. "Have you any idea how many people come through here? And how do they watch her without her knowin'. This place was built for secrecy. No, Nat. That ain't gonna happen. It ain't possible."

Nat perched on the edge of the desk. "Fine, what about offering fifty dollars to anyone who sees her talking to anyone not employed here?"

"How about takin' your money and shovin' it right up your—"

"Now, Pearl," Jake cut in, "that ain't ladylike."

"I'm only a lady in my spare time, and I don't get a lot of that." Her chair creaked as she leaned back. "I'll have even less time if I play this dumb game and it's worth a whole lot more than fifty stinkin' dollars. Find another whorehouse to ask questions in. This one's special."

"Aw, come on, Pearl. Just a few weeks?"

"Two, at most, and just do your best." Nat smiled his most charming smile. "We're trying to find out what happened to Bessie and Dora. Won't your girls be pleased to think you did something?" Nat walked around the desk and wrapped his arms around her thick waist and gave her a squeeze. "Two-and-a-half, and I'll throw in a night with Jake."

Pearl pushed him away. "Don't be disgustin'. He's like my nephew. Fine, two-and-a-half weeks, but she works as hard as anyone else here—and if I catch her usin' anythin' she learns here for anythin' other than findin' the girls, I'll skin her alive myself."

Nat kissed her cheek. "You're a star, Pearl. She'll be good as gold and work like a slave."

"I will not. I have a job to do." They all turned toward the slight figure in the doorway dressed in a simple skirt and white blouse, her dark hair gathered in a bun. "Not only that, I'm recovering from an injury."

"Deal's off. I ain't havin' a maid who talks back," snorted Pearl.

Jake turned. "How long have you been there?"

Abigail ignored him and appealed direct to Pearl. "Look, I need to get in here to get background on the girls. You don't have to like me, you don't even have to see me, but I want to help that poor boy of Dora's. Can you imagine what it must be like growing up knowing your mother has disappeared and no one cares enough to even search for her?"

Pearl gave small harrumph as Abigail continued. "That damages a boy. What kind of future do you think he'll have with that kind of anger? He could end up, well—" she flung an arm out toward Nat and Jake, "like them."

"Hey!" cried an indignant Jake.

Pearl bristled. "He could do worse."

"Sure, yes, I don't want to talk to your customers, just the staff. They'll know most about Bessie and Dora." She walked over and looked straight into Pearl's pale blue eyes. "Please. I'm asking you woman to woman. What's the worst that can happen? If I don't find out anything, I'll just walk away. Nobody's any worse off."

Pearl let out a rasping sigh of impatience. "Why does this matter to you?"

"I care about people. You might not have seen that in the law before, but I'm not your usual town sheriff, am I?"

"I can't trust you."

"Mrs. Dubois, you can't trust anyone here, and you know it. As soon as I learned the fake Innocents were killers, I prioritized them. You saw me do it. If someone is killing women around here I can't think of anything more urgent, can you? We are both women. Stealing matters, but not as much as murder."

Pearl simmered. "You empty all the chamber pots every mornin'. You work the kitchens and the latrines. Nowhere else. If I see you anywhere else, I'll kick your bony ass outta here, and I got a kick like a mule. Got that?"

"Did she hear us, Nat?"

He shrugged. "Dunno, Jake. Probably. She's got ears like a hungry watchdog, that one."

"So, she knows we're watchin' her." Jake leaned on the post and gazed out into the yard. "Remind me why we're not ridin' outta here and headin' straight back to Ghost Canyon?"

"Because we owe Bessie and Dora?" Nat sighed. "Not to mention Pearl."

"Yeah. That's the problem. We always told Pearl we'd have her back if she needed us. This loyalty stuff ain't all it's cracked up to be when you could be facin' twenty years inside."

"I know." The dark eyes slid sideways. "When folks have seen you at your worst, and still stick by you, you don't let them go."

"At their worst?" mused the older man. "You mean like covered in dried puke, blood, and I don't even want to think what else? That's about as bad as it gets."

"I'm not talking about Abi."

"I know you ain't talkin' about Abi. That's what worries me." Jake turned and examined his nephew. "She's a challenge to you, and you can never resist a challenge."

"She's no challenge to me," snorted Nat. "Women are good at getting gossip out of other women, and Pinkerton's smart enough to use that. There's no reason I can't do the same. Anyway, I'm talking about the people who cared for us when we were cold and hungry. Pearl is real cut up about this." The dark eyes stared into Jake's. "And so are you. Dora was special to you." He put up a hand to ward of objections. "I'm not saying you were in love, or anything like that. You were real fond of her. You were friends."

Jake glanced at the ground with a heavy sigh. "Friendship's about the only honesty I've ever seen in my whole shitty life. That boy's got nobody. He'll end up in an orphanage until he can be sold as cheap labor to a farmer. Dora would've hated that. He's smart. She was tryin' to buy him the chance of a future by gettin' him an education. It'll waste his whole life."

"So, we use Abi to find out what the women around here know. Stuff we can't get them to talk to us about. We at least try to get him justice. It's better than nothing."

"Yeah, right. Then we go; far away from here, and her, and we don't see Pearl for a real long time. This ain't good, Nat. We can't mess with the law up close like this. It's a dangerous game." Jake pushed himself upright, his gaze following the boy carrying the bucket of coal from the shed. "Hey, you!" He called over to the lad. "Do you work here?"

A pair of bright eyes blinked their way, from a not-so-bright-face face covered in soot. "Sure. Can I help you, mister? Clean your boots for you?"

"They need it, but no thanks. What's your name?"

"Henry."

"I'm guessin' you do odd jobs and polish boots, Huh? Do you want to earn thirty dollars?"

The boy's face lit up, his hazel eyes standing out in his soot-covered face. "Thirty dollars?" The head tilted in suspicion. "What d'ya want me to do?"

"I want to ask you about that maid who came here today. The one with the dark hair?"

"Abi? Sure. I've seen her."

"Yeah," the gunman pulled out a banknote. "Well, I want you to watch her real close, and let me know if she passes a note to anyone or gets one delivered. It might be done real sneaky-like, so you're gonna have to watch real close. I can give you ten now, and the rest when you get me the information I want. Give it to Pearl, and tell her to contact Mr. Black urgently. Have you got that?" The urchin reached out a filthy hand, only for the note to be snatched just out of reach. "What have you got to do?"

"Tell Miss Pearl if Abi gets a note or leaves one for someone else."

"And my name?"

"Mr. Black."

"Good for you." Jake arched his brows. "There'll be an extra twenty if you can find out the name of the person she's passin' notes to. His name, description, and where he's stayin'. You know what that adds up to don't you?"

The boy's lips moved in tandem with his computation. "Ten,

then twenty, then another—that's lots! Wow. Are you sure, mister? There are ladies in there who are much prettier. Lulu has great big lovely—"

"I'm sure," Jake cut in.

"—eyes," Henry carried on.

"It's Abi," Jake asserted. "You tell me as soon as she speaks to anyone outside this place. Got that?"

"Sure," Henry nodded. "You got it, mister. Are you sure Miss Pearl is alright with this?"

"Yup. We're very old friends. In fact, I used to do your job here."

"Yah, did? It's great here, innit? I don't know why you'd ever leave."

A smile twitched at Jake's lips. "Sometimes, I wonder that myself. Good to meet you, Henry."

"And you, Mr. Black," Henry hauled his bucket of coal into the building. "See ya."

"Black?" Nat queried.

Jake shrugged. "One of the aliases I use now and again. I like to keep them simple."

"Nah," Nat shook his head. "I prefer a complicated alias. Common names always seem too false to me. I want something that doesn't sound like you could make it up on the spot."

♦ ◇ ♦

The distant mountains formed a jagged fortress of slate gray against the horizon, encircling the rugged land with spiked castellations. The countryside below was too wide to be called a valley and lacked the expanse of a plain, but the scrubby, graveled land cut out by glaciers was vast enough to lose any number of homesteads among the many trees and rivers cutting through the rough, stony sod.

This was the haystack Nat and Jake had to search for the

missing needles, but where to start was a daunting question. Bessie and Dora had traveled out here and disappeared, along with a wagon and team of horses. One glance at the terrain told anyone with any sense it was not their decision. The men had pored over maps, garnering information from Pearl and her security man about the whereabouts of other cabins in the area, some abandoned after their stakes failed to produce a living, let alone the fortunes in gold the prospectors dreamed of; while others were still inhabited by men still scratching a living. That gave them about a tenth of the picture. Two of Pearl's security men took one-half, and they took the other. None of them were sure they'd ever see Bessie or Dora again, but they had to try.

The low sun blinded them when they loped into the tumbledown homestead. A curious jackrabbit blinked at them from the edge of the clearing, the spoon-like ears twitching at every unfamiliar sound in this peaceful area. It decided against the pleasure of their company and hopped off, bobbing its fluffy tail through the long grass until it disappeared into the shrubbery.

"This'll have to be the last one for the day," Jake scanned the sky. "We'll lose light in a few hours."

"Yeah, we'll search, then we might as well camp here for the night when we're done," Nat agreed. "It shouldn't take long. It doesn't look like anyone's lived here for years."

"Yeah," Jake sighed, "or even been here. They could have abandoned the roads and used the horses, I guess."

"Why would two women do that?" Nat shook his head. "No, we stick to places they could have taken a wagon. If that doesn't work, we don't even know where to start."

"I guess so. I'll take the barn and the woodshed. You take the back of the house. If the place isn't in too bad a way we could spend a night indoors."

Nat paused. "I think we're searching for bodies now, Jake."

Jake turned to fix his partner with a stony stare. "I've been lookin' for bodies from the moment I left town. Dora would never leave her boy alone. He was her whole world."

Nat sighed and gave a joyless smile. "Yeah. She was different."

"I liked her spirit and her humor. She loved so fierce it shone." He dropped his head. "She always reminded me of my ma. Now that she's died young, she reminds me of her even more."

"It's been over a week. We've come up with zero."

"Yup," Jake kicked out at nothing in particular, "and I'll be damned if I'll see another woman's murder go unrevenged."

A caustic grin played around Nat' lips. "Unrevenged? Is that a word?"

The gunman strode over to the barn calling over his shoulder. "Dunno. If it ain't, it sure as hell *should* be."

"She sure hates you. What've you done?" The question came from the slim black woman who sat across the table from Abigail as they snatched a few minutes to drink their coffee at the kitchen table.

"I've no idea. She just doesn't seem to like me. I probably won't stay very long."

"She ain't too forgivin' if you do somethin' wrong. You need to talk as smooth as a toad's belly once you upset her, but it's worth it. The money's real good here." Seraphina's brow creased. "You seem familiar. Where do I know you from?"

"I've no idea. Have you ever shopped downtown? Could you have seen me there?" Abigail smiled at Seraphina's expressive simile but saw an opportunity lurking in the background and changed the subject. "Do you think she's hoping for a career change? She's short-handed now those other two girls ran off. She asked me and I refused."

Seraphina shuddered. "Somethin' bad happened to them. They'd never ran off before. They'd never do that."

"Really? What? What do you think happened?"

"I think it was natives, or outlaws, or maybe they had an enemy?" The girl's mind ran with wild schemes from dime novels.

"An enemy? *Did* they have an enemy? Are there natives around here?"

"Nooo. That's just me thinkin' out loud. Everyone loved them." She giggled. "Some more than others. A couple in particular, loved them three or four times a week and twice on pay day."

Abigail grinned. "Perhaps someone got jealous?"

"I doubt it. Bessie's been around for years. She'd have gone off with anyone who wanted to make an honest woman of her. Dora, she loved Ben Middleton, but he's already married."

"Ben Middleton? Could it have been his wife?" Abigail widened her eyes and tried to make it sound conspiratorial. This wasn't likely scenario, but it was a technique she used often to get gossipy women to open up to her.

"What?" chortled Seraphina. "Liz Middleton? She weighs about eighty pounds soakin' wet. Dora would have flattened her, and Bessie could lay out a miner in a fight. I saw her do it once with my own two eyes."

Abigail nodded, noting that a slight build never stopped Helene Jegado who poisoned at least thirty-six people before being caught and executed. "Do you think? No. It couldn't be. Could it?"

"What?" Seraphina leaned forward, being drawn in without even realizing it. Abigail's voice dropped to a whisper as her eyes widened with mock horror. "What if Ben Middleton did it? What if his wife gave him a hard time?"

Seraphina bellowed with laughter as she rocked back and forth. "Ben? Have you seen him? He's been blind this last three years. Dora had a soft heart and looked after him. There's no way he could have gone out after a wagon and taken two women. He can barely get about town."

"How can he afford—well, Dora's services?"

"He works as a musician. Teaches and tunes pianos by day and plays the bars in the evenin's. He plays around here sometimes. His wife thought he was workin' when he saw Dora." She stretched her neck forward. "Between you and me, I think Dora often did him for free. I'd often catch them sneakin' off together, or him comin' out of her room at dawn."

"Dora must have loved him."

"I guess. She was sweet, real sweet."

"I cleaned their rooms," Abi pressed. "It gave me the creeps, thinking of them dead somewhere. Dora had a telegram from someone who signed themselves 'R.D.'. She was going to meet them the day after she disappeared. Who could that have been?"

"'R.D.'?" Seraphina shook her head. "I've no idea. She never said anythin'. "

"Abi! Where are you, girl?" Pearl's voice could screech through every floor of the building when she put her mind to it and it had the cadence of finger nails on a blackboard. "There you are." She appeared at the doorway in a black peignoir covering substantial, industrial-looking lingerie. "We got a party comin' in and there's a whole sack of potatoes to peel. Get to it."

◆ ◇ ◆

The woman prodded the Station Master with a sharp forefinger. "My hat box. It's gone." He stared up and down the platform, bustling with people arriving from San Francisco, and shrugged. "Hat box? Where did you lose it?"

"I put it on the rack above my head when we left San

Francisco, and now it's gone. Somebody must have stolen it." Her accusing stare followed a woman walking by with a huge hatbox, her sharp nose leading her way as the woman headed for the gate to town. "I thought that was mine for a moment there."

"Did you see anyone take it?"

"No," she turned to her husband. "Did you see anything, Bob?"

"If I had, I would have stopped them, dear. I was reading."

She harrumphed. "Don't I know it. You've had your nose in that book since we left. I could hardly get a word out of you."

"It was a pleasant journey, dear," her husband paused. "Until now."

The platform cleared of passengers leaving no more than a few stragglers. "Well, that's everyone." The Station Master shrugged. "If it's not on the train and we didn't see it get taken away by anyone, I guess we'll have to submit a report. Come with me." They followed the man into the office where a tall, gangly man spoke through gapped teeth.

"I'm here to collect a telegram I'm expecting. From R.D. to R.D. They told me it would be in about now, and to be here to collect it at one-thirty, precisely. The name's Rigby Daintree."

"Sure," the clerk rifled through a drawer and handed over an envelope. "Here you go, sir."

"Mrs. Davies," the woman brushed passed the thin man. "Pardon me, but I just had a hat box stolen. Can you believe it?" She turned back to the clerk. "Mary Davies. I'll be staying at the hotel in town if you find anything. I'll be checking in directly after I leave here."

"The Three Trees Hotel," Daintree replied. "I'm staying there myself. I'm sure I'll see you there." Daintree opened the envelope and glanced inside, satisfied with the contents. He tipped his hat politely and headed for the door. "See you later, Mr. and Mrs. Davies. I hope you find your hatbox."

♦ ◊ ♦

The next day, a weary Nat dismounted and scanned the landscape of yet another tumble-down cabin, the last on their list as they looped their way back to town after a fruitless search. Their flagging spirits dropped as both men stopped and stared at the ground.

"Somethin' heavy's been here," Jake crouched to examine the dual ruts cut into the soil. "And it was recent. It's driven the grass into the soil. Judgin' by the fact the broken grass is dead, it's been more'n a few days ago."

They both checked out the shabby building, the dilapidated wood siding as gray and dismal as the somber sky which hung over them like a pall. "The house doesn't look like it's been used for years. The logs have even lost most of their chinking."

Nat strode over to the porch and mounted the steps, hesitating at the door. It swung open with a grating creak and he stepped inside, engulfed in the darkness of the interior. His eyes adjusted to the poor light filtering in through the grimy windows, until he could see the details in the poor habitation. The chimney hooks and spit were straight out of his own childhood home.

He turned at a noise, just in time to spot a little masked bandit of a raccoon make a dash for the door. The place had no more than the skeletal remains of basic furniture, and rotten, faded fabric still hung at the windows. His practiced eye told him the dust on the floorboards showed no sign of being disturbed, so he dismissed the idea of anything being hidden beneath them. There was nothing else to see here, so he clunked over the rough planks to the door and walked back outside.

Jake appeared out of what was left of the barn as Nat stepped out of the cabin. He met his nephew's questioning gaze with a negating shake of the head. "Nothin', Nat?"

The dark eyes dropped to the ground, a frown creasing Nat's brow as he followed the ruts out to the perimeter with a sinking heart. He stepped back to ground level, wandering along the length of the tracks until they reached out to the circular, squat, stone wall. "Nat—"

"I know, Jake."

"The well? Oh, dear Lord. Not the well."

"We have to check," Nat agreed, approaching the cover. He paused, holding his tense uncle's gaze with fearful eyes. "We've got to."

He reached out and pulled back the wooden cover and an ominous cloud of insects flew out, forming a hideous murmuration of necrosis, carrying the stench of rotting flesh with them as they spiraled and danced in mid-air in a macabre whirl. Nat steeled himself to peer over the edge, into the black, dank, darkness below.

The stink hit him full in the face and he spun around, grasping his guts as he vomited on the grass.

Knowing blue eyes melded anger and grief with an air of resignation. "We gotta get help, Nat. They need a decent burial. They need someone to do just one decent thing for them for one time in their whole miserable lives."

Nat straightened, gulping away the acid and tears of his convulsion. He nodded. "Yeah. And if that woman has got nothing useful for us to go on, we'll get Pearl to ride her out of town on a rail. She's had long enough to meddle. This isn't a game." He glanced toward the well. "Women shouldn't be involved in this stuff."

Chapter Nine

A soft, brown hand snaked through the blond curls as Marisol caressed the man in a professional act of welcome. He smiled, his eyes flowing over her golden skin, the color of running molasses, before he pulled himself back to the business at hand with an internal groan.

"Sorry, darlin'. I want that one, Pearl." Jake pointed at Abigail who loitered by the kitchen door. She gave a little start of anxiety.

This was not the deal. If she appeared to be turning tricks, she would alienate the girls here, and other men might demand her too. She shook her head. "No. I'm a maid. I'm not available."

"I gotta insist, darlin'. My money is good, and I want her, Pearl. I'll pay extra. Double." His eyes burned into her trying to get her to understand how much he needed her to spend time alone with him. Seraphina was ensconced in the kitchen baking bread for the next morning and he had hung around too long as it was.

Pearl paused, understanding the importance of Jake's visit. "I think you should consider it, darlin'. He's good lookin' and pays well. If you were thinkin' of startin' out, it'd be a good introduction." Her eyes narrowed, pressing home the point. "In fact, if you want to stay here you'd better learn to do as you're told. Talk to him. All I ask is for you to consider it."

Abigail dropped her head, picking up on the subtext. How could she do this without annoying the girls who were already eyeing her with hostile suspicion? They were paid by the customer, like piecework, and a maid taking a well-paying client was taking the bread from their mouths. "I'll talk to him alone before I decide."

She walked into one of the rooms with him, the assorted stares of the working girls penetrating her back like arrows. As the door closed behind him she gave a snort of annoyance. "This is not helping. Those girls hate me now."

He strolled over to her as he pulled off his hat trying to take account of normal proprieties even in these strange circumstances. "We've found the bodies. I had to let you know and we ain't been able to get you on your own. The cook never leaves the kitchen."

"No! How did they die?"

Jake shrugged. "I dunno. Does it matter? They're dead. We found them in a well."

"It matters. It can tell you a lot about who did it. I need to see the bodies."

"Abi, they've been in a well for over a week. That ain't a good idea. They stink."

"Of course they stink. That's no reason for not doing a proper job." She fixed him with the patient smile of someone used to handling objections. "It's nothing I haven't seen before, Mr. Conroy. I haven't spent the last four years as a school teacher."

He glanced down, still not happy women should be involved in the things his every instinct taught him to protect them from. "This ain't right, Abi. You shouldn't be in a place like this, and you shouldn't be lookin' at things like that. You're a nice girl."

Determined brown eyes burned into his. "Thank you, but Dora was a nice girl. She was also very unlucky. She didn't deserve to die because of that, Mr. Conroy. We owe both her and Bessie."

His face softened in way she hadn't seen since she first

regained consciousness in the cabin. "Call me Jake."

She smiled, realizing this was a turning point for a man who would have cheerfully strangled her not so long ago. "Jake, where are they now?"

"At the funeral parlor. The doc's gonna examine them tomorrow."

She nodded. "I need to go there. I want to see them."

"Are you mad? Besides, it's locked. I came here to ask what you've found out."

"I'll tell you after I've seen the bodies," she stripped off her apron and thrust her head out of the window. "At least we're on the ground floor. That helps. And since when did a locked door stop you two?"

"I ain't never broken into an undertaker's. Anyway, locks are Nat's department."

She grinned at him as she swung a leg over the sill. "Good job I'm here, then. Come on. You can keep watch."

"Abi, I came to talk to you—"

But she had already slipped off into the night.

Jake glanced around as Abigail pulled something from her hair and prodded and probing around in the lock. It wasn't easy. The back door to the undertaker's sat in deep, dark shadow, so it was difficult to see what she was doing. As she had guessed, it was a cheap, cursory security measure as most people did their level best to keep out of a funeral parlor, not break in.

"A hair pin?" Jake muttered under his breath. "Are you kiddin'? You've read too many dime novels. It ain't that easy."

The whites of her eyes caught the poor light as she glanced at him, still working on the door. "I'll get us in."

She wasn't about to disclose to him she always kept a small lock pick in her hair as the truce was only temporary and this information may jeopardize any future attempts to bring them in. It was missed as Pearl tended to her, mistaking it for a hairpin in her innocence of the tools of housebreaking; well, as much as a madam in a brothel could ever be called innocent.

The knob turned with a satisfying squeak as Jake muttered in admiration under his breath. "You're wasted in the law, Abi."

"Come on, and be quiet."

"Why? We ain't gonna wake anyone."

She snickered through the gloom as she sought a candle. "Let's hope not, eh?"

Jake glanced around the room with a shudder. He had seen death in so many guises but something about the way the bodies were laid out made them appear as though they were sleeping, and when coupled with the blank, gray undertones, a crawling tingle crept under his skin. His eyes fixed on an open coffin. It was a little girl, aged about ten. Her eyes were closed but her skin looked like white porcelain whilst the ordered blond ringlets lay at either side of her face, arranged under the pink ribbons in her hair. The velvet dress would have been her Sunday best. She looked perfect; as beautiful as the angel she had become. There was not a mark on her, no sign of why she had died. Her death appeared to be arbitrary and pointless, but Jake understood how empty the life of her parents would be from this point, and a sharp pain speared his already scarred heart.

His breathing came in short, sharp gasps, and his fingers tingled. The sense of terrible foreboding washed over him; a terrible legacy which had followed him from his childhood trauma; the day his family were killed. His head swam and every nerve in his body was alight; ready to fight, ready to flee—but actually frozen. The vision of his sister's broken body loomed into his mind's eye, and the sounds from the past rang in his ears.

He felt Abigail's warm hand slide into his, shaking him from his creeping nightmare. She spoke with steady reassurance, frowning at the trembling stiffness of the man known as a ruthless gunman. "Come on, Jake. Don't think too hard about this, that's the trick here. Easy does it. You're fine."

"Hmmm."

"Breathe. Stop and breathe deeply. I know. It takes us all like this to start with, but the dead tell tales. You just have to learn how to read them. That's how we help them." She gave him a reassuring squeeze. "It's also how we help those they leave behind." She paused and rubbed his arm. "Are you alright?"

He took a sharp juddering intake of breath. "It's kids. It always gets me when it's kids."

He shook himself out of his trance and followed her into the back room.

"Whoa." He pulled back his head as the stench hit him like a wall. His eyes watered and, surprisingly, so did his mouth as his stomach turned over.

"Shhhh."

"The smell. How can you stand the smell?"

"You just get on with it. It'll pass. I'm guessing they're in here. You can stay at the door if you want."

She strode over and pulled back the sheet on the first body as a swollen purple, red, and black congested mass of rotting flesh came into view. "Who was the tallest? We'll never identify them from facial features."

She pulled back the other sheet and examining them, comparing the rotting cadavers.

Jake winced. "Bessie." He glanced at the traces of the dyed red hair on the nearest body before he continued, staying as near the door as possible. "Dora was blonde."

Abigail nodded as she held the candle close, running her eyes over the bodies, examining the limbs, the engorged faces and the obvious bullet hole in the forehead of the larger woman. Her body inspection seemed to take forever before she was satisfied. She then covered the bodies back up to the neck with the sheets. "I've almost seen enough. I just need to check a couple of things."

"I saw enough half-an-hour ago."

"Do you have a knife, or something sharp I can use?"

Horror flashed over his face. "You ain't cuttin' them open?"

She shook her head. "No. I think I can get evidence. I need some paper or something to scrape the fingernails onto, too." She glanced over at the desk just outside the door. "There's some out there. Can you get me a few sheets?"

She took the knife and scraped under the nails, depositing the residue on the sheet of paper. "They have broken nails. I'd need my microscope to be sure, but this seems to be human skin," she glanced at Jake. "They fought for their lives, both of them."

"They were scared?" Jake's voice chilled in anger.

"I'm afraid so."

"So how does this help us? This is even worse."

"It means the murderer, or murderers, will be scarred for a little while where they were scratched," Abigail replied. "It helps, as long as we can get them quickly enough. It's evidence." She held the candle as she used the knife to move the engorged flesh around the neck before she nodded to herself.

Abigail strode over to the sink and scrubbed at her hands with coal tar soap, and finished by pouring pure alcohol over her fingers and rubbing it in. She blew out the candle with a huff, snuffing out any more conversation and made her way to the back door.

They closed it behind them and crept into the alley where she paused. "Can I come back to the cabin tonight? Right now?"

Jake glinted at her with suspicion swirling behind his eyes as his hand crept to his gun. "Why?"

She smiled, recognizing the gesture. "Relax. It's not a trap. I think I've found out everything I can at Pearl's. I need to take another tack and find out about the "respectable" people in this town. I can't do that in a brothel."

He shrugged. "Sure, but why right away? What did you find out in there that meant you have to leave?"

"The smell. I can take the smell in there, but I can't take another morning of emptying all the chamber pots at Pearl's. She can do that herself."

"Well, Nat wanted to know what you'd got. I guess you can tell him yourself."

♦ ◊ ♦

Nat's eyebrows rose in surprise as they walked into the cabin. "Abi? What's wrong? Why are you back here?"

"I don't want to stay at Pearl's anymore. I need to move on."

Jake closed the cabin door. "She examined the bodies, Nat. Handled them and everything. It don't seem right to me."

"Move on? What do you mean, *move on*? You lost interest? If you have, the truce is off."

She gave a shrug of irritation as she hooked him with an angry glare. "Do your worst. Whilst you're huffing and puffing, I have work to do. Do you have any paper and ink?"

He narrowed his eyes as she sat at the table. "Sure, yes. You looked at the bodies? Why?"

"Bessie was shot in the head, but Dora was strangled. Double murders don't usually use different methods unless there's more than one killer." She slumped and gazed off, lost in her thoughts. "Poor Dora. I think Bessie was killed quite quickly, but Dora would have suffered."

The men exchanged a glance. "How could you tell Dora was strangled?"

"The ligature was still around her neck. It was being covered by rotting flesh and adipocere. The rope was a thin one, triple woven a common type, so that's no help. "

Nat frowned. "Adi—what?"

"Adipocere. The body can react with water to form a thick, soapy substance, but that's not important. I think we could be looking for more than one killer, people acting together. Bessie probably had to be killed quickly because I've heard she was a good fighter. I heard she once laid out a miner with one punch."

"So? More than one killer?" Jake thought back to the German boy with the twisted mouth, remembering the stocky, grizzled father who lurked in the background.

"Maybe. You can't assume anything. Bessie could have been killed first to terrify and control Dora or simply to get her out of the way. I'm keeping an open mind. There might have been another reason to kill her by a different method. To punish her perhaps?"

Nat crossed his arms. "If it's too open you'll never narrow anything down."

"I know. That's why I need the paper, to write it up and see what leaps out at me. I also need to get a different perspective on them and find out more about the respectable people they had dealings with." She shrugged. "I've never understood why prostitutes are considered worse than the men who use them. If there's one thing I can't stand it's a hypocrite."

Nat stood over her and peered at the scramble of notes. "What the hell is that?"

She glanced at him out of the corner of her eye with a smirk. "It's Gaelic, the Scottish language. You didn't think I would write in English, did you? I don't want to let you get a grasp on how I work. Not the way your mind works. These notes are for me—you don't need to see or understand them."

He gave a grunt and strode over to the chair at the far side of the table and threw himself down. "You really mean to bring us in, don't you Abi?"

She gave him a small, regretful shrug. "You know I do, Mr. Quinn. It's not personal. It's my job."

An intense look flickered over his face before it dimpled into a cold smile. "So, what have you found out?"

"Bessie was almost fifty, or anything up to that, depending on her mood that day. She was born in Louisville and her folks were dirt poor. She married years ago and he left her with two kids. No one seems to know anything about them. Her clientele has been dropping off lately, and Pearl had to reduce her fees. She tried to get out, to find a man, but she only found bad luck, lots of terrible luck." Abigail sighed and glanced at her paper.

"Dora? She was pretty, fun, clever, and desperate. She came from Boston. No one knows much about her folks, but it looks like she ran away from home to get married to Phil Benson. They had a boy together, David, who's now eight. Her husband died in a mining accident three years ago. Poverty drove her to work at Pearl's out of desperation. She was doing better than Bessie, and had a few regulars." She darted a meaningful look at Jake before she continued. "Her favorite seems to be a blind musician called Ben Middleton. I haven't found out much about him yet, but as there was a shooting involved, I think we can eliminate him acting on his own, but not if he was with someone else. "

"So?" Nat sat back on his chair. "We already knew that stuff."

"They set out about ten, had a reading with Anna Schmidt and the Schmidts claim they left about two to return. They were never seen again, until their bodies were found. No sign of the wagon or horses, though. Pearl told me Dora was excited about money coming her way. She was looking forward to a new future. That's why she wanted a reading."

Nat put his hands behind his head and gave hear rueful look. "That's it? That's all you've got. I'm not impressed."

"This isn't about impressing you, Mr. Quinn." Abigail retorted. "Were you aware two different sets of people have been trying to adopt Dora's son since he went into the Juvenile Asylum? The man who works there says he's never seen interest like it in just over a week. It's unprecedented. I spoke to a politician friend of his tonight before Jake came. The other woman who enquired kicked up quite the fuss about the boy already being allocated to someone else. He gets collected next week when the paperwork is completed. I also found a telegram arranging a meeting with someone with the initials of R.D. on the day she died. I don't think that's a coincidence. It was from Boston."

Both men sat upright with a start.

"Her son?" said Nat.

"Yes. That's why I'm here. I have a job for you if you're up for it. Bring him here, by force if necessary. Someone wants that little boy very badly, and I'm not sure they have his best interests at heart."

Jake shook his head. "I can't scare a kid, Abi. He's only eight."

"You'll find a way. I sure of it." She gave him a reassuring smile. "There's a side to you which is very gentle."

Nat stood and fixed her with a wide grin. "Miss MacKay, you wouldn't be asking us to break the law, now, would you?"

She tilted her chin in challenge. "Nope. I'm asking you to protect a *child*. If you won't do it, I will."

He folded his arms. "And what if he doesn't want to come?"

"Persuade him, Mr. Quinn." She glared at him with frosty eyes. "You'll find a way through his resistance. That's your specialty, as I remember."

"Give me one reason why we don't get you driven out of town as an informant at a brothel," Nat demanded. "All you've got is gossip, and now you want us to break the law for you? How do I know it's not a trap?"

"A trap? This concerns a little boy, not you." She stood. "I gave you my word, and that means something. You think your way is the only one, Mr. Quinn? Why do you think a man a smart as Alan Pinkerton would waste money on us if we didn't get results?"

Nat arched a brow. "Men have all kinds of reasons for wanting women around, Abi. It usually has nothing to do with their minds."

"What exactly do you mean by that?" she demanded.

"Oh, come on. You can't be that naïve. Men use women all the time." He paused. "I'll bet you're not paid as well as the men. In my gang everyone gets an equal share. Do you get paid the same as the men?"

She bridled at him. "Mr. Quinn, when you see me fall for that sort of manipulation you will also see hell freeze over. Are you reneging on your promise to help solve this? Fine. I'll leave here and do this alone, but I'll not forget how little your word is worth."

Jake strode over to the door. "You're not goin' anywhere, Abi. It's past midnight, and we're miles from town. It ain't safe. You take the bed, and we'll sleep on the floor." He eyed them both with weary blue eyes. "And no arguments. Dealin' with you two is like tryin' to make a knot outta fog. We all want the same thing, so why the Sam Hill are you feudin' like hillbillies on moonshine?" He pointed over at the bedstead. "Bed. Now! We'll discuss this in the mornin'."

"But—"

"No buts, Abi. It's time to turn in. There's no question about us helpin', but we ain't just at your beck and call. We decide as a *team*—or not at all. I get you ain't used to that any more than he is, but it's about time you learned teamwork ain't just about bein' smart and tellin' people what do all the time. Got that?"

She bit into her lip. "You're right. I'm not communicating

with you as well as I should." She glanced over at Nat. "In the morning, then? I fully accept there are things you're better at than me. All I ask is you give me the same credit. I got good stuff at Pearl's."

Jake gave a gasp of exasperation. "He ain't saying you're stupid, woman. He's scared for you and too dumb to tell you outright."

"Oh," Abigail's eyes widened, glancing at the outlaw leader who glared at his uncle. "Well, there's no need to be. This is my choice."

"Enough." The gunman rolled out his bedroll. "It's late. You two can talk, or not, in the mornin'. If you have any consideration at all, you'll do it when I'm not here."

Chapter Ten

Nat watched Abigail as she sat on the porch, enjoying the weak morning sun, musing over the cloud of scribblings on her paper; a list of words in arcane writing, with thoughts which shot off in circled bubbles in all directions. Her impenetrable language lay scattered over the page in what had to be more organized than it looked. It appeared completely disordered with vowels and consonants arranged in nonsensical groups, but the arrows tracking one to the other showed she had some kind of structure to her investigation. Nat cursed her for not cooperating, but also had to admit he didn't blame her. He stood in the doorway admiring the graceful curve of her waist and the little curls on the nape of her long neck. It was so inviting and kissable, but he shook himself back to reality. That was madness. She might as well be the biggest, hairy-assed, smelliest, pot-bellied lawman he ever met because she'd stick him inside as soon as look at him. Jake had never been more right. He loved a challenge, but Abigail MacKay was a step too far, no matter how provoking. She could destroy his whole life, or even brutally end it. He shifted his weight, a floor board creaking in protest, alerting her to his presence. She turned, her feline eyes smoldering in the hinterlands between smile and question.

"Good morning, Mr. Quinn."

"'Mornin', Abi." He strolled over and leaned on the rail. "Looking over your notes, I see. Has anything occurred to you?"

"Only the obvious. What about you?"

He rolled his eyes. "Still not telling me anything? Look, we're either working together or we're not. If you're going to cut us out the whole time, you might as well go and leave this to us."

"Leave it to you?" Her brows met in consternation. "Why would I let a bunch of criminals take over a murder investigation?" Her dark eyes simmered with suspicion. "Are you planning on killing them? I won't help you murder someone."

His jaw firmed. "Haven't you learned anything about me? I thought you were supposed to be bright. I'd only kill to save a life. I handed the man who killed that railway guard over to the law."

"That guard wasn't a friend. Dora matters to Jake. This isn't the same."

"True, but I'm still not a killer. Don't get me wrong, I'll watch the hanging from a safe distance. It takes a special kind of evil to murder two defenseless women. I won't be sorry for them, but I'll leave killing to the law."

She nodded. "I know what you mean, but what about Jake?"

"He's never killed anyone who didn't try to kill him first, and each and every one of them was already a violent criminal. We survive, is all. Our world is violent and brutal." He sighed and crossed his long legs. "We need to come to an agreement, or this isn't going to work. You communicate with us, we share information; we work as a team. You want us to get the boy, we'll do it, but we need to know what you plan on doing while we do our bit. Don't you think this is risky for us, too?"

She nodded. "Fair enough. I plan on trying to speak to people who knew Dora before she became a prostitute, when she was a respectable married woman. They may have an idea why she hoped to come into money. They might also cast light on who R.D. is and why he sent her a telegram. I also want to know more about the people trying to adopt the boy."

"A telegram? Yes, they must be from out of the area," Nat frowned.

"It came from Boston." Abigail ticked off Celtic gobbledygook on her list. "So I plan on checking into the hotel after that. Let's see who's arrived who has those initials."

Nat's eyes narrowed. "On your own?"

"I've spent the last four years living in hotel rooms all over the country, Mr. Quinn. I don't make a habit of collecting random people to keep me company."

"That's as may be, but there's a killer on the loose, and he kills women."

She gave a huff of irritation and climbed to her feet. "Mr. Quinn. You met me in the most unfortunate of circumstances, but—"

"You can say that again."

She pursed her lips before she continued, "—but I am generally very professional. I am very grateful to both of you. You saved my life. I have no doubt about that, but it doesn't mean you have any hold on me or my actions. I am offering to help to pay my debt to you. I have dealt with killers before, quite a number of them. You need to let me do my job my way. I'm obligated to you. I really am—"

His voice dropped to a growl. "Are you?"

Her brow creased. "Of course I am. You're very humane men. You need to stop looking at me as a woman. I am a person doing a job. Anything which can happen to me can happen to a man."

His eyes blazed out from beneath the brown hair flopping onto his forehead. "Not everything, Abi."

She arched a brow. "Now you're being naïve, Mr. Quinn. That's not true, either."

He tilted his head, his cheek pitting with a joyless dimple. "See? You shouldn't know things like that. It's not right."

"But I do, so let's deal with reality, shall we?"

"I'm trying to make you face it, Abi. This is a dangerous world. I don't want you on my conscience." She sighed and walked back toward the door, but his hand shot out and grasped her arm. "I'm not finished."

She sucked in a breath and winced as he hit her injury. His face softened and eyes widened in dismay. His hand slid to her forearm in a gentle stroke. "Dammit! I'm sorry. I forgot. Did I hurt you?"

Her generous mouth slipped into her lopsided smile. "Only when you underestimated me. Look, can we start over? You stop being so suspicious and I'll share more. I'm not going to turn you in until this is over. I gave you my word, and I meant it. I'm after the killers, and want to pay my debt. You have to trust me at least a little. How about you go and look into the boy's safety and I'll speak to the women? You can't complain about me speaking to ordinary people. Women who drink tea?"

He nodded. "I guess. Just one question. Why don't you just flood this place with Pinkertons and solve this thing?"

She bit into her lip. "I suppose there's no harm in telling you. The area commander is dead set against having a woman working here at all. He'll glory in my failure. I won't take you two back to him, but there's no shame in it, because none of his men brought you in, either. If I can arrest the killers, at least I won't go back empty-handed. I'll still have done better than his men. You have no idea what it's like being a woman in that world. I have to prove myself constantly."

His jaw hardened. "So this isn't about paying us back?"

"Oh, yes. It is, and I understand the need to be doing something when you lose a loved one. That's how I became a Pinkerton; but if you weren't involved, I'd use local law enforcement before the local Pinkerton office. I have something to prove to them, too. This way, it's two birds with one stone. This isn't all concerning the two of you."

"It looks like you've got something to prove to everyone," his face gleamed with devilment. "I may not have a solution to you being a woman in a man's world, but I sure do admire the problem."

Her head dropped to stare at the hand still wrapped around her forearm. "Are you quite finished, Mr. Quinn?"

He released her, holding her gaze in an intense stare. "Not even a little, Miss MacKay."

She swallowed the charge spiraling in her chest. "No. I think you are. We have enough to deal with. We don't need to complicate things any further."

Nat Quinn and Jake Conroy watched the woman standing at the gate of the school yard. They wore their business suits once more, pressed and brushed down, so they looked a million miles away from the members of the outlaw fraternity.

"It's a good job you put your foot down with Abi this mornin'." Jake tried to look casual as he watched the woman with the wide-brimmed bonnet linger by the wall. "Otherwise, she'd be the one followin' these folks all the way from the orphanage to the school house in the freezin' cold."

"It made sense for us to do it," Nat frowned. "She's gone to find out about Dora's family from the townsfolk. Gossip is something women do better than us."

Jake chuckled. "Huh? Have you ever sat in the bunkhouse with the rest of the gang when Ghost Canyon is snowed in? It's like a quiltin' bee gone bad. Real bad."

The bell rang and the woman walked through the gate, heading straight for the building and the teacher standing in the doorway, pausing only to slow down and stare at the blond boy practicing his pitching with his classmates.

"You go. I'll watch the street." Jake muttered, his blue eyes searching for impending danger.

As he approached, Nat could hear the woman remonstrating with the pretty schoolteacher. "He has to come now. The train leaves in half-an-hour."

"The train, ma'am? What train would that be?"

Both women turned to look at the handsome man with the smiling brown eyes who blocked the path. The older woman answered, her sharp nose as good an indicator of her nature as her piercing eyes. "I can't see what business that is of yours, sir," she turned away to address the teacher again, but Nat stepped forward.

"Ma'am, I work for the Juvenile Asylum as an investigator. I would like you to explain what your interests in that boy are."

The woman took a heavy gulp and drank in the authoritative stance and the stony face which brooked no argument.

"I—"

The teacher stepped into the void as the woman floundered in front of them. "She says she's David's aunt."

His dark eyebrows flicked up in query. "I happen to know he had no family declared by his mother before she died, ma'am. I think you best come with me so we can look into this more deeply. We can't allow children to go off with just anyone, can we?"

"Since when?" the woman snorted.

"Since Henry Bergh formed a society to protect animals. There's been a lot of pressure to protect children, too. Handing them over to reputable local businessmen is one thing," Nat answered. "Letting them go off with just anyone is another thing entirely. The Society pays people like me to look after their welfare. The law is changing on children, ma'am."

"What Society?"

"The Schenectady Children's Union, ma'am. We work all over the country looking after people who can't look after themselves."

"I've never heard of it."

Nat shrugged. Of course she hadn't heard of it. He'd just invented it. "I don't care. We make sure orphanages check out people before children are handed over to them. You can't take him until you are checked." He threw an appealing look at the teacher. "Can you make sure the child stays here until we look into this?"

"Of course." The young teacher cast anxious eyes across the school yard. "David Benson. Come here right away." The small blond boy dropped his ball, enormous cornflower blue eyes widening to enormous globes of hurt. "Awww, Miss. Do I have to? I ain't done nothin' wrong."

"Yes!" She had barked with a harder edge than she intended as her fear for a child in her care hit her. She bit the words back, shaking her head with regret before she spoke with a welcoming smile, pasted on to combat her anxiety. "Come here, David. I need a good boy to help me sort the chalks." Her eyes brightened. "I have pie. We could have some while you help me."

"Apple?"

"Yes. You can have a big piece," she cast her gaze to an older boy in the yard. "John Peterson! I want you to make sure no children leave this yard while I go inside. Nobody should leave with anyone other than me or this gentleman. It's important. Any adults demanding a child leave should be challenged by all you big boys and someone must come and get me immediately. Am I clear?"

"Challenged? Even with catapults?" John asked, his eyes wide with hope.

"You cannot do anything without warnings, John. But no children can leave. None."

The boy's face brightened and he waved over his partners in crime. He had never had such power, and he intended to execute it in the most robust fashion. "Yes, Miss. Nobody leaves."

Nat held the woman's arm in an iron grip. "Come with me, ma'am. I have a few questions I want to ask you."

She pulled back, but Nat dragged her. She planted her feet apart and tried to stand her ground, but it was like trying to fight the wind, and before she knew it, she stood back outside the gate, face to face with Jake. His harsh glare threatened more than just an interview.

She stood rooted to the ground, her eyes darting between both men as she seemed to rally her courage. "Who are you? You don't work for a charity."

"It doesn't matter who we work for. What do you want with that boy?" Nat demanded.

"I'm his aunt."

"The boy has no family," Nat reiterated.

"He does. I'm his father's sister. I'm not going to let that boy end up in an orphanage just because his parents were too pig-headed to ask for help."

Nat and Jake shared a look of uncertainty. This woman was determined and stood up to them as though very sure of her ground.

"What's your name?" asked Nat.

"My name is Helena Hislop. Philip Benson was my brother. We've been looking on Dora from afar for many years, since Philip died. She would take nothing from us. She hated us since my father disinherited Philip for marrying a scullery maid; for running off with her."

Nat sighed. "You can't just take him, ma'am."

"Why not? We tried to adopt, but they want to go through official channels and he's in that place all the while. Have you seen it? Do you know what the inside of an orphanage is like? It's terrible."

"Why did they refuse?" asked Nat.

"Because he's already been claimed by someone else and is going to him next week. They offered me the pick of the rest, but it's not the same as blood, is it? Let the other man take *his* pick."

Nat threw her a sympathetic smile. "Ma'am, we can't let you take him. I'll make sure he's well cared for. Convince them you want him and do it right."

She glared at the lump in Jake's jacket. "I won't be intimidated by a thug with a gun."

"Yes, ma'am, but I'd take my colleague's advice if I were you. This ain't the way. Do it the proper way. Go to court."

She sniffed and took out a fluttering lace edged handkerchief and dabbed at her red rimmed eyes. "I loved my brother so much. I miss him every day. I would love to have given Dora and David a home, but she was stubborn. All I want now is to look after the boy. Is that so terrible?"

Nat released her arm. "Go to court to force it through if you want him now, but we can't let you steal a child."

"Thank you," she sniffed. "Mr.—"

"Smith," Jake replied with a knowing twinkle at his nephew. "Smith and Black."

They watched the woman's receding back as Nat turned to his uncle. "You believe that?"

Jake's eyes hardened. "Not one word. I knew Dora, and she'd have said something if anyone had tried to give her and her boy a home. Do you think pride in makin' it up with a relative would have stopped her when she was driven to sellin' herself?"

"Then why'd you let her go?" Nat demanded.

"What were we supposed to do? Shoot her down in the street?"

"Should we follow her?" Nat paused deciding against it. "Nah. She's seen us both and might get the law involved. The boy needs to be safe, that's the main thing." He glared after the thwarted woman. "I'll see her again without taking stupid risks. Let's get the boy."

♦ ◊ ♦

Abigail slipped into the room without a sound. Sash windows without a jamming mechanism were stupidly easy to open, and she would never have them in her home when she had one. Her existence was even more nomadic than The Innocents at the moment, and they didn't have any consistent base the law knew of.

She moved like a cat, creeping on her toes, carrying a bull's eye lantern with shutters so she could focus the light where needed or shut it out if required. These were called dark lights and were an essential tool for the average night-time thief, but they were just as useful to the law.

She stopped at the large mahogany desk and placed the dark light on the top before she rummaged through the desk, the top drawer catching against the brass lock. She held her breath. The information she wanted was most likely to be in the desk. She stood upright to remove her picklock from her hair and froze as a hand clamped over her mouth and a strong arm snaked around her body.

"Abi," Nat's voice hissed in her ear. "I'm disappointed in you. You're supposed to be an example to us criminal types." He released her mouth but continued to hold her against him as he whispered; his rich, dark-brown voice drifting through her senses as her stomach did a little flip. "You've got criminal tendencies. Someone should take you in hand. Want me to do it? I'd be real gentle this time."

She stiffened and shrugged him off swirling round to face the wide smile caught the low beams from the dark light. "What are you doing here?"

"Looking for the paperwork for David. What are *you* doing here?"

"The same." He shook his head. "Why didn't you tell me? We could have come together, made an evening of it. I'd have brought flowers and maybe some wine—"

"Can we get on with the job at hand?" Her brows knitted together. "Do you think it's in the safe?"

"Could be. I haven't had time to look. This is what I meant about sharing information. There's no need for both of us to be here. We're duplicating work."

"You didn't tell me either, Mr. Quinn."

"Because you were supposed to be checking into the hotel to talk to townspeople," his eyes glinted in the darkness. "You never said a word about coming here."

"Can we discuss this later? There are more pressing matters to deal with, don't you think?"

"Oh, yes. We'll discuss this. You and I need another talk."

"Is that how you intimidate your gang members, Mr. Quinn? It may not have occurred to you, throwing me out of your gang is no punishment."

"You have so little imagination. Imagine more." He folded his arms and leaned closer. His breath hit her face as he murmured in a rich velvet baritone. "I dare you."

Her breathing quickened before she shook herself back to business. "You smell of apples. Don't leave the cores lying about. We can get evidence from them."

He sighed. "Do you ever let yourself just be a woman?"

"Not when I'm breaking and entering." She cast out a hand

toward the desk. "You do the safe and I'll do the drawers."

The lights in his eyes switched from devilment to intrigue. "Three of them are locked."

She crooked an eyebrow at him. "I'll manage."

A huge grin spread over his face. "Oh, Abi. I knew you were something special when I met you. How about you do the safe and *I'll* do the drawers?"

Uncertainty flickered over her face. "I'll do the drawers."

He nodded, a secret smile playing around his lips. Another limit had been established, to be stored away in his encyclopedic mind. This could be useful in the future.

He turned as she pulled open the top drawer and dragged out a ledger. "That was quick."

"Was it?" She replied with a lick of innocence in her voice. She flicked through the thick vellum pages. "This is it." She hissed. "Mr. and Mrs. Mellor, Boston."

"Mellor? She told me the name was Hislop."

"And Mr. Andrew Burton. He made a donation of a hundred and fifty dollars." Abigail pursed her lips. "That's one expensive orphan. I can't read the address."

"No problem," he ripped the page from the book and it into his shirt. "We got all the time in the world now."

"You can't do that. It's theft."

"Yeah? You stand here after breaking in and try to lecture me?" he grasped her hand and pulled her towards the window. "Out you go. We'll discuss this back at the cabin."

"Where is he?" Abigail stared around the cabin. "I asked you to bring the boy here."

Jake stared at her. "I might be helpin' you, but I ain't about to leap into action because you issue an order, Abi. We ain't got time to babysit. He's bein' well-taken care of."

"Who by?"

"Friends. A real nice family. They got two girls who are spoilin' him to death. I think the youngest has a crush on him. It's so sweet it's sickening."

"He'd better not be in a foul hideout with a bunch of criminals."

"He'd be safer there than anywhere in this town," Nat dropped into a seat. "But he's not."

"And no one can find him?" Abigail appeared mollified.

"Can you?" Nat demanded in an open challenge. "Feel free to start right now."

She smiled. "Good. I need to go into town tomorrow. I have an appointment to meet some of the local women to find out more about the Middletons and Dora's past. I'm sure she's the key to this. I'll be staying at the hotel after that."

"You think they'll mix with a woman who used to work in a brothel? It ain't gonna work."

She flicked up an eyebrow. "I'll make it work, Jake. I also need to send a telegram to get Dora and her husband's past checked out in Boston for me. Once I've done that, there's just one thing left to do."

"What's that?" Jake put the coffee pot on the stove.

"I need to go alone for a psychic reading with the Schmidts."

The men exchanged a glance. "I can't allow that, Abi," Nat replied.

Her dark eyes gave an adversarial flash. "You can't stop me, Mr. Quinn."

"Can't I? I'm not the best man to push, Abi. Jake'll testify to that."

Her stomach fluttered as she realized he was issuing a serious warning. "I need to experience what they did that day. It's the only way I can find out what the Schmidts had to do with it, if anything."

"It's too dangerous. You going into town and asking questions is one thing, a stunt like this, off into the countryside on your own is another thing entirely. Two women have already been killed doing the exact same thing."

Her generous lips pulled into a smile. "I didn't know you cared, Mr. Quinn." She stood and strode over to face him. "It's my job. I've chosen to do it."

"Yeah? And do you think the murderers are gonna look after you like we did?"

She paused. "That's never happened before."

"And if we hadn't come along nothing would have ever happened again; except, maybe, your funeral." He leaned back on his chair and shook his head. "Nope. I won't allow it."

"So? Have you never had a close shave? This is a risky business. When you're no longer prepared to accept that, it's time to get out."

His answer was an impassive, hard stare.

"You looked after me, and I'm very grateful. I'm doing this for you, as well as Bessie and Dora. I need to thank you, but this isn't your decision. If I don't go alone, I won't get the real story."

"Don't try to tell me what I can and can't decide." The brown eyes glittered dangerously. "I can promise you won't win that way." He folded his arms and held her gaze. "You can go to the Schmidts' place, but we're comin' with you. You're not doing this without back up, and I won't hear another word about it."

"That'll be pointless. I can't arrive with a pair of gunfighters. I'll learn nothing."

"They won't see us. But we're backing you up," Nat replied.

She turned to Jake. "My stars, how can you work with him?" she huffed in exasperation.

Jake narrowed his eyes to the gleam of hard flint. "If he

hadn't said it I would've. I'm not about to let anyone take a risk like that, either. Not even him, and I know he can take care of himself. You've got a lot to learn about teamwork, Abi."

She paused. "Fine. They usually send me in alone. I'm not used to working with others, and when I do, men often need convincing of my abilities. It's a battle I've fought for years, even before I became a Pinkerton." She glanced from one to the other. "I'll trust you as long as no one sees I've brought back up."

"They won't. We know what we're doin'." Jake fixed on her as though she were a simple child. "There are lots of women on our side of the law, and none of us doubt they're good at what they do. We don't work to the same rules as everyone else. Results count, nothin' else. Don't pull that *woman* stuff on me."

"Thanks," she rubbed her face in defeat. "I'm turning in. I have to get up at dawn to get to town in the morning, if that's alright with you two?"

"As long as you really are goin' to town and not headin' out to the Schmidts' place, you can do what you want." Jake's brow furrowed. "What's the matter with you? First, you ride into the night after criminals on your own, and now you want to follow in the footsteps of two women who were murdered, and with even less back up than they had? Are you crazy?"

She stared back at him, mute and defiant, with eyes so dark he couldn't even make out the pupils. He frowned, sensing he'd hit a nerve.

"Abi? What's wrong?"

"Nothing," she pasted on a watery smile. "I just don't have any responsibilities; no family to worry about, so I don't consider the dangers enough. You're right. I need to be less impulsive. Goodnight."

She stepped over to the brass bed and pulled over the blanket which had been rigged up as a curtain to afford a measure of privacy.

Nat gestured with his head, inviting Jake outside to the porch. He waited until the door closed behind him. "What was all that about?"

"It's like she doesn't care about her own life. It comes last to everythin' else. That's a real deep hurt. She says she ain't got any family." Jake leaned on the rail. "Do you think somethin' happened? Somethin' like ours?"

"That's what I wondered," Nat folded his arms and stared out into the night. "And if we can believe her, she usually works alone. That could be important to understanding how Pinkerton aims at bringing us in."

"Yeah, there ain't many women out there like that; out there on their own, that's for sure. They should be easy to spot; people with no connections." The blue eyes glittered through the night. "Now I've just got to work out if it's strength—or a weakness."

"It's both, Jake. It depends on the situation. But now that I know, I can use it."

Chapter Eleven

Nat's brown eyes opened a crack at the sound of a splash of Abigail's washing behind the curtained-off area. The swish of fabric and the rumpling of materials as she got dressed followed. He glanced over at his uncle, who signaled his annoyance at being awakened before dawn in a flash of bleary blue eyes before he turned over and pulled a blanket over his head. She peeped around the curtain, but Nat feigned sleep and listened to her pad over to the door.

He waited for it to creak closed and followed her out to the porch where she sat buttoning her boots. The gray crepuscular twilight added silver tones to the morning chill and made the whites of her eyes gleam like mother-of-pearl as she turned her head around to face him.

"Creeping off, Abi? You know we can't let you negotiate your way to town without a blindfold. We need to keep this place private."

"Och, for heaven's sake. Can we stop this charade? If I haven't been able to work out the way by now I should be watered twice a week. I've known where we are for ages."

"I should've guessed." He arched a brow and gave her a wry grin. "We haven't had that talk yet, though."

"Talk?"

"The one I promised when you broke into the orphanage last night. The one about going it alone."

She tilted her head. "You mean when *you* went it alone and I walked in on you? It's too early to analyze irony."

"And yet, you're still doing it. Where are you going?"

"Would you believe, to the outhouse? You go there alone, too. If you want us all to go together, I have a problem with that."

"If you mean you're going there first before you take a horse and head off, yes. I would." He leaned on the rail blocking her way. "This can't go on. We need to be more honest with each other. I think we're risking more than you are."

She stared at him, her chocolate-brown eyes glistening with frankness. "I'm a head smaller than both of you and I'm out here alone. How can you say that?"

"Because I proved it to you. I took you to my limit as well as yours," he folded his arms. "I haven't seen anything like that from you."

She blinked in surprise. "I'm not going to ravish you, Mr. Quinn, no matter how nicely you ask."

He smiled in spite of himself. "Now let's not be rash and just go dismissing things out of hand. All I mean is, we only have your word for what you might do to us. One of the drawbacks of my profession are people's words don't count for much. I need more."

She stood. "Such as what? Don't you think I could have walked right over to the sheriff's office when I was at Pearl's? I didn't have to come back with Jake after the funeral parlor, either. I could have followed him with a posse. At some point, you're going to have to accept that all I've done is try to find out who murdered Dora and Bessie."

He paused, his intense stare glittering in the half light. "So where are you off to now?"

"To town. I need to speak to the women, and I need to access the wigs I have hidden there. You said yourself I can't see them looking like anyone who worked at a brothel. Is that a problem? You could come, too, and ask around to see if anyone has been trying to sell any stolen goods. The people who buy them will talk to you better than they'll talk to me."

He rubbed his face, his tawny bed-hair standing out on end. "Abi, I worry about you."

She smiled, her eyes warming. "That's sweet of you, Mr. Quinn. I must confess to having a creeping affection for you two. You are throwing your lives away, living like this."

"What else can we do? You get into a bad crowd when you're young and it gives you a life sentence. There's no statute of limitations in Wyoming. We'll be wanted as long as we live."

"I'm sure someone as ingenious as you could come up with something. Just go away, lie low, and reinvent yourself. Give this up."

He shrugged. "Maybe someday? When there's something to stop for, huh? I guess that's something we have in common. Neither of us cares too much about the future. I've seen that in a few reckless young men, but I've got to admit I've never seen it in a woman." His jaw tensed. "Why? What happened to you?"

The playfulness shut down, locked out by an impenetrable shield of darkness in the eyes. "Why must something have happened to me? Why can't women be adventurous?"

He shook his head, giving his mind time to run and analyze as he examined her. "Nope. I've seen that in plenty of women, but you take it to a whole other level. You do things experienced men would refuse to do. None of my gang would have trailed the Pattersons alone, and I wouldn't expect them to. Why would you do it?" He stared at the top of her head as she gazed at the floor. He took her chin in a crooked finger and lifted it so she faced him once more, speaking with delicate softness. "Don't you have anyone? Nobody at all?"

The absent eyes gathered mettle full of sparking lights in their depths. She raised her head away from the caressing forefinger. "Wasn't it you who told me you'd keep out of my family if I kept out of yours? I'm holding you to that, Mr. Quinn."

He frowned. "But you didn't. You're here with my only relative."

"Well, you would say that, wouldn't you? I could say the same, but would you believe me?"

"Yes. If you told me you were alone in the world, I'd believe it."

Her brow crinkled. "But not when I tell you I promise not to hand you in until this is over? You saved my life. I know what could have happened. I owe this to you and Jake. Then, we'll be even."

"Even?" He sighed. "If that's all this is, you can leave with no hard feelings. I'd have done it for anyone. So would you."

"Yes." A smile ghosted over her face. "But I still want you to know I'll help. It's what I do, and I do it for everyone. Nobody else will investigate it and you can't access the Pinkerton records if we need them. I'm staying, and I'm going to catch these people."

"We," he corrected. "*We're* going to catch them."

"Wee? That reminds me." Her eyes widened and she sidestepped him, trotting down the steps with a flash of white petticoat. "I'll be back in a minute."

He scowled and stepped out to follow her, stopped by a voice coming from the doorway behind him.

"Leave her be. She said she was goin' for a wee. She's gone to the outhouse," Jake leaned against the door jamb and smirked. "You've really forgotten all the Irish stuff, haven't you? The Scots say it, too. Your Ma would be ashamed of you chasin' a woman to the latrines."

"Eavesdropping, Jake?" Nat frowned. "You're better than that."

"No, I ain't, and my bladder *certainly* ain't." He pushed himself upright and walked back into the cabin calling behind him. "Let me know when she's done. I'm next."

♦ ◊ ♦

It was about ten o'clock in the morning when Abigail retrieved her trunk from the stored luggage area of Bannen's Railway station. She needed privacy to change her appearance and she set off to the rail yard to find a quiet corner as the public restrooms were little more than unsanitary latrines.

All of Abigail's wigs were human hair and were of the highest order. They were almost indistinguishable from a coiffured head, and she held a good variety of them for use at the drop of a hat. The first female Pinkerton had been an actress, and she promulgated the skills of her profession through the department. The women were trained with a theatrical make-up artist and had an infinite collection of prosthetics: noses, teeth, wrinkled neck skin formed elderly dewlaps which, when applied by her expert hand, meant even their own mothers wouldn't recognize them.

When the train from Topeka pulled in at twelve minutes after eleven, nobody paid any attention to the stout, middle-aged woman dressed in widow's weeds and carrying a carpet bag, who followed the porter. He pushed ahead with her large trunk on a trolley. Abigail understood how invisible unattractive middle-aged women were in society, and she exploited this sad truth whenever it suited her purposes. The women of Bannen would never associate her with the slim, curly-haired maid who had worked at the brothel, or the mousey Irish girl who ran off. She needed to look respectable.

"Porter." Her tones rang out in a clear, perfect American accent. All her Celtic vowels and rolled consonants gone.

"Can you direct me to a respectable boarding house?"

♦ ◊ ♦

"I'm hoping to find something out about the whereabouts of my son. He fell out with his father many years ago and we became estranged." She took a sip of tea from her flowered, china cup as she fixed the other woman with a pained expression. "You know how men are, and we women can do little to move them when they make up their minds. My David died six months ago, and I've decided it was time to reach reconciliation. I had heard he and his wife were in this area. I was told you could help."

Mrs. Leyton's eyes widened in sympathy. "I do know. We women just have to deal with it all. What was it? Money?"

Abigail shook her head. "Women. He fell in love with one of the servants. My David wouldn't have it, so they ran away together. David cut them off."

A pair of rheumy blue eyes opened in sympathy as the matron noted her new boarder had servants; plural. How gracious. How wealthy. How pleased was she to have this interesting arrival in town in her boardinghouse and to be in the vortex of the new storm of gossip about to sweep through Bannen? She leaned forward to get more details. "What's your son's name?"

"Philip. Philip Benson. His wife is Dora; Dora Blythe, as was."

She watched as the landlady took a great gulp of air and put down her tea cup. "I'm sorry, so sorry."

"Why?

"I don't know how to tell you this. He lived here."

"Has he left? Do you know where?"

"Oh, Mrs. Benson."

"What?"

"Your son is dead, and so is his wife."

Abigail sat in total silence as she shook the cup in the saucer so violently, Mrs. Leyton removed them from her hands, concerned she might chip her valued tea set. "When? How? Was there some kind of dreadful accident? What happened? Why did nobody tell us?"

"Your son died about three years ago. There was an explosion in the mine he worked in. Another man was seriously injured in the accident, but he survived. He was blinded."

Abigail swooned and fanned herself. "That poor girl. All on her own."

"She had a son. He's also called David. He's eight now."

Mrs. Leyton watched as she dabbed her eyes with a handkerchief. "He called him after his father. Oh, where is he? I must see him."

A stiff, pregnant pause stilled the room. "Dora is also dead. She became—" the woman groped for a sensitive way to tell this woman her daughter-in-law was driven into prostitution by poverty, "a working woman, a soiled dove, a fallen angel. She went missing not so long ago. They found her body just the other day in the most dreadful circumstances."

Abigail rasped her nose on her handkerchief, trying not to laugh at the woman's purple prose. When she had contained herself, she spoke in a voice cracking with amusement which could be mistaken for emotion. "The child? What happened to the child?"

"He went missing after being put into care."

"The poor baby. What are the authorities doing?"

"I'm not sure."

A hard edge crept into her voice. "Well. That's about to change. What kind of town is this where people are killed and children disappear and no one cares?"

"It's a very nice town, Mrs. Benson. I'm sure the sheriff will help you."

"I'm sure of it, too. He'll deal with this, or I'll have his badge."

♦◊♦

"Mrs. Benson" sat opposite the sheriff, her normal Scottish accent back in play. "I have here a letter of authority from Alan

Pinkerton himself. Please contact the agency by telegraph if you wish to verify my identity. I'd never normally carry this in deep cover, but I need to speak to you about a few things which necessitate supporting documentation." She leaned forward. "Please check. In fact, I insist upon it. I'll wait."

◆◇◆

Jake patted the neck of the sorrel who nickered and pawed at the straw, eager for the humans to stop talking and pay attention to her. She was hungry, and the stableman just stood there with the sack by his feet as he yammered away with this other human. Her ears flicked back and she dropped her head, stretching out her neck to nip at the bag. The stableman snatched it back. "Here now, Meggy. I'll give that to you when I'm good and ready."

"She's hungry," Jake laughed. "Feed her. I'm the same when I need to eat and folks are yakkin' away."

The old man nodded and emptied the sack into her tub and scattered over extra grains, apples and carrots. He watched the velvet nose drop into the food and grinned. "There ya go. I should get some peace now, huh?" He raised his head to face the visitor. "She's a character, that one. Belongs to a gent stayin' over at the hotel. You might wanna meet him. He sells novelties, and decided rentin' was too expensive and bought her." The stableman reached into his back pocket and fanned out a pack of cards. "Have you ever seen the like of this?"

Jake stared at an array of nude, or barely-clad, women in lewd poses. "If you think they're good you should see the ace of spades." The stableman shuffled. "Of course they needed her to be dark 'cause it was ace of spades, but wait'll ya see her. She should be in a travelin' show. I ain't never seen the like."

Jake shook his head. "I prefer the real thing."

"That's easy for you to say at your age, young fella." He stuffed the cards back into his back pocket. "When you get to my age, it's all a man's got to do to while away a long evenin'." He raised his beetled brows. "What did you want again?"

"It ain't a game of cards, that's for sure." Jake chuckled.

The old man laughed and pointed over to a bale of hay. He walked over to it and kicked it, causing the rising dust to dance in the golden sunbeams. He sat. "Folks sellin' stolen horses, you say?"

"Yeah," Jake joined him on the bale. "Pearl said you'd know if anyone did that around here."

"She's right. I would. What's your interest in this thing?"

"I was kinda fond of Dora," Jake replied, his face solemn, but his blue eyes flashing. "The law's doing nothin'."

"I know," the old man nodded his craggy head. "This ain't the town to sell stolen horseflesh, especially if it belonged to anyone local before it was took. Now, from what hear, they'd take them to a town about forty miles from here called Paris. It's a real dirty place, and it ain't got no sheriff. You can buy and sell anythin' there, and I mean anythin'—even people. Have you ever heard of it?"

Jake's face registered *faux* shock. "I've heard of it. They say outlaws can kick back there without worryin' about arrest. It must be a real hole."

"Oh, it is. I ain't never been there, but I've got a theory the bushwackers round here come out of Paris. I think they ride out from there and hit poor innocent folks before they head back. They're always that side of town."

"There's been bushwackin's?"

"Oh, yes," the stableman agreed. "They've been goin' on well nigh fifteen years, now. Ain't nobody ever been killed, though. I guess it was just a matter of time."

"Any descriptions? Are they all the same outfit, or just random?"

"It used to be just one man, back in the day, but now it's usually three men. I guess word got around it was easy pickin's or the first one got old and needed back up."

"How often do these happen?"

"I dunno," the old man creaked to a standing position, his hand propping his lower back with both hands. "Four, maybe five times a year? I ain't never paid too much attention to it. It's always strangers passin' through. Families, and the like. They go for easy targets, so the locals go armed with plenty of men or use the train. I'm sure it comes straight outta Paris 'cause it's full of them low-life cowards."

"And if I went to Paris? Is there anyone you think I should speak to?" murmured Jake.

"You can't go there, son. It's dangerous."

"I have no choice. I'm goin'. Who should I speak to?"

The old man looked at the straw-covered floor, scratching behind his ear. "I wouldn't, son. I really wouldn't."

"I'm thirty-six, and nobody's son," snapped Jake.

The stableman turned in surprise at the sudden anger in the younger man's voice. "Easy, I didn't mean nuthin' by it. I'm just worried for ya. If you have to go, take backup—lots of it. Five or more men. It's a treacherous place. I also don't count on you gettin' any answers."

"But you know the name of the man we should speak to?" Jake pressed.

"No. I only got rumors."

"Rumors are enough. I want a name. Where do I start?"

"Ethan. Ethan Green. He'll buy horses from anywhere." The older man scowled. "Don't take that attitude with him. He'll shoot you quick as look at you."

Jake stood. "I'll take my chances." He reached into his waistcoat pocket and pulled out a few notes. "Thanks for your help. He'll never hear from me where I got his name."

The stableman watched Jake turn and stroll out of the building. He walked over and stroked the mare's ears. "A nice young fella, Meggy. What a shame he'll never make it outta Paris alive."

Chapter Twelve

The man glowered at her from under tufted brows, which, when combined with his wiry frame and dun-colored hair, gave him the look of an irritated Jack Russell Terrier. He discarded the reply from the Pinkerton Agency with a mute shake of the head at the madness of the modern world and slumped into the seat opposite, glaring at her in open challenge.

"An old woman? Are they kiddin' me? I ain't got any knittin' patterns in this office."

"I don't think I need to tell you I require the utmost discretion in this case. You can tell no one who I am. Mr. Pinkerton will take the matter up with the state governor himself if it gets out. You're the only person who knows. It couldn't come from anywhere else."

"I can't spare no men to look into the death of two whores. We're stretched enough looking after the respectable folks. I guess Pinkerton ain't got any spare, either, to send the likes of you."

Abigail swallowed her distaste for the man. "I'm not asking for men or any other resources, Mr. Thompson. I simply want to know a few things. At worst, you can collect evidence which needs a badge behind it."

"Such as what?"

"Let's start with crime in the area. Has anyone else been killed in circumstances which are similar, regardless of how they made a living?"

"Of course not. What kind of town do you think I'm running,

here?"

She fixed him with intense brown eyes. "Since you ask, one in which the brutal murder of two women and a kidnapping of an innocent child doesn't even merit you attempting to leave the office. That's not good in anyone's book. I was taught justice is blind, but you also seem to want to make her as deaf and dumb, too."

He half-stood, leaning on the desk as he glared at her with beady eyes. "It's a good job you're an old woman or I'd make you regret that remark. What the hell are they doin' employin' an old baggage like you?"

Abigail smiled to herself but understood she was getting more respect than she would get if he knew she was only twenty-four. "People say things around old ladies they won't say to a man with a star. It's a matter of getting results, and you will be judged on whether you help or hinder me in getting them. Now, killings in the area, please?"

He muttered under his breath as he brought out a large ledger. "There've been occasional bushwackin's, but nothin' like the whores. There are shootouts and a few stabbin's in bars. There may be a fella or two who've slapped their wives a bit too hard and ended up in the cells for the night. This is a good town."

"How occasional are the bushwhackings?"

"A few a year. Nobody killed before the whores though, except for old man Schmidt. They've been goin' on for over fifteen years now. It could be as long as twenty. I'd have to check."

"Schmidt?"

"Yeah lives out—"

"I know where he lives." Her brow furrowed. "When and how did he die?"

The sheriff examined her in open surprise, bemused by her local knowledge. "He got shot. His body was found just on the outskirts of town the day before yesterday. Are you talkin' about the same one? The one with the boy who's a bit simple?"

Abigail paused in thought before she spoke. "Through the forehead?"

"Yeah. How'd you know?"

She nodded. "I didn't. I guessed. I need to see the body."

"Why? It's just an old man in a box. There ain't no clues there."

"I need to see if he put up a fight."

Thompson shrugged. "Suit yourself. I'll get my deputy to take you over to the undertaker's office, but I don't get it."

"Do you have descriptions of the bushwhackers?"

"Three men, heavy-set, masked. One little. I ain't got nothin' more."

"Has Kurt always been simple?"

"Always," he nodded. "The teacher couldn't even teach him in the school when they arrived here. He's real backward, but pleasant enough. Smiley, but simple. He ain't no bother."

"Any pattern in the robberies?"

The lawman shook his head. "Random. There are all kinds of victims, just folks passin' through. There weren't hardly anyone local until Schmidt."

"Or until the women. What would make these robbers suddenly kill?" She nodded, knowing he thought he was being far from helpful and confronting her with a show of dumb insolence. "I have a job for you. I want to know if Dora or Bessie sent telegrams to anyone. If so, to whom. I want details for everything they sent; details of the contents, the replies which came back, everything. There was a telegram in Dora's room dated the week before she was killed saying someone with the initials R.D. would visit. Find out about that."

"How the hell did you find that out?"

Abigail pulled a censorious face. She enjoyed playing a part, especially when she could wind up the feckless or judgmental.

"Language, young man."

His lips curled into a snarl. "I told you, old ladies have a way of getting people to help them. Please understand if you underestimate people it only ever makes it easier from them to get one over on you. I would prefer that we work together. If we don't, I can make you look like an incompetent fool by pointing out to the governor you could have found all this out for yourself—but didn't bother. "

"I'll get on it." He grumbled, muttering through a grudging breath.

"One more thing. I need a description of anyone who made enquiries about adopting David Benson and anything else they have on them, all the supporting documents. Anything at all, no matter how small." She stood and walked over to the door. "Shall we say, tomorrow? None of that should be hard to get for a man wearing a badge."

Sheriff Thompson glowered at her receding back as she walked out. If they had sent a man, he could fight him, even provoke him into drawing—but what was he supposed to do with an old woman? Call her out in the street and beat her to a pulp? No, he needed to get her out of town as fast as possible.

◆◇◆

Nat and Jake sat in Pearl's drawing room in a black mood. "Where the hell is she? She told us she was comin' back to town. She said she'd meet us here an hour ago."

"No one's seen her since she left here," Pearl relaxed into a cushion. "That suits me just fine. If I *never* see her again it'll be too soon."

"I don't like this," muttered Jake. "She's vanished off the face of the earth. Do you think she's headed out to the Schmidts on her own?"

"She's ornery enough to do just that," Nat muttered.

"She said she'd be talkin' to townsfolk, women and people who knew Dora before she fell on hard times."

Nat nodded. "Let's get over to the Middletons and see what they know. That's one of the places she said she was going. We'll take another turn about town and see if we can see her. If not we're heading out to the Schmidts. That damned woman is as stubborn as a hungry mule."

"Good luck, boys," Pearl watched them leave with a sigh. "Time to get back to work. Appetites never cease, and there's money to be made in caterin' to them. If you need any more back up from my boys, just ask."

The two men strode out into the caustic sunlight and glanced around the streets of Bannen. Nat nodded over to an alley. "Middleton lives along here."

◆◊◆

The ramshackle building testified to the poverty of the Middleton family. The blistered green paint on the clapboard finish was peeling and the front yard sprouted dominating weeds which arrogantly defied the pecking of the skinny chickens darting around. They flicked their scrawny necks back and forth as they scuttled away from the visitors to what was little more than a glorified hut. Jake paused as a stout woman in her sixties dressed in black passed them and carried on through the alley toward the main street.

"What?" Nat hissed. "What's wrong?"

He shook his head and glanced back seeing everything and nothing. "I dunno. There's something wrong, but I can't put my finger on it."

They both glanced around, searching for danger with a practiced eye, but everything remained resolutely normal. Children played, washing dried on the lines, an old woman walked on, and birds flew overhead. "I guess someone just walked over my grave," said Jake.

Nat frowned and glanced around once again. He trusted Jake's instincts, and he had regretted any occasion where he had dismissed his intuition as mere fancy. "Let's get on in case someone's following us. We'll leave the back way."

◆◇◆

"What do you want?" The blind man faced them, his head inclined at an unnatural angle to maximize his ability to hear. One eye was sealed behind a twisted crater, hidden behind the impenetrable scars ravaging his face. His nose was hideously twisted and the light-brown hair sat in tufts over the now healed, but contracted flesh of white and purple mottled scalp. The other eye had the appearance of an abominable, unseeing marble, rolling back in his skull.

"Sir? We are friends of Dora Benson. We're trying to find out what happened to her. Can we talk to you?" Nat's politeness echoed his cool smile. "You knew her from your work as the pianist at Pearl's."

Ben Middleton shook his unseeing head in frustration. "Talk to me? What the hell's going on here? I just told those women where to go. Why'd you think I'd do any different for you?"

"Women?"

"Yeah. They've just gone. You must have seen them unless you're blind, too. Two of them. One was Scottish."

Nat darted a look at Jake. That had to be Abigail. They exchanged a smile knowing she was out there; somewhere. But why hadn't they seen her?

"No, sir." Jake cut in. "We know nothin' about that. I've known Dora for about two years and I was shocked to find out she'd been killed. I was even more shocked to find out the law are doin' nothin' about it. I want to help, if I can."

Nat looked into the man's distorted face. The explosion

which killed Dora's husband was violent, and Ben Middleton had been lucky to survive. Middleton's thin lips opened again.

"One of them said she was Phil's mother, but I was having none of it. I knew she weren't, and sent them off with a flea in their ears. Threatened them with the law if she didn't clear off."

"Phil Benson's mother?" Nat processed this information as his stomach sank. "A fraud? How would you know she wasn't who she said she was?"

"None o' your business," barked Ben Middleton.

"Sir, one of those ladies is a friend of ours, and she has now gone missing. If she's goin' around with someone who's not who they say they are, I'm worried. How would you know the other woman was an imposter?"

"I just do. She's dead. Phil told me so. Now, get the hell out of here."

"Sir," Jake interjected. "Can we speak to your wife?"

"She ain't here. She works in the laundry."

Nat frowned. "You have an Eastern accent. Where are you from?"

The man gave an urgent huff of irritation and tried to close the door but Jake wedged his foot through the gap.

"Mister. Everyone at Pearl's says you and Dora were real close. Don't you want to help her? Don't you think you owe it to her son, at least?"

He hesitated. "David?"

"Yes. We've known Pearl since we were boys. Ask us anythin' about her or Dora if you doubt who we are. Please?"

Ben's shoulders sagged and his voice softened. "I can't help you. I was real fond of Dora and I would take the boy if I could afford to, but we're hand to mouth as it is. I don't know who killed her. All I know is she was real excited about something and said it would change her life. I don't know anything more than that. She said it would be a surprise. She deserved it. I got a pittance from the mine for being injured, but she got nothing 'cause Phil died; not a penny, because they blamed him for the explosion. The insurance wouldn't pay her for him. That was a crock, too. I was there and it wasn't his fault, but he wasn't here to speak for himself."

"Coming into money? When did she say that?" Nat and Jake exchanged a glance.

"A few days before she died," Middleton shook his head. "If I knew who killed her, I'd be shouting it in the streets. I damn myself to hell that I couldn't do more for her or her boy. She shouldn't have had to do that. That place, those men. The very thought of it broke me. She had nobody. Dora's folks were dead, she lost her husband, and Phil's brother died years ago. She had nowhere to turn."

They both heard the emotion catch in his voice. Jake reached out and touched his hand. "Thank you, sir," his voice was soft, trying to reassure. "Can we let you know if we find anything? Will that help?"

The unseeing head twitched. "You'd do that?"

"Yes, sir. We will." Middleton proffered a hand and Jake took it and shook it in agreement. "I can promise we'll do our best for her and her boy. If you need us, tell Pearl. She can find us for you."

"Thanks. I will," Middleton replied. "What's your names?"

"Pearl calls us her boys. Just tell her that. She gave us a roof when we were little."

"Yeah, Pearl's like that. She collects waifs and strays. That why I play there. Good ta meet ya, boys," Middleton drew the door shut leaving them standing looking at the peeling paint. Nat strode out as soon as the door closed.

"Where are you goin'?" demanded Jake.

"I'm gonna find those women who were here. One of them's Abi. The other's a fraud, and I want to speak to her."

"We only saw one woman. The old lady."

Their eyes locked as they spoke in unison. "What has she done with Abi?"

♦◇♦

They saw her in the distance and she sure moved fast for an old lady.

"That's her." Nat gestured with his head. "She was the only one walking away. Abi's got to be in one of the buildings in the lane."

They quickened their pace, gaining ground on her, but they had to be careful. Two young men couldn't be seen to be browbeating an elderly woman in the street. They timed their approach, splitting so Jake could approach her from the front after ducking down another alley and overtaking her as she reached the main street.

She saw Jake coming, wondering how he had got in front of her; time to cross the road, and fast. As she stood at the sidewalk ready to step into the busy road, a gloved hand curled around her left wrist.

"Ma'am. I'd like to talk to you, if you don't mind. We just saw you leavin' the Middletons' place." It was Nat. He had closed in from behind in a pincer movement.

She switched to her American accent as she glared through her veil at the hand holding her wrist. Abigail was determined not to let these criminals know how good she was with disguises. Every secret asset gave her the element of surprise. "I don't have time young man."

Nat hung on as he nodded to Jake they had the right woman. "Ma'am, we want to know where our friend is. You were with her at the Middleton place. Two women walked away from the house, but only one reached the main street."

"I know nothing about your friend," she pushed her way forward but Jake swung an arm around her waist and they deftly negotiated her back into the alley behind. She fought, but they held an arm each as they lifted her a few inches from the ground. Her only way out was to cry out for help, but she was in no position to raise her profile. She was pushed against the wall and Jake leaned with his hand over her head and lowered his face to hers with burning blue eyes.

"Ma'am? I want to know where our friend is please."

Abigail swallowed a knot of irritation. They clearly didn't recognize her, she needed to misdirect them. She didn't want them to know how skilled she was with disguises. "She's in the sheriff's office."

Nat wasn't buying it. "That's the other end of the main street. How'd she get there faster than you?"

Abigail shrugged. "She's younger than me. She's quicker."

"You move pretty well for a woman your age." Nat examined her, his scrutiny making her uncomfortable. At least the light in the alley was poor so any faults in her makeup were going unnoticed under her veil. "I've had enough of this. Let me go. Right now, or I'll call for the sheriff."

"Ma'am, what's your name? Maybe we *should* call the sheriff… A woman is missin' and you ain't helpin'?" Jake's demand was growing more instant. His eyes narrowed. "Calling the law is a better option than stayin' down an alley with two angry men. You got a choice. Pick one."

She nodded her head with genuine reluctance. The game was up. "I'm flattered gentlemen; very flattered. You care." She had switched to her own voice and watched as confusion crowded their faces. "Yes. It's me."

"Abi?"

She nodded. Her secret was out.

Nat sucked in a breath. "What the—"

"For heaven's sake, Jake. Let me go. It's me, Abigail."

Her eyes darted from one to the other behind the pebble glasses. "I believe there's a restaurant a few doors away. Let's talk there."

◆◇◆

They sat at the table as they gawked at her disguise. Neither of them had ever seen the like in their lives.

"Och, for heaven's sake. Stop staring at me. Have you never seen an old lady before?"

"I ain't never gonna look at them in the same way again, that's for sure. How did you do that? He said there were two women," Jake replied.

"He's blind, Jake." Nat grinned at him. "She used two different voices."

"Ah." Jake flushed in shame.

"You do one hell of a disguise Abi. You got any others?"

"No. Who's got the time?"

His eyes danced with mischievous lights as he sat back and grinned pensively. "Yeah. Right."

"Why were you pretendin' to be Dora's mother-in-law?" asked Jake.

She dropped her gaze as the pretty waitress came over to the table. Jake lit up like a Christmas tree as he beamed his most charming smile.

The receptive girl peered through her coy lashes. "What'll it be?"

"Coffee please, and pie? You got any pie?"

"Sure. Apple or Cherry?"

"Apple." Both men spoke together.

The waitress's coquettish grin was still aimed at the males. "And your mother?"

Abigail lifted her head and smiled. "Ooh, cherry please, but they're not my sons."

"No?"

She leaned forward and grasped Jake's hand. "He's my husband."

Jake spluttered and tried to pull his hand away but she held on tight.

"Don't be embarrassed, darling," she grinned before turning

back to the waitress. "My father thought he married me for my money, but I know better. You don't get passion like that between the balance sheets."

The young woman gaped in amazement at the crone who seemed to satisfy the virile, handsome young man more than half her age. Jake colored from the neck up as Abigail pushed her glasses back up her nose with one finger and coughed into her handkerchief.

"Errr, yes." The waitress murmured before she walked away as Jake hissed as Abigail.

"What did you do that for? She smiled at me. She liked me." Abigail leaned forward as Nat chortled into his napkin.

"Because you were strong-arming me in the alley. Did you think I'd let you off scott-free?"

His eyes fixed on her. "I swear, Abi! She thinks I like little old ladies for their money. When this is all over—"

She finished his sentence for him. "You'll laugh about this. Look, they're all looking out from the kitchen. They're laughing. Everyone else thinks it's funny."

"Back to business," muttered Nat as he swallowed his mirth. "Why did you pretend to be Mrs. Benson?"

"Because it was the best way to get people to open up to me. I've learned nothing new except Ben Middleton seems to know the real Mrs. Benson. That raises another question. How does he know her?"

"He told us she was dead."

"Hmmm, still. He seemed really certain, and people estranged from their family often just claim they're dead to avoid questions. Phil Benson fits the bill, but Ben Middleton had the air of someone who knew firsthand, and not just anecdotally. I'm going to look into his past, too. It's better to get facts than run on assumptions."

The waitress arrived with their order.

"Thank you, dear," Abigail smiled and watched the girl beat a hasty retreat from their table. "Old man Schmidt has been murdered, in another violent bushwhacking." Abigail glanced from one man to the other. "I went to see the body. He was shot in the forehead without putting up any fight that I could see. Because of the powder burns, it had to be point blank range."

"Shot?" Jake's brow creased. "Well, I guess that kills my theory. I thought it *was* the Schmidts. I spoke to the stableman today and he reckons the robberies come from Paris. He gave me a lead on someone who might know who buys and sells stolen property there."

"So we go to Paris?" Abigail suggested.

The men shared an incredulous look.

"We ain't takin' a respectable woman to Paris, Abi. We'll go alone," Jake snorted.

"You'll just cramp our style," Nat agreed. "We need to go there alone."

She pursed her lips and spoke after a considered pause. "Fair enough. I'm sure I can find something useful to do here. I'll look into the prospective adopters."

"I hope you mean that." Nat narrowed his eyes in suspicion. "I guess we've done all we can in Bannen except to get the psychic reading."

"We're closing in. We need to look at the page from the ledger and see what we can decipher from it. I'm going to check into the hotel tonight as the old lady. I can't go without this heavy disguise just yet." She paused and stroked Jake's hand. "Darling, do you prefer me like this? I could hold onto it?"

His hard fist gripped her hand. "Do that again and I'll crush your fingers," he hissed.

The waitress passed by and her eyes fixed on the man's long fingers wrapped around the old woman's hand before she stared straight into his eyes with a look of total disdain. His heart sank as she walked away, shaking her head while Nat and Abigail choked with laughter.

Chapter Thirteen

"Mrs. Earnestine Cadwallader," Abigail stood at the desk of the hotel in full little-old-lady regalia. "What rooms do you have available?"

The clerk's round spectacles twinkled. "For you, and Mr. Cadwallader, I can offer you our best double room. It's a corner room, right at the front and gets the sun first thing in the morning. Windows on both sides."

He stretched to look over her shoulder. His brow creased at the size of her enormous trunk. "Is that yours, ma'am?"

"Yes, but it isn't heavy, though."

"It'll need two men to carry it upstairs just for the size alone. Is your husband getting the rest of the luggage?"

"My husband died years ago, and there's no more luggage."

"Well, that's a relief," the clerk's eyes widened as he realized what he'd just said. "About the luggage, not your husband. I'm so sorry for your loss."

"Thank you, but as it happened fifteen years ago, I'm not in deep mourning," Abigail inclined her head benignly.

"She's traveling with her son," Nat's baritone voice drifted from behind her as an arm slipped around her thick waist and dropped a light kiss on her surprised cheek. "A double room, you say? Perhaps a twin would be better?"

She swiveled around to glare at him, but he stared ahead at the clerk, a charming smile beaming sweetness and light like an annoying beacon through a window in the dead of night which disturbed sleep. "Can you help?"

"Well," the clerk began as he pored over his register, "number five can be converted into a suite with twin beds adjoining by opening the double doors in between. It's a little more expensive but—"

"We'll take it," Nat announced. "Shall we say three nights in advance for cash? We may need more."

"That will do very nicely, Mr. Cadwallader. Can you complete the register?"

Nat fixed Abigail with a keen eye while still grinning at the desk clerk. "Sure." He picked up the pen and scribbled in an exaggerated expansive scrawl. "Nathaniel Cadwallader."

He turned to Abigail. "Mother, dear. Would you like to sign?"

"That won't be necessary. We only need the signature of the head of the household."

The clerk clicked his fingers and the bellboy appeared, his jaw dropping in dismay at the sight of a trunk just inches shorter than himself. The clerk pointed to the stairs. "Johnny, get Bert and take the luggage to number five."

Johnny frowned scratching his head at the enormous trunk. "We moved West in somethin' smaller'n that."

Nat led his 'mother' toward the stairs. "There'll be a generous tip in it for you, son. Women don't travel light. You know what they're like."

"I thought I did," muttered Johnny, "but this one seems to come with a box of spares."

Nat threw open the double doors between the two rooms and nodded in appreciation.

"Over here, sir?" Johnny and a waiter placed the trunk by the dresser.

"Perfect," Nat fished out a tip and tossed a few coins to

both men.

"Thanks."

The doors closed behind the lad and Abigail's mouth opened, but Nat placed a finger on his lips and padded over to the door. He took a cautious glance outside before locking it. He reached into his pocket jammed a door wedge in place, then walked to the adjoining room and forced a chair under the door handle.

"Can't be too careful, can we? This way, nobody can force their way in and surprise us."

"Do you always wedge the door shut?"

"Sure, I do. Locks can be unlocked. This buys us more time to get away if we need it."

"Mr. Quinn, I have no intention of 'getting away'. If you don't feel safe here you should have gone back to the cabin instead of muscling your way in. What were you thinking?"

He turned back to her, the sunlight from the window catching his chestnut hair, lighting it with golden-red tones. "I thought there was no need for you to spend a night here without protection. It's too late for us to head off Paris tonight and we've got to stay somewhere. This is perfect. It's the right side of town."

"You just want to poke around in my chest." She flushed bright red as she realized what she had just said.

Nat laughed and wandered over to the trunk. "You're not wrong. Are you offering a key, or do I have to force my way in?"

"I'm offering nothing. My possessions are private."

"I think you've got a whole wardrobe of disguises in there; everything from boys to old men. Am I right?"

She shook her head. "This isn't helping. People talk more freely to an old woman alone."

He leaned on the trunk crooking one leg casually. "I'm not going to get in the way of chatting. You'll be surprised at how people take to me. They find me very personable," he patted the luggage. "They rarely come with as much baggage as you."

"Are you just going to stand there making puns?"

"You started it," he picked up his saddle bags and took them through to the twin room. He closed the double doors, smiling through the crack. "I'm going to get changed for dinner. No peeking unless you really have to. In which case, you're welcome to come join me."

♦◊♦

The old lady settled herself in the lounge, smiling at the people enjoying a pre-dinner drink. Her attentive son soon arrived with a glass of sherry and a whiskey for himself. "Here you go, Mother," Nat sat on the sofa beside her and crossed one leg over the other, propping his ankle on his knee.

Abigail leaned forward. "Are you staying here, Mr.—?"

"Rigby Daintree. Yes, ma'am. I'm a traveling salesman." He leaned forward with a gapped-tooth smile. "Novelties and curiosities. They're very popular."

"How interesting. Is there much call for such things in the West?"

The skeletal-thin man nodded. "Sure is. I've been doin' very well."

The old woman's gray head inclined with interest. "How long have you been here?"

"Oh, a couple of weeks."

"What kind of curiosities? They must sell well to keep you here."

"Ahem," all eyes turned to the small, dapper man at the other end of the lounge who hooked Nat with a warning glance. "This is your mother? Those curiosities aren't fit to be seen by a decent woman."

The man's graying hair had been bright red, given the traces of gold flashing through the silver, and his little polished feet barely touched the floor. In another outfit, he could be mistaken for an aging leprechaun. "You're going to get yourself shot if you keep offering that trash of yours to ladies, Daintree."

Nat darted a warning glance to Daintree and smiled gratefully at the little man. "Thank you, sir."

"Tiberius Ulysses F. Dunbar, at your service." He gave a twinkle of previously unseen charm. "A bit of a mouthful, I admit, but there's something about Irish mothers; the poorer they are, the grander the name they give their offspring. As you can probably guess from my extravagant moniker, my sainted mother was as dirt poor as they come. She wasn't the religious type; she preferred the classical over a congregation of saints. People call me Tibby."

"What does the F. stand for?" All heads turned as Jake walked into the lounge and took a seat beside Nat.

"Nothing. She thought an initial sounded good, so she threw one in. All my life people have been volunteering their versions. They vary between the very unoriginal to the obscene." Tibby appraised Jake with shrewd blue eyes. "And your name sir?"

"Jake Black. And this is my partner Nathaniel Cadwallader. The lady is Nat's mother. She's taking the chance to travel with us to visit relatives."

"What line of work are you gentlemen in?" asked Tibby.

"We work for a charity," Nat toyed with his glass. "It's a charity that helps place orphans without exploitation. We inspect processes and establishments. And you, Mr. Dunbar?"

"Politics. I advise people on how best to run their campaigns."

"That's a job?" Nat grinned. "Who knew?"

"Yes. Who knew yours was a job, either? It takes me away from home a lot, much to Mrs. Dunbar's delight." Tibby sat back in his chair. "I'm a constant disappointment to her. I think she hoped I'd drink myself into the grave like her father, but I haven't mastered that either, so I work away from home."

"Goodness! That's terrible," Abigail's eyes widened.

"Tell me about it," Tibby chuckled. "It wasn't even his grave. There was a terrible to-do pulling him back out. Don't drink until after the funeral, that's my advice."

"I think you are messing with me, young man," laughed Abigail.

"Guilty as charged, madam," the little man relaxed back in his chair. "A few laughs always help the evening pass far more quickly."

All eyes turned to the couple who walked into the room. The woman's curt nod to the company was an obvious dismissal. They took a seat in the corner as the man walked over to the waiter.

"Good evening. I was beginning to think I was the only lady," beamed Abigail. "How do you do? Mrs. Earnestine Cadwallader. I'm traveling with my son and his friend."

The woman didn't respond, so Abigail pushed the issue. "And you are?"

"Mrs. Richards, Victoria Richards. And this is my husband, Denham."

The husband returned with a frown at nobody in particular. "Victoria. Enough."

"The lady asked."

"We like to keep ourselves to ourselves, madam." The husband tugged at the creases of his trousers to stop them bagging at the knees as he sat. "We don't mean to be rude."

"I completely understand," Abigail pressed regardless. "You don't *mean* to be. That's fine. It's just that I'm so pleased to have a lady to talk to." A dull stare met her questions. "It's boring here for a lady. Perhaps your wife could point me to any ladies' meetings and associations? Have you been here long? Is there much for a lady to do?"

"Vicky doesn't mix well. She's shy." Nat and Jake shared a

look of amusement as the husband glared at Abigail. "My wife isn't available for your entertainment."

"Of course, sir," Abigail's smile buried fierceness amid the brightness. "I've encountered many ladies like your lovely wife. I can understand why you would guard her closely. You cherish her so much it hurts. And you, Mr. Richards? What do you do?"

"I came here to be the headmaster of the new school they are building. The accommodation isn't completed yet, so they put us up at the hotel. It wasn't what was promised. I'm not amused. "

"Nobody could tell. How long have you been here?" asked Abigail. She caught her breath as the waiter arrived and the man stretched out an arm to receive the drinks. His cuffs slid back and revealed a myriad of vermillion tracks, deep red and newly-healed scars.

"Since the beginning of last month. It is not what I expected at all."

"What did you do to your arm, Mr. Richards?"

He averted his eyes, tugging at his cuffs before glaring at Abigail for daring to encroach on his privacy. "Nothing which concerns you, madam. Please stop bothering us."

The room fell into an icy silence and Mrs. Richards stared at her feet. Her husband stood. "Come, Victoria. We will sit in the dining room."

"I don't think they're ready for us yet, Denham."

"I don't care. They can lay tables around us," he stood, beckoning abruptly with his fingers. "Victoria. Come."

She stood, following her husband. Abigail watched the cowed eyes and stiff posture in the woman and relented. She turned her attention back to Tibby. The little man arched his brows and smiled around the room. "That was fun, wasn't it? Makes you glad you're not at school where people like that rule anymore, huh?" He turned back to Abigail. "At least we have some conversation around here. How long are you staying?"

"I'm tired of traveling," Abigail replied as all heads turned to watch the waiter fold back the doors to announce dinner. "I will rest here for a few days before moving on to San Francisco. My son has work in the area."

"I've been here a few weeks," Tibby replied. "I came in on the train where the guard got shot. The one which was held up. Very scary."

"You were?" gaped Abigail. "You must have been terrified."

"Not very, more shocked." Tibby shook his head, a rueful moue on his expressive face. "I'm glad they put them behind bars so fast."

"It was The Innocents. Wasn't it?" Daintree ventured.

"Imposters," Jake murmured. "The Innocents never kill."

"They'll steal from ya, though," Daintree continued. "Ain't ya worried about bringing your mother out here?"

"I don't scare easily, young man. In any case, I can't see a gang of criminals in having any interest in a little old lady. I'm far from wealthy." She smiled at Daintree. "So they frighten you?"

"No. I was just thinking of you."

"Well, there's a first," chortled Tibby. "In all the weeks I've known you, I've never seen you think about anyone but yourself, Daintree." He turned to the waiter who stood by the doors to the dining room. Tibby lowered himself to the ground and walked over to Abigail, proffering an arm. "It looks like dinner is served. May I escort you in, madam?"

She stood towering over the man by a good three inches as she took his arm.

"You may. How refreshing to find a gentleman out here. Thank you, Mr. Dunbar."

"I was always taught to be respectful to my elders, madam. It's just that it's getting harder and harder to find one by the day."

◆ ◇ ◆

A thin-faced, fair-haired man strode into the dining room and glowered at the large communal table in surprise.

"Ah, Davies." Tibby waved the man over. "There you are. Isn't your wife with you? We kept you both chairs."

"One table?" Davies queried in disbelief.

"Yeah, Mrs. Cadwallader insisted," muttered Daintree. "Wants us all to get to know one another on her first night here. I don't see why you should get away with it."

"You have a wife with you?" Abigail trilled.

Davies nodded, his face sullen. "Mary isn't coming to dinner. She's having one of her headaches. They're giving her a tray in her room."

"Oh, how sad. Then you must join us," she insisted. "We can't have you eating alone. Move over gentlemen, there's plenty of room."

The place filled with the echoes of clattering dishes, tinkling cutlery, and scraping chairs, leaving the new arrival very little choice but to join the table.

"So, here we all are," Abigail beamed around the table. "You have all been here for weeks and know one another well, so I'm glad to get the chance to get acquainted with you before my son goes off to work for a couple of days. I won't feel so alone now. It can be so hard to join a social group once they are already gelled, don't you think?"

"I wouldn't exactly describe us a *social group*," Davies replied. "More a bunch of people thrown together."

"Kinda like a salad," grinned Tibby. "Or a carriage accident."

"Or a prison," Daintree added.

"I wouldn't know," Tibby replied. "Have you been inside, Daintree?"

"Of course not," the thin man snapped. "What kind of question is that?"

"You brought it up," Tibby turned back to the new arrival. "The missus is out of sorts? The family business not doing so well?"

Davies shrugged. "Yeah, well. You know how women are. Just a lot of fuss about nothing."

"A hole is nothing, until you break your neck in it." Tibby sat back, allowing the waiter to serve the soup. "Does that mean you'll be leaving soon?"

"No. We haven't finished here yet."

Davies sighed. "There's one more thing to wrap up."

"What exactly is your business?" Abigail asked.

Davies glared at her. "It's a family matter. It's private."

"I see," she smiled, clasping her hands together, showing off the fingerless lace gloves which disguised her youthful skin. "I didn't mean to intrude. We were talking about criminals earlier. Have you encountered any outlaws while you've been out here? Mr. Dunbar was on a train which was robbed. Where are you from?"

"No, I've seen nothing like that," Davies picked up a bread roll. "We came in from San Francisco. It's been just fine."

Tibby turned and frowned at Davies but stretched across him and stabbed a bread roll with his fork. "I certainly found the robbery more than I cared to have happen in a day. Wasn't that enough dishonesty for a lifetime?"

"I didn't see it," Davies dipped his bread in his soup and nodded at Nat and Jake. "Who are these two?"

"This is my son, Nathaniel, and his colleague, Jake," Abigail smiled. "They'll be leaving me here for a couple of days while they attend to work. How long do your wife's incapacities generally last?"

Davies shrugged. "She'll be fine tomorrow, I guess."

"Then I may see her after all?" Her eyes brightened. "I shall look forward to it. Another lady to chat with." She scanned the people gathered around the table. "I'm sure you men will soon tire of an old lady's company. I shall call on her. Please tell her."

♦ ◊ ♦

They watched the thin rubber strips stretch her skin as she stripped them away and peeled away the gum which clung like a parasite. Gradually, the young woman emerged from the prosthetics and part-masks and rubbed her skin fresh and clear. She wiped away the greasepaint from the remaining skin until she was pink and youthful once more.

"So, we have a collection of people who were here in town when Dora and Bessie were murdered. Tibby is very amusing. He doesn't look big enough to overpower Bessie, though, so if he did it he was most certainly acting with someone else. He and Davies don't seem to like one another very much, nor does Daintree. Daintree is interesting. He must have saturated the area in those novelties by now? He can't be earning enough to pay his hotel bill."

Jake's blue eyes examined the cosmetic process with fascination. "I'd never believe it was you unless I saw it with my own two eyes, Abi."

"Then perhaps you should consider giving up a life of crime, Jake?" Abigail replied. "This is just a taste of what we can do to bring in criminals nowadays. Detection is becoming more and more sophisticated."

"So are criminals," grinned Nat. He picked at the rubber pieces and tested the elasticity. "You've taught me an important lesson, though. We need to stop showing our faces. Maybe we could use this stuff?"

She reached over and took it from him, but he held onto the end, stretching it until it released with a snap. "Honestly, you're like an overgrown child. Sophisticated?"

"So these people were all here visiting the town at the time of the murders. R.D. the telegram said," Jake leaned back on the double bed. "Rigby Daintree?"

"There are a lot of 'D's," Nat agreed. "Tibby's name is

Dunbar, and Davies' name is Bob. Robert, or something like that? That's if they're using their real names at all."

"Yes, there's only one way to find out." Abigail collected her makeup and returned it to a leather case. "I must have a look around their rooms."

"What if they catch you?" Nat frowned.

She arched a brow. "Will they know all the hotel's maids, or even if there's now a new one?"

"That's one of the most sneaky and underhanded things you've ever suggested." Nat's eyes sparkled. "I like it."

"I thought you'd appreciate it. How long will it take you to get to Paris?"

"We'll leave at dawn and should get there by the evening if we keep a decent pace," Jake pondered. "We should get back by the following night."

"I'll get the hotel to keep you some food," Abigail opened the connecting doors and gestured for them to leave. "It'll be interesting to see what we all come up with over the next couple of days. I've been to Paris. Keep your wits about you."

Chapter Fourteen

Jake Conroy's eyes narrowed as he approached the stables in the optimistically named town of Paris. It shared little with its namesake. It was not a bustling cultural centre or a Mecca for the gourmands, and certainly did not support the arts. It did have a whole main street dedicated to whores, brothels, and the more prosaic pursuits. It had enough vice simmering in the background to rival any city, and more than enough crime to scare the casual traveler.

Business was done in this bright place full of shady people, and if anyone wanted to sell stolen horses after a murder, this was the most likely place within fifty miles of Bannen. Few would dare to ask questions in a place like this, but Nat Quinn and Jake Conroy were not easy to intimidate.

A large bear of a man was sorting through tack when the two young men walked in. He made a fast assessment of them as being in their late twenties, with eyes older than their faces. He noted their tied-down guns and judged them as showy, but missed their deliberate and measured body language. They were clean, groomed, and wholesome as far as his unpracticed eye could see. To him, they were fair game.

"Howdy, boys. How can I help?"

"Are you Ethan Green?"

A man with uneven eyes and a face full of stubble raised his head at Jake's question. He emerged from the shadows at the end of the barn.

"Who wants to know?"

Nat fixed him with a smile. "I'm lookin' for information. I'm ready to pay."

"Don't do information, just horseflesh."

"This relates to horseflesh. One paint, one sorrel, about two weeks ago. I want to know who sold them. I'm not interested in getting them back or in any charges relating to stolen horses. Just want know who sold them."

The man arched a pair of dark, bushy eyebrows and glanced from one to the other. "I can't help."

Jake shot a glance to Nat before he spoke. "We were told you could."

The man turned his back and continued to work. "Who told you a dumb thing like that?"

"Jess Schofield, he's a business associate of ours. Do you want to tell him he's dumb?" asked Jake. "Jess can be kind of unpredictable, though. Rather you than me."

The man turned at the familiar name, not knowing he was simply one of the young men's criminal contacts.

"You the law?"

Jake's derisive laugh told the man all he needed to know. "Do we look like the law?"

"You don't, but your friend here—"

Nat cut in. "We're not the law."

"Look, we need to find out who sold those horses. We ain't interested in what you might have done with them. We want to know who sold them."

The man wiped his fleshy face and gave them a considered look. "You said you were ready to pay?"

"Sure. We got fifty dollars."

The man pocketed the money and led them to a stall at the back of the stables. A black and white horse stood there, idly munching on hay as it raised its ears in interest at the strangers. "The other one was sold."

"Who brought them in?" Nat asked.

The man's malignant smirk spread. "I got no idea. I weren't here."

The shadows in the joyless dimple echoed the shadows in the dark eyes. "Think harder about that answer. You took our money. We want an answer."

"Too late, boys. You can look on this as a lesson? Find out what you're payin' for first."

"Don't want teachin'. We want information." Jake's calm tone also held a warning. His posture had changed. He stood more erect and one arm grabbed the other across his body, a precursor to his action to anyone who familiar with him, but the man carried on blithely unaware of the dangers ahead.

"Look, boys. I suggest you move on. You got all you're gonna get here."

Jake fixed him with ice-blue eyes. "We ain't goin' nowhere until you give us the answer we're lookin for, mister."

The man's hand crept to his gun as he glared at the young men, a self-satisfied smirk on his face. A muscle flexed on the gunman's jaw and the eyes narrowed to stilettos of ice. "I wouldn't do that if I were you. I don't want to draw, but if you go for that gun, I'll have to go for mine."

"I don't need advice from the likes of you, sonny. Now, get outta my place."

"My partner told you we're not going anywhere until we get the truth. Now just answer our questions, and we'll be on our way."

The stableman's face reddened. "I don't like bein' called a liar, boy. Get outta here now, while the goin's good."

"Nope," Jake replied with the simple crispness of new snow.

The man's plump, stubby fingers moved toward his gun as Nat groaned. Would people never learn? Why did they always want to do things the hard way?

"What the—"

The gun seemed to leap into Jake's hand before the man's

clumsy fist had moved more than a few inches.

Nat's smile was sweet reason itself as he stepped forward and removed the man's weapon. "Now, why don't you answer my friend's question?"

"I ain't never seen anythin' like it." The man's mouth gaped open, displaying a fine set of discolored teeth.

"You ain't seen nothin' yet," growled Jake. "Tell us what we want to know before you don't get to see anythin' ever again."

"There's only one man who can draw like that. You must be him—"

Blue eyes skewered the stableman. "I came here askin' questions, not answerin' them. The name."

"I ain't got a name, just a description."

"That's a start," Nat replied.

"Young lad. Blond, blue eyes."

"German? A simple boy? What age?" demanded Nat.

"Nope, sharp as a tack and American. About nineteen." The man relaxed. "I didn't realize it was you two. I would've told you straight off if you'd told me who you were."

Jake holstered his gun but kept the man pinned with his flint-like gaze. "We still ain't told you who we are."

"I been around enough. I can guess. I ain't got a name but the boy sells horses here regular. I'll get you a name, but I ain't got it now. I'm always happy to do business with the likes of you. Anything for Quinn and Con—"

"No names." Nat cut him off. "We'd appreciate that. When do you expect him back?"

"Dunno, whenever he's got somethin' to sell. It's usually late on when he comes. Like you are now."

"We'll be back." Nat dropped the man's gun into a bucket of water. "Just to make sure you don't shoot us in the back." They turned to walk out as a call made them turn. "There was somethin' else. The boy had a scar on his mouth, a kind of a cleft lip. He sells clothes and jewelry too. See Goldman the pawnbroker. He buys most everything. He went there after me."

◆ ◇ ◆

Abigail tapped at the door, only her knuckles visible in her little-old-lady fingerless lace gloves. The door opened and Bob Davies scowled at the matron bearing a little cake box. "You? From last night?"

"Mrs. Cadwallader. Yes. I've come to see how your wife is."

A female voice called from behind the door blocking her view. "Who is it?"

"It's that woman I told you about last night."

"Oh. What does she want?"

"To bring you cake and offer an oasis of civilized female conversation in this wilderness of cowboys and mud," Abigail said. "I won't stay more than an hour. I promise."

"Oh." The door swept aside and a woman with a pointed nose and mousey hair smiled at her. The woman clutched an embroidered oriental gown over her corseted figure. "How sweet of you. I'm not dressed, though."

"You've been indisposed. I wouldn't expect you to be. Please, relax," Abigail didn't wait to for an invitation and swept in. "Is it megrim disorder? I was a martyr to that in my younger years, every month, regular as clockwork. Since my time of life things have been much better."

"Every month? Time of life? Oh, good Lord," Davies groaned. "I'm going out if you're going to talk about that sort of stuff." He snatched his hat and jammed it on his head. "I'll see you in about an hour, Mary."

Abigail watched him leave with a glimmer of satisfaction and settled on the chair. She opened the box with delicate fingertips and proffered it to Mrs. Davies. "German bakers are the best, aren't they? When I saw the name Pfister over the shop, I knew I'd find something wonderful. When I lived in New York I always found the French made the cakes look so much more beautiful, but you had to go to a German bakery to get the best flavors."

"Ooh," Mrs. Davies's eyes widened at the beautiful pastries in the box. "You live in New York?"

"We used to. We moved to Chicago. I'm on my way to see my sister in San Francisco. She followed her daughter out there. What is it like? Your husband said you'd come from there."

"It's big, enormous. It's growing so fast."

"Well, everywhere is, isn't it? We live in such interesting times." Abigail unpacked a delicious morsel and handed it to her companion on a little cardboard tray covered in a doily, noting the cicatricial flesh where the extravagant gown fell away from Mrs. Davies's arms in wide swaths of silk. "Where would you suggest I visit while I'm there? What should I see?"

"Well, there's the shops," she replied. "Your sister will have a view on where to take you. I am boring and enjoy Woodward's gardens. I grow roses. I'm quite the enthusiast. Robert always says I should move on to chrysanthemums. Roses scratch so, don't they?" She rubbed at the marks before allowing the sleeves to drop back to her wrists. "My arms are quite shredded, not to mention my gardening clothes. Just look at them. How long has it been since you saw her?"

"Oh, it must be getting on for twenty years! I'm so excited," Abigail smiled. "She followed her daughter when she married and moved west. I've missed her so."

"Bob said your son works for charity? Cruelty to children?"

"Yes," Abigail nodded, adding for mischief's sake, "but they're against it, you know."

"How interesting." Mrs. Davies munched on her pastry. "What do they do when they find cruelty?"

"They prosecute if they can't take the child to safety. I've seen my Nat preparing for all kinds of court cases. The charity pays the costs. I'm very proud of him doing such good work."

"Do they leave the child with the parents after that?"

"Goodness me, no," Abigail replied. "They can be made a

ward of court, or taken into care. He has people he can place children with until a more permanent solution is found when there's no suitable place in an orphanage."

"Does he have those everywhere? Here, for instance?"

"I think the charity does. Why?"

Mrs. Davies shrugged. "I just wondered. It seems a great thing to do. How do you become one of the people who help children?"

"I genuinely don't know," Abigail observed the woman intently. "I suppose one would contact the charity. Do you want me to ask my son? Are you interested in helping?"

"I might be. Perhaps if I could meet someone who does it, I could decide. Maybe someone here?"

"I can certainly ask him about it," Abigail dabbed at the corners of her mouth with her napkin. "How lovely of you to think of the children. Shall you be coming to dinner tonight?"

"You told my husband you'd be alone tonight?"

"I will. Nat has business out of town. It would be wonderful to have another lady to dine with."

"Then I must. I can't leave you sitting alone. Can I, Mrs. Cadwallader?"

"It's a date. Shall we say around seven-thirty?"

"Indeed." Mrs. Davies stood to walk her guest to the door. "I'll meet you in the lounge."

The cheerful bell over the shop door tinkled, announcing the arrival of the two men who blinked around the shadows of the dark emporium crowded with goods, looking for assistance. Furious barking and growling punctuated the air, and the sound of something big and hairy throwing itself against the back door was hard to miss. A voice drifted out of the black corners.

"Good evening, gentlemen. How can I help you?"

"Are you Goldman? Ethan Green gave us your name and told us you could help us?" Nat blinked as his eyes became accustomed to the dimness, but he still couldn't see who spoke through the umbrage in the store.

"Did he? What are you selling?"

"Buying. Information," Nat answered.

A figure ghosted out of the shadows, his dark waistcoat and sleeve protectors seemingly dissipating into the gloom behind him. "You've come to the wrong place. My clients are assured of complete privacy."

"Even killers?" Jake demanded.

"I know nothing about any crimes, sir." The man shook his head, his odd, pale-brown, frizzy hair stiff and motionless in its neo-classical cut. "I just buy and sell. I ask no questions, and I answer even less."

"It would have been a boy with a twisted lip. Sometime soon after the twenty-fifth of last month."

"I suggest you leave, gentlemen."

"How much will it take?" Nat asked. "We're not interested in any charges, getting the stuff back, or anything other than finding the man who killed our friend. We'll keep you out of it."

"I shall ask once more, gentlemen," the metallic click of a gun behind them made their blood run cold, "then I'll let my sons take over." Goldman's mild tone belied the hardness of his pebble eyes. "You don't think I run a place like this in Paris without backup, do you? I've never been robbed. Never. We're vigilant and deal with people who do not comply with store policy." His cold smile added to the grim aspect. "A few have been killed trying, though; but this is a town where nobody asks too many questions and the authorities don't quibble too much about the explanations."

The partners exchanged a silent conversation in a glance. "Fine," Jake shrugged. "We wanted information, but we know when we're beat." He gestured with his head toward the door.

"C'mon. I need a drink."

"But—"

"No buts. I ain't losin' my life over a dumb vendetta about a woman. When I do, it's gonna be somethin' worthwhile, like a jealous husband or a hernia from carryin' all my money. Git!"

Nat blinked away his anger, his mouth firming into an angry line before turning on his heel and pulling open the door.

Jake placed a hand on his shoulder, but Nat threw it off, yelling in his face. "Get away from me you coward! I'm leaving. Make your own way back." He stormed off, leaving Jake to share a look of embarrassment with the shopkeeper.

"It's a wise course of action. Go after him. Buy him a drink. Young men can be such hotheads. It's good to see you have more of a level head."

Jake's curt nod was his only reply. He left; his pace rising to a trot to catch up with his nephew. He spread his hands as if remonstrating with the younger man, but the content of the conversation didn't match what the casual observer saw. It was all show.

Nat's eyes remained fixed ahead. "Do you think they bought it?"

Jake's arms waved as though shouting. "I don't see why they wouldn't. I would have."

"Good, they won't be expecting us back later," Nat's eyes gleamed with venal lights. "So, they've never been broken into? They've never come up against us before. Where's the doctor's office?"

He strode on ahead, while Jake's hands dropped to his hips, watching his nephew stride on ahead. He could feel the eyes from the shop boring into his back. They could act normal again once they turned the corner knowing they wouldn't be alerted to the imminent break-in, so he shook his head as though resigned to something and stalked after Nat.

◆ ◊ ◆

The dark-haired young woman carried her apron. An unknown face could be mistaken as a new guest by anyone, but staff would question her if they saw her dressed as a maid in their establishment. It would go on when she was inside a room in case the occupant interrupted her in action. It always surprised her how people dismissed a woman doing mundane work, but it was a useful tool.

She stopped outside number twelve, her dark eyes darting from side to side as she tinkered with the lock. It clicked. One more look around and the handle turned in her hand. She was in. Abigail had already watched the gangly man leave the hotel from her room, and the side windows of the corner room were useful to watch him progress up the main street. She had no idea where Daintree was going, but she suspected the saloon was involved, due to the smell of his breath yesterday evening.

She closed and locked the door behind her and donned her apron as a disguise. There were two bags in the room; a cheap, cardboard suitcase with leather-corners and a carpet bag. She moved in on the carpet bag first. It was unlocked and made easy pickings. Her brow creased as she flicked open a box full of calling cards; the names and occupations varied; from journeyman tailor to lawyer. There were numerous names and identities, and unlike her own false papers, were not hidden in any hidden lining or compartment. She replaced the box and rifled through numerous papers finding a telegram from D.B to R.D. dated ten days before the murders. It offered a meeting in Bannen. She frowned and thrust it into her pocket. There was nothing more of any interest in the carpet bag, so she turned her attentions to the suitcase.

It was also unlocked, and a quick run around the lining told her there were no hidden compartments or false bottoms. The bag appeared too cheap for that, anyway. It contained a few shirts, paper collars, nightshirts, and underwear. All things she could have expected, but the cardboard accordion file at the bottom caught her attention. She untied the string and drew in a breath at the contents. There were letters about a family inheritance and the name Benson was mentioned. There were far too many of them to read here and now.

Time for a split-second decision. She pulled up her skirts and slid the folder into the large pouch in her petticoats. The clothes were replaced and the suitcase snapped closed. She unlocked the door and a quick check in the hall showed it was all clear. She stripped off her apron and jammed it under her arm, the lock pick tinkering in the keyhole to secure the door behind her.

Abigail heaved a sigh of relief and made for the staircase, her heart leaping into her mouth at the sight of Daintree's gangly form rounding the corner to climb back to his floor. He paused, smiling in surprise at the young woman descending the stairs toward him. His lips stretched into a gap-toothed grin and a hand slid up to remove his hat.

"Good afternoon, miss. You're new here, aren't you?"

For no reason at all, other than sheer devilment, her accent went to the Deep South. "Why, yes. I am, sir." She smiled through coquettish lashes as she crossed him on her way down. "Shall I see you at dinner?"

"Maybe you will. The name's Daintree."

"Pleased to meet you, Mr. Daintree. Until tonight." She slipped out of sight and quickened her pace, onto the landing below, thanking her lucky stars she had thought to leave her own door unlocked. She stepped inside and turned the key, still leaning against the firm, cool wood in relief. Her heart thumped so loud she was sure it must be audible in the hallway.

There was a thrill to be got from burglary, but try as she might, she could feel nothing but on edge when breaking and entering. She grudgingly admired Nat Quinn's insouciance in such circumstances, but she'd never reach that level of nonchalance. She pressed her ear to the door and listened hard. All was quiet, but she suspected that would not last for long, not when Daintree discovered his file missing.

She kicked the wedge back under the door and sat in front of the mirror. Time to get back into makeup in case anyone raised the alarm; there had to be no sign of the young dark-haired woman in the building if anyone came to her door, and that could happen any time.

Gas bottles, bearing the legend 'S.S. White Dental Manufacturing Company of Philadelphia' hissed through the rubber tubes, one jammed into the keyhole, the rest under the door.

"Is this necessary?" muttered Jake.

Nat turned wide eyes on his uncle. "Those dogs sounded enormous judging by the thumps as they threw themselves at the door earlier. There's a reason why they've never been broken into. They leave the dogs running about the shop at night and the minute they hear anyone cutting glass or picking a lock, they'll go crazy. There are no gaps in the door to throw in drugged meat. What choice do I have?"

"So there's just four bottles of that stuff. Is there enough to fill the whole place?"

"We don't want to fill the whole place. We'd be knocked out when we went in." Nat pointed to the bottles at his feet. "That shop is about twenty feet square and about eight foot high. I note things like that. I reckon the dogs' noses will only be about three feet from the floor at most. For the gas to hit the dogs' noses, I need to account for a total volume of air of one hundred and sixty-four thousand five hundred and sixty-nine pints of air to fill one-third of that with gas in the lower part of the room. It's heavier than air, so the room will fill from the bottom up—one-third is fifty-four thousand eight hundred and fifty-six. According to the books, that's the dosage: a ratio of one part nitrous oxide to two parts air to knock you out. So one-third of the bottom part of the room is only eighteen thousand two hundred and eighty-five," Nat paused. "Roughly estimated."

"Huh? So we ain't knockin' out the family?" Jake asked. "The ones with the guns? 'Cause that'd be kinda handy."

"We're knocking out the ones who'll wake the men with guns," Nat whispered. "There's ninety-six pints of gas here and it's heavier than air, so it'll fall to the floor level. That means we have two hundred and eighty-eight pints of air to gas to be an effective dose. That'll knock out the dogs." He paused. "I hope."

"Quit saying it'll knock out the dogs! You threw all those numbers at me deliberately because you knew we had nowhere near enough." Jake's eyes narrowed. "I worked to put you through school because they said you were real smart, but even I can work out we've got nowhere near enough. Maybe you should have been Pearl's boot boy and *I* should've gone to school."

"It's all I could steal," Nat shrugged. "I took ether and chloroform, too. And chloral hydrate. It could come in handy one day."

"You're gonna chloroform a dog? A great big bitin', slaverin' beast? Its nose is right next to the teeth. Are you loco?"

"Probably," the shadows caught Nat's dimples. "I'm hoping it won't make them too dopey to eat the drugged steak I brought, though."

Jake dropped his head into his hands. "We're mincemeat."

"No, we're not. If they don't get knocked sideways by the gas, we don't break in."

The gunman shook his head. "Nat, check the pipes. I think the gas is goin' to your head."

♦◊♦

The lock pick tinkered at the back door of the pawnbrokers. Jake frowned at the sound of whimpering and snuffling coming from inside. Nat turned a glittering glance back to his uncle who rolled his eyes. Sure, the watchdogs were quieter, but they were still awake. One of the hounds could launch itself at their throats as soon as they opened the door. Jake delivered a warning look and pulled out his gun.

Nat arched his brows and pulled out a packet of greaseproof paper. "I think the gas has made them dopey."

"Dopey enough to join the gang and let you lead them?" Jake asked.

"I'm hoping the combination of gas and the smell of steak'll make them forget to be territorial."

"I hope it wasn't expensive steak?" hissed Jake.

"It's drugged. Liver and tripe, too. I got a bit of everything. What do they like best?"

Jake scowled. "They lick their own butts. Anything'll do."

"Here goes. Let's hope the gas made them groggy enough not to bark." Nat opened the door a crack and tossed the meat inside, snapping it closed again. The sound of snuffling and slobbering caused his cheeks to dimple.

"Now, we wait."

Chapter Fifteen

Nat and Jake picked their way back across the scrubby open land, heading due south towards Bannen under a caustic sun and a biting wind. The two horsemen set off at dawn to put as much space between them and any pursuit as possible after breaking into the pawnbroker's store. They felt comfortable enough to walk the horses for a spell.

"He kept real good records, that Goldman," mused Jake. "He's gonna miss his book."

"Yup. It won't stop people from claiming their goods, though," Nat chuckled. "They'll have all the information on their ticket. It's gonna cost him."

"He'll know we did it. Green'll talk, and he guessed who we are."

"Then he'll know better'n to cross The Innocents next time he meets us," Nat retorted.

"*If* he meets us," Jake snickered. "We're not dumb enough to mix with criminals in our down time. That's how you get turned in."

"It seems a boy's been selling horses and jewelry, and anything he could get his hands on for years in Paris. Even clothes, if they're good quality. He sold the horses late on the twenty-fifth, the same date the women were killed, the same date John Smith sold valuable jewelry. He was the only one selling stuff in three days, so it had to be him. Everyone else was buying or pawning. I found the name John Smith every couple of months. Green told us he was heading over to

Goldman's after him, and Goldman's records bear that out. "

"It'll be interestin' to see if John Smith's sales coincide with all the other bushwackin's," Jake's mouth firmed into a hard line. "Hittin' poor folks and takin' everythin' they've got is the lowest of the low. At least we only steal from banks and railroads, not strugglin' families."

"He sold a lot of jewelry according to the book. Where would Dora and Bessie get anything like that?"

"They wouldn't, unless they came into money. The girls at Pearl's wear cheap jewelry made of paste and glass." Jake sighed. "Dora talked about that. It's all fallin' into place. It could be the reason they got targeted."

"The blond boy, could it be Kurt Schmidt?"

"Pearl says they've lived outside of town for years. It sounds like Kurt with the scarred lip but he sure ain't smart and he hardly speaks any English. I think he struggles with his own folks' language, let alone anythin' else. Everyone who knows him says he couldn't even pretend to be smart for ten minutes."

"And he was American. Scars on lips are pretty common. Some are born with a hare lip and others are injuries. I guess we've got to take a leaf out of Abi's book and keep an open mind." Nat kicked his mount into action. "C'mon. Let's see if she's got anything better than this ledger."

Jake's eyes narrowed at the mention of Abigail's name. Nat was getting too involved. The sooner they got to the end of this thing, the better. Perhaps this was enough evidence for her to act on. He nudged his horse forward and followed his nephew into the rocky vastness stretching out before them.

Nat and Jake were earlier than she thought they would be. Abigail met them striding across from the stables toward the hotel, dusty and tired. Nat's smile shone with affection and caught her in a hug. Jake scowled at the warmth in what was supposed to be a contrived relationship.

Nat's eyes gleamed. "Did you miss me, Mom?"

She glanced over at Jake's stony countenance. "I missed both of you. I'm glad you're both back safe and sound." She shook off Nat and embraced Jake in welcome. "Did you get anything?"

"A pawnbroker's ledger. It shows the same boy with the twisted lip who sold Dora and Bessie's horses sold jewelry that day. It itemizes it, too."

Abigail's frown was concealed beneath the old lady prosthetics. "The book describes the person selling it as the boy with the twisted lip?"

"No, but the stableman said he was heading there next after selling the horses and we have the records of what he sold. Nobody else sold within three days," Nat replied. "The John Smith selling the stuff had to be him."

"It's a start," she nodded, "and the level of proof required by courts is higher, but this is great. This gives us information on where to apply pressure to get witnesses."

Nat looked crestfallen. "People don't talk in places like Paris. You're lucky to get anything."

"Honestly, this is good. I've got something similar. Come on, and I'll show you." She caught Nat by the hand and pulled him to the hotel.

"I need to wash," Jake hung back with a sullen frown. "We've had a long ride. Are you goin' to the bath house, Nat?" He paused, commenting pointedly at Abigail. "We'll see you later, Mrs. Cadwallader."

"Oh, right," she nodded. "You'll want a rest, too. I'll get sandwiches sent to your room. You relax. We've got plenty of time." She turned away eyeing Jake's reaction with caution. "I'll see you later."

♦ ◇ ♦

Jake worked his way through a pile of sandwiches, his stocking feet propped on the edge of the bed while Nat examined the telegram and the documents in the file.

"So, let me get this straight," Nat mused. "A person called D.B. sent a telegram to R.D. offering a meeting in Bannen on the fifteenth. Dora Benson was murdered on the twenty-fifth. On top of that, Daintree has a whole pile of correspondence about an inheritance in the Benson family." He frowned, pulling out a letter covered in spidery writing. "This one suggests Phil Benson didn't die in the mine accident and is due to inherit from his father." His brow lined with a frown. "Why would they think that? Dora would never have had to work in a brothel if her husband was still alive."

"Could he have deserted her?" Abigail asked. "It happens all the time."

All eyes turned to Jake who thought hard. "Nope. Not the way she talked about him. She was destroyed when he died. Anyway, what about the people who saw him go into the mine? There were other people caught up in the blast, too. They saw him."

"What about a false name?" she mused. "What if the man she thought she was married to was using a false identity? What if he was killed in the mine accident using her husband's name and he's still alive somewhere?"

Jake chewed, mulling it over. "Why would he do that?"

"Why do any of us do it?" she replied. "He could have just picked a name at random to change his identity. He may have used the name already on the marriage license to support a new identity after Dora was deserted."

"Nope." Nat shuffled through more papers. "Everyone knows Dora was a servant in the Benson home in Boston, and she and Phil ran away to get married. I don't think there's any doubt about who either of them were."

Abigail scratched her head under the wig. "Could she have picked up with anyone else in between? A substitute husband?"

"You never knew her," growled Jake. "She was one of the most decent people I ever met. She loved her family, and that's why she sold herself—to give her son a roof over his head and an education. If anyone was lyin', it weren't her. Got that?"

She nodded. "But whoever sent that telegram was so sure."

"Abi, did you notice the telegram about Phil still being alive was from R.D. TO R.D." Nat held up the paper. It says it was sent from WUTRAVBURO BH, then there are numbers," Nat glanced over at her, a questioning frown on his face. "It was sent to R. Daintree at an address in Scollay Square, Boston."

"That's Western Union Travel Bureau. The code is in Boston, but I can't remember which one. We can find out. Scollay Square is in a pretty seedy part of town near the waterfront. It's been flooded with poor Irish and Italian immigrants for years now." She bit into her lip. "I never noticed that on the paperwork. Boston to Boston? So people in Boston have been questioning whether Phil Benson is alive and hiding in Bannen? That's very interesting."

"So who died in the mine?" snarled Jake.

Abigail nodded. "It was an explosion, so a look at the face wouldn't help, not judging by the blind pianist. He was caught in it, too. He was blinded and disfigured."

"Dora was honest. She loved her husband and everyone who worked at the mine saw him go in and a body come out. Why would he fake his death, watch his family struggle, and still not claim any inheritance? It makes no sense." Jake lifted another sandwich. "Whoever thinks Phil Benson's still alive is an idiot. He's dead."

"I will have to contact the Boston office to look into this for me," Abigail stood. "While I was dressed like this I got the sheriff to look into the telegrams Dora sent." Jake's foot dropped off the bed at the mention of the word 'sheriff'. "He should have them by now. I'll go and see him while you two rest."

"Now, wait a minute. You went to the sheriff?" demanded Nat.

"Of course I did. I needed the weight of a badge to get the telegrams. They don't just hand them over to anyone. I had to steal these. I went there before you even saw me in this disguise and you're still free as a bird." She tilted her head and smiled at the tense men. "Don't you think he'd have been over by now if I'd turned you in? Go and sleep. Goodness, you two wouldn't recognize honesty if it smacked you in the face."

"The people we mix with are as crooked as a barrelful of fish hooks, and plenty of them would smack you in the face as soon as look at you. You ain't exactly honest yourself, Abi," retorted Jake. "We had to scare the truth outta you."

"I'm doing it professionally."

"So are we," Nat snorted. "This isn't a game."

She huffed in derision. "Well, you have a choice to make don't you? You can have a rest or you can get your cowardly arses over to the stables and hightail it out of here. I'm going to the sheriff's office. I have work to do."

"Abi!" Nat's eyes widened. "I've never heard you use language like that before."

"You've heard me say that and a lot worse, I just don't generally do it in English." She paused at the door on her way out, "but this time, I want you to understand me clearly enough to decide who I am. Pick a damned side, once and for all."

Sheriff Thompson rolled his eyes at the sight of the middle-aged woman prodding the deputy out of her way with her umbrella. "You again?"

"Yes, Mr. Thompson. Me again. I told you I'd be back. How did you get on? Did you get anything?"

Thompson reached into his drawer and pulled out a sheaf of papers. "I wondered when you would show for this. You made it sound real urgent and then you go disappearin' on me for days."

"Yes, I'm sorry about that. I have been very busy." Abigail sat and shuffled through the telegrams, pausing at one in particular. "Is this everything?"

Thompson raised his chin in challenge. "'Course it is. We're professionals."

"Thank you, Sheriff. I'm very grateful." She folded them and put them in the bag dangling from her wrist. "What information did you get about the people seeking to adopt David?"

He sat back in his chair, the legs creaking in protest. "Yeah, I spoke to Martin at the Juvenile Asylum. Somebody ripped the page out of his book so he lost the records, but he remembers they were from Boston and called Mellor. Husband and wife they were, and real mad the boy had already been given to someone else."

"Could he describe these people?"

"Real average, he said. An older woman," he nodded toward Abigail, "not as old as you, mind. Just a bit past it. He was kinda baldin' and she was kinda plain. That's it. He couldn't even remember what color of hair she had. She wore a hat."

"And the man who was awarded the boy?"

"He was a big man, real big. A fine white moustache and spoke real well. Impressive, he said."

"How big?" asked Abigail.

"Martin said he was at least a six-foot-seven."

"This man is six-foot-seven? He'd be noticeable around here. In fact, he'd be noticeable around anywhere."

"That's what he said." Thompson shrugged. "There was somethin' else. He had a finger missin'," Thompson pointed to his middle finger, "right here on the right hand. Right off from the knuckle he said. There weren't no stub."

"Well, I must keep an eye out for him." Abigail stood and thrust out a hand. "Thank you so much for all your help. I will make sure Alan Pinkerton is informed how helpful you have been. I know it must be very difficult working with someone as out of the ordinary as me. Your efforts will be reported back to the governor."

Thompson paused, and took the hand with reluctance. He cleared his throat. "Yeah, are we done now?"

"For the time being. We now have a considerable amount of evidence. We just need to put it together. That's the hard bit, huh?"

"I wouldn't know, ma'am. I usually just catch them in the act."

"Very efficient of you, Sheriff." She strolled over to the door and nodded a farewell. "I'll try to take a leaf out of your book."

She strolled along the sidewalk considering whether to go back to the hotel. Something about Jake's demeanor worried her. If Jake and Nat were resting, there'd be a wedge under the door and she'd have to wake them to get in. They might be long gone, given Jake's attitude. She sighed and decided to give them the benefit of the doubt, but uncertainty still ate away at a corner of her mind. If the truce was off, would they take the law into their own hands? And if they did, who would be the suspect?

She resolved to take time to compose the telegram to the Pinkertons to get the connections to Boston investigated, but as it had to be compiled in code, it would take formulating. Time for refreshment and a seat in a local restaurant.

◆ ◊ ◆

She sipped her coffee, pausing intermittently to glance at the code book from her reticule, filling her notes with a series of numbers which equated to the action required to get the information she needed.

The names and addresses were a simple transposed code. The telegrams were sent to an innocuous address to prevent agents in the field from being identified. It needed to be a long message due to the amount of information required and she plodded through it, concentrating on the details as much as possible.

Admin had never been her strong point, so she checked and double-checked to make sure her message was accurate, buoyed by copious amounts of coffee and the restaurant's delicious Railroad Cake.

The view from the window was a distraction from the tedium of the most boring part of her job. Three old men sat on the other side of the road, long on beards and short on teeth. They chatted over unknowable events before deliberating and spitting on the planks, much to the disgust of most of the female passers-by who scuttled by, lifting their skirts with looks of disdain. The little man who stopped to chat drew Abigail's attention.

The small, impeccably-groomed man shared an anecdote which made the old-timers roar with laughter. That wasn't surprising in itself, but the passerby was Tibby Dunbar, and the old-timers all pointed in unison off to the west. Where were they sending him, and what had he asked?

Abigail made a final check of her document. A lengthy check to make sure she had things right, and then sat back to enjoy her coffee and cake. She glanced at the check and pulled out cash before scraping the chair back and leaving the restaurant. She stepped onto the road looking both ways, approaching the huddle of old men across the road.

"Excuse me. I think I just saw you talk to a friend of mine."

Her hand at just over shoulder level indicated Tibby's short stature. "Gray hair, a smart coat, and big, round eyes. Have you any idea where he went?"

A grizzled old man with a single white tooth mugged at her with an elastic face with the texture of a well-used paper bag. "That little fella with the stick? Kinda like a store-bought pixie?"

"That's the one. Can you tell me which way he went?"

"He asked where the orphanage was," responded his leather-faced friend. "We told him."

"Oh," Abigail hid her surprise. "Is it far? I can try to catch him."

"It's right outta town," the first man replied, "about two miles that way."

"Two miles?" She shrugged. "I think I'll leave him to it and finish my shopping. Thank you, gentlemen."

A crescendo of laughter greeted the title. "Gentlemen? Ain't nobody ever called me one of them."

"Really? I've found you very helpful. Good day to you."

She clattered off along the wooden sidewalk toward the telegraph office. She not only had a long message to send, she also had to find out which station had the code BH. This visit would take time. Once she was finished there, she had to find out why Tiberius F. Dunbar was so interested in the local orphanage.

She strolled away from the telegraph office musing on the information she had received. the 'BH' telegraph code related to the commercial telegraph office in the old Boston Advertiser building in Washington Street. It was at the heart of the bustling business area and although Scollay Square was a mere five miles away, it might as well be on a different planet from the wealthy, forward-thrusting, modern street 'garden squares'; an exercise in town planning meant to emulate the best modern design ideas of places like Bath and London. The waterfront area was a poor and impenetrable rookery for crime and want. The divisions in the city were stark.

She glanced at her pocket watch. Almost five. Surely, Tibby would be on his way back by now? She headed out toward the orphanage to see if she could walk him back and have a conversation with him, so she pulled her wrap closer and headed out of town on the main street.

She paused, backing off to the buildings at the edge of town, observing the little man who stood at the white picket fence talking to the schoolteacher, his walking stick propped over his shoulder like a rifle at salute. The orphanage, and now, the school? He was very gregarious. It was possible he had just stopped to speak to a pretty girl and had no ulterior motives, but she had to check. She turned and walked back up Main Street, dipping into the next alley, where she could double around the back to circle around the back of the school.

It wasn't long before she had concealed herself, waiting until Tibby gave the woman a cheery doff of his hat and strode back into town. Abigail allowed him a couple of minutes to get on his way before she joined the main highway and hailed the schoolteacher who was heading back into the schoolhouse.

"Excuse me? Can you help? Was that my friend, Mr. Dunbar? I've been looking for him."

The schoolteacher nodded, her cornflower blue eyes still twinkling with amusement. "Why yes, it was. He's very diverting, isn't he?"

"Very," Abigail agreed. "He's wonderful company. What were you two talking about?"

"Oh, many things. He can talk on many subjects and make

them so fascinating, but he was interested in whether I could help him with his research. I couldn't, of course. It's not my area, and I haven't been here long. He had to look at the records. The new headmaster wanted him today. Can you imagine charging for public records? The school board weren't pleased when I passed that on to them."

"Research?" Abigail's brows arched.

"Yes. About orphans in the area, old pupils, that kind of thing. I've spent time allowing him to go through the old records. He's very thorough."

Abigail glanced at the teacher's hands, scarred and scored by the remains of deep scratches. "Oh, my. What happened to you?"

The teacher rolled her eyes. "The Adams and the Powell girls. Honestly. They're like feuding hillbillies. They behave like wild animals. I've had to suspend Clara Powell. You should have seen them two weeks ago. Those girls are terrible. That new headmaster was no help, either. If anything he made things worse."

"I'm glad they're healing well. I had no idea your work was so hazardous."

"Few people do, but out here in the frontier, some of children have been allowed to run wild for far too long. They take it ill when I try to instill some discipline."

Abigail's brown eyes fixed on the receding back of dapper little man heading back to the hotel. "Ah, yes. His work on orphans. Have a good evening. I must try to catch him before he gets too far ahead."

Chapter Sixteen

The key turned in the lock and the door to their rooms swung open, unwedged and unhindered by any obstacles. Abigail walked over to the connecting doors and tapped. There was no reply, so she grasped the brass knob and turned it tentatively. The double doors swung open revealing a tidy, empty room; the beds were made and there was no sign of any bags.

She sucked in a breath, caught unawares by the sudden sense of dark emptiness engulfing her. She wandered over to the window, not sure why she went there. It wasn't as though she would see them from the room. Nat Quinn and Jake Conroy would be long gone. Had she been a fool to think these criminals would have worked to find a murderer? Possibly, but at least she had discharged her debt to them for saving her life. She tried to help, it wasn't her fault they rejected it. Irritation wormed through her disappointment. They had been so very close to a resolution, but it was still feasible she could still pull this off on her own? The hollowness, however, was about more than just the case.

The realization suddenly hit her that she'd been living again. Really living. Not just wading through the minutiae of existence as she'd been doing for the last few years. Visions of lost faces flashed across her mind's eye, along with survivor's guilt and a sense of loss. It seemed wrong to embrace any kind of satisfaction in the face of so much death, but she'd done it without even noticing. Life crept up on her and dragged her back in while she waded through nothingness. Was this recovery? Did the gnawing ache in her breast fade from black to shades of gray until it was light enough to reveal who she now was? Did she even *know* who she now was?

She swung around at a sound behind her. "Nat?"

He stood in the doorway in the same suit he wore at their first meeting, the crisp lines showcasing his broad shoulders and slim hips. The greasy stain was long gone. His cheeks dimpled at the confusion in her eyes. "Yes. Who were you expecting?"

"I—nobody."

"Nobody? We're sharing a suite."

She walked over to the door and cast out a hand towards the room. "It's empty. I thought you'd gone."

"So? We tidied. We're not animals."

"Your bags are gone."

He produced a key from his waistcoat pocket. "They're in the wardrobe. Saddlebags don't have locks. That wardrobe won't stop a determined intruder, but it'll slow the average snoop." He paused and examined her, full of curiosity. "What's wrong?"

"Nothing," she shook herself out of the blues. "I got the impression you might leave. Jake was quite cold earlier. I think he's had enough of this."

His brow creased. "He's fine. He's in the lounge having a drink. We saw you pass by on your way back to the room. He wants Dora's killer found as much as anyone. You're imagining things."

"Am I? I hope so. I think we're getting close, now. I've got a few things more, but we can't go through the new telegrams in the lounge."

"Good, we thought we'd have an early dinner and turn in. We're going to the Schmidt's for that psychic reading tomorrow, and thought we'd start out just after dawn. We can look at them later."

He proffered an arm with a twinkling smile. "May I escort you to dinner, Mother?"

Her smile reached into her eyes at last as she took his arm. "You may. Let's go eat."

They strolled across the landing, but he paused at the top of the stairs. "So? Did you miss me?"

"When?"

"When you thought I'd gone. Did you miss me? You seemed kinda sad."

She dropped her head, looking through her lashes. "I was surprised, that's all."

He laughed. "Tell the truth. You missed me." His scrutiny melded with a grimace. "Although I can't tell you how uncomfortable it makes me having this conversation with you looking like a sixty-year-old." He paused. "You missed me. I know you did."

Her breath caught in her words, betraying the emotion she beat down. "I confess I've enjoyed working with people for a change."

He tilted his head. "Is that it? You can't even look at me. For what it's worth, I will miss you when this is over. A lot."

She gulped back the butterflies spiraling in her stomach and steeled herself to return his gaze. "Yes. I'll miss you, but right now, we're missing dinner and Jake's probably wondering where we are. Let's go."

She linked arms with 'her son' and they continued on down the stairs until they turned the corner and found Bob Davies blocking their way. A swish of skirts disappeared around the corner and bustled along the corridor to the back of the hotel.

"Just going to dinner?" asked Davies.

Abigail nodded. "Yes, will we see you and Mary there?"

"Not tonight," he cast out a hand toward the corridor his wife had just vacated. "We were out earlier, and we've already eaten. She's gone to use the necessary."

"Is she quite well? She seems to be heading for the outhouse at quite a speed. Should I go to her?"

"She's fine," Davies replied. "Mary always walks like that. She isn't one for wasting time, my wife."

Nat stared hard at the man blocking their way on the staircase. "Do you mind?"

"Oh," Davies's nervous chuckle rolled in his chest. "Sorry. I said I'd wait for her here. I wasn't thinking." He stepped aside with a sweeping arm. "Enjoy your meal, and if we don't see you before you leave tomorrow, have a safe journey."

"Thank you," Abigail nodded as they strode past him. "And please tell Mary I was asking about her."

A shrill scream cut through the air, followed by thumps and bumps. Both Nat and Jake burst through the double doors into Abigail's room, where she was already out of bed with an ear to the floor. "It's the floor below us," she hissed.

"It's like someone's being murdered," muttered Jake. "Let's get down there."

"It sounds like a woman." Abigail grimaced in frustration. "I need to make up. I'll be there as fast as I can. You go."

They clattered downstairs and were joined by Davies and Tibby, who stood nearby in an extravagant silk dressing gown.

"I think it's the Richardses," Tibby explained. "My room is next door, and I hear them arguing quite a lot."

Furniture crashed from within the room as the night manager rushed forward with a set of master keys on a huge ring. They jingled in the lock as more staff arrived, pulling on jackets and sharing looks of concern with one another at the increased intensity of the screams. The manager's futile ramming of key after key in the lock was infuriating. This went on for what seemed like an eternity against a backdrop of screams, curses, and thumps.

"Get that door open or I'm shootin' the lock off," yelled Jake.

"I'm doin' my best," the manager tried another key, then yet another. "This is a big place."

The sudden silence made the hairs on the back of everyone's necks rise.

"Get out of my way," Nat barked. He pushed the manager aside and stuck something in the lock, his shoulders rising in tension against the cacophony inside. One final click, and Nat pushed open the door, allowing the staff to rush in.

"A very interesting skill you have there. What did you say you did for a living?" Nat turned to the appraising stare of the little man in the vivid robe. "Not many people can do that," said Tibby.

"I used to be a locksmith," Nat replied. "It's a standard double action lever lock. Easy, if you know what you're doing." He turned and strode into the room.

A struggling Richards fought and bellowed, held by two members of staff while his wife sat on the bed, her arched back wracking with heaving sobs. Jake laid a comforting hand on her shoulder. "Are you hurt? What did he do, ma'am?"

She sat with her head in her right hand and shook her head. The night manager pointed at the bell boy, dressed in his uniform pants over long underwear. "Johnny, go fetch the law then run and get the doc."

The boy nodded snappily and bolted from the room. The manager turned to Nat. "She needs a woman to see to her. Would your mother be able to help?"

"I'm sure of it," he headed for the door. "She was all for coming here with us, but I told her to stay put. I'll go fetch her."

♦ ◇ ♦

'Mrs. Cadwallader' entered the room having donned a cotton robe over her expansive figure. A pair of embroidered slippers peeped out from the hem as she bustled over to the distressed woman. She sat on the bed beside Mrs. Richards and spoke softly but with authority, examining the twisted, deformed arm with mute alarm.

"Has anyone called a doctor?"

"He's on his way."

"Get me a pillow." Abigail took it and nestled it on the woman's lap. "Victoria, put your arm on there. It's not high enough, get me another." She rearranged the support. "There, oh, my. I know. It hurts. I think it's broken. Let's rest it on here and keep it supported until the doctor comes, shall we?" She turned to the men. "Can you get me some laudanum?"

The woman gasped in pain as the limb settled on the downy cushion.

"We'll get you something for the pain, shall we?" Abigail stroked back unruly hair from the woman's face, noting the livid finger marks on her throat and the swollen eye, congested and closing. "What happened? You can tell us. We can all see you've had a fight."

Jake stepped in to grab Richards's swinging arm, landing a punch on the man's soft belly. "You ain't fightin' a woman anymore, you coward."

The man's wife wailed in distress, and Abigail frowned. "Get him out of here. You're upsetting her," she returned to her patient, assessing her replies. "Were you unconscious at all?"

Victoria shook her head. "No. I wished I was when he swung me about and I heard the arm break. But no, I wasn't unconscious."

Abigail's stomach turned over at the very thought. "You poor thing. What brought this on?" She glanced at the bellboy who arrived with the laudanum and measured out a dose. "Here take this. It'll help with the pain." She watched the woman swallow the drug. "I don't want to give you too much before the doctor sees you. What happened? Why did he do this?"

"Denham's been fired, something about financial irregularities. He was so angry when he came back. I just knew things would blow up. They've already replaced him. We have to leave right away."

"Does he blow up often?" Abigail asked, fixing her with gentle brown eyes.

Mrs. Richards hesitated. "Sometimes. It's never been as bad as this, though. I thought he'd kill me this time. They called the sheriff. What will happen to him?"

"He'll be fine," Abigail's voice hardened. "His kind always are. We will make sure you're well-looked after. Where's that doctor?" She paused, but decided this was her only chance to ask, so pressed on. "Mrs. Richards? Did you scratch your husband a couple of weeks ago?"

She darted a guilty glance at Abigail. "Why?"

"I saw the scratches on his hands. They were newly-healed but still very red, indicating they were very deep. Somebody scratched him. Was it you, Victoria?"

She shook her head and opened her mouth to speak but was cut off by a man at the door. "You called for a doctor?"

Abigail gulped back her frustration and stepped back to make way for medical help. The doctor strode over and appraised the injured woman, noting the deformity in her left arm. He stepped forward deposited his leather bag on the floor. "What's your name?"

"Victoria. Victoria Richards."

"Well, Mrs. Richards." He examined the swollen eye before pulling up the eyelid on the healthy one and gazing into it. "I'm Dr. Walsh, and that arm is broken. I'm going to have to splint it."

"Broken?" Mrs. Richards blanched.

"I'm afraid so. I have to deal with it or you might lose the arm. It's a displaced fracture, and I need to get the bones back in position and stabilized. I will get the men to carry you very carefully downstairs after I get your arm secured in a splint. We'll take you over to my office. Please don't worry. Dealing with a lot of farmers and ranchers means I'm very experienced with broken bones. I'll have you as good as new before you know it. I promise."

"I gave her a dose of laudanum, Doctor," Abigail stood. "I thought you should know. Ten drops."

"Thank you, madam. I can take over from here. Can you ask a couple of men to fetch a stretcher from my office?"

They all rose early the next morning, but the disturbed night etched tiredness across their pale, pinched faces and made spirits flag. Abigail was no longer in disguise, and she wore a simple dark green riding habit. She had snuck off to the railway station to ensure her precious chest was booked back into left luggage while the men checked out of the hotel.

Jake's sharp blue eyes watched his nephew's every move and stolen glances. The days spent with the rotund matron seemed to exemplify the difference between the disguise and Abigail's lithe figure, and he had noted his nephew's dark eyes in their hungry exploration of her lubricious sway and enticing curves. The younger man was being drawn in by her reckless headlong run at life. Nat had always been drawn to danger and sensation, and it was Jake's mission to damp that down. Abigail was dangerous, and he was ruing the day he had agreed to nurse her at the cabin. He should have left her to Pearl. He bit back his feelings and carried on. Once today was over, Jake had determined they would leave. Nat just didn't know it yet.

♦◊♦

The Schmidt place sat about ten miles from town. It was just far enough to convince tired travelers to stay there close to nightfall rather than try to make it into town before it got too late to travel in unknown country. Tiredness could be the only reason anyone would stay at this bleak, stark place. Homey, it was not.

Jake saw a lone figure in the distance, riding away from them, leading two horses behind. He was too far away to identify much, he guessed the rider was male because this wasn't the kind of country where women would ride alone. The man rode from the wild land which led to the rocky lowlands of the mountains out toward Paris. This was not an area for anyone to take the air. It was full of bears, mountain lions, and wild men. Nat threw Jake a look, knowing it would take someone quite confident in their ability to defend themselves before they'd ride out in country like this.

"I want you to stay here, Abi. Hang back." Jake shot over his shoulder. "We're goin' to talk to him."

Jake recognized the figure as they approached.

It was the German boy with the twisted mouth from the Schmidt's place. Kurt Schmidt paused, clearly recognizing the blond one who had come to their house looking for the two women who had disappeared. He stopped and gave a crooked smile. "Guten Morgen."

"You speak English, boy?" Nat asked.

"He didn't speak any when I was at their place, just his sister. Don't trust him. He followed me out."

Nat shuffled in his saddle. "How we gonna find out what he's doin' out here?"

Kurt grinned at them.

"Why's he got two horses with him when he's riding alone?" Jake asked, his suspicions rising.

Nat rode over to him and pointed to one of his bags. *"What's in there?"* he yelled.

"He ain't deaf, Nat. He's German," Jake snickered.

Nat stretched out a hand and gestured with his fingers, indicating he wanted the bag, but Kurt gave him an empty stare and did nothing. Nat rode right up to him and took hold of the bag, but Kurt shook his head and pulled back. When he saw the chilling look in Nat's dark eyes, he reluctantly let go.

"What's this? A dress?" demanded Nat, pulling out the contents.

"Must be his sister's. She's real pretty," Jake answered. Scarlet silk and ribbons tumbled and unwound their way out of the bag.

"Doesn't look much like a farm girl's dress," said Nat, looking at the low cut front of the evening gown.

Jake scanned the length and matched it to the petite redhead he had met. "Too big for her, too."

The German boy looked even more uneasy as Nat put a hand out to take another bag. Jake caught the keen look in the boy's eyes and a flash of movement as the boy went for a gun, but his lightning reflexes felled him with a single shot through the shoulder. He toppled to the ground with an ominous thump, uttering a soft groan. Nat glanced back at Abigail and threw Jake a worried look before he jumped from his horse to check the boy.

"Help me," he groaned.

They glanced at one another in surprise. "I thought you didn't speak English, boy," barked Jake.

"I do, please help me. The pain is terrible—"

They exchanged glances, the description of the blond young man with a twisted lip given to them at the stables in Paris consolidating in their minds now that they'd discovered the boy spoke perfect English with an American accent.

Abigail thundered up on her horse and leaped to the ground to tend to the wounded youth, throwing an accusing look at Jake. "What have you done?"

The boy's eyes flickered and rolled in his head as he passed out with a hollow groan.

"What did you do?" she raged.

His glare was cold. "He's Kurt Schmidt. He was gonna shoot Nat. I had to."

"What? The sheriff told me he's simple. He wouldn't have meant any harm."

"He's dangerous. He was going to kill. I saw the look in his eyes."

"How could you? Did you think I'd just watch you shoot a boy and do nothing?"

Nat bent over the lad. "He's passed out. We need to get him into town."

"He speaks perfect English, so he now fits the description of the boy who sold the missin' horses in Paris. He's the one who sold Bessie and Dora's horses," Jake dismounted.

"That's no reason to shoot him. You didn't have to. You can outdraw a farm boy." Abigail's hard stare held Jake's glower. "Even I could outdraw a farm boy!"

Jake's glare chilled, every word a jab. "I did what I had to do."

She met his gaze, refusing to be intimidated. "I won't be hanging back again. I'll be right up front to see exactly what you do and how you do it," her eyes narrowed. "And I'll remember it all."

Jake strode over to her, his eyes boring right through her as the truce started to disintegrate before their very eyes. "I was tryin' to protect you both. If you don't want to accept that, we're headin' for trouble, lady."

Abigail tilted her head back so she could match the much taller man. "You'll shoot me too? Go ahead. Let's see where that gets you."

He remained tense, scowling at her in silence. He drew in a breath and opened his mouth to reply before Nat's call distracted him. "Jake, look at this."

Nat had opened the other bag. Another dress, this time a child's in blue silk spilled out along with jewelry, trinkets and books. The dress was splattered in blood. "The books are in English, so I'm guessing they're not his." He opened it. "A family Bible, embossed in silver, name of Clark."

Abigail ran forward to look at the garment in shock as a bitter Jake looked daggers at her back. "I told you he was dangerous. Are there any children at the Schmidts' place?"

"No." She watched a muscle in Jake's granite jaw flicker as realization set in. "I'm sorry."

"You went with your instincts," he shrugged, not meeting her eyes, "just like I had to."

She understood this comment was laden with meaning beyond this incident, but he was cold. His gentle side had gone. Had she killed it?

"No," she insisted. "I'm sorry. I truly am. "

Jake ignored her and took off his hat, running his hand through his tousled hair before strolling over to Nat who stood staring at the sad collection of belongings.

"Where'd he come from?" He raised his head and gazed out toward the pass, the expanse of sky reflecting in his deep blue eyes. "Let's get over there. I'll tie him on his horse."

It didn't take them long to see smoke in the distance as they retraced Kurt's route. The small fire sat in the dip cut out of the landscape by the river as it wound its way through the valley. A horseless wagon sat beside the small, smoldering pile, where a woman and a man lay on the ground covered in blood. A small, almost naked girl wandered around the site, bawling her heart out as the sharp stones cut into her little soft feet. She could have been no more than two-years old and the thin mountain sun had already beaten onto her bare skin making it raw and angry. The contents of various bags lay scattered around the area with fabrics fluttering in the breeze in a scene of utter devastation. Abigail sucked in a breath of horror and leaped down to her, but Jake was faster and snatched the girl in his arms before she reached her, cuddling her close.

"Hey, my baby. You're fine now."

He clutched at a piece of cloth and wrapped her in it, covering her sunburn before he sat with her and hugged her to his hard chest. "Get me some water."

He glanced over at the toddler's parents and adjusted his position so she was shielded from the horror as Nat handed him his canteen so the thirsty child could drink. "Here, darlin', be a good girl and drink this while the lady sees to your ma and pa." Abigail watched him rock the girl back and forth with a gentle hum before soaking fabric and bathing her cut feet as the child screamed in protest. "Ssshh, darlin'. Let me sort those for you. I'll make it all better."

Abigail frowned, struck by his gentle patience before she turned away and took the woman's hand, looking closely into her face. "She's still breathing."

"So's he," yelled Nat. "Jake, help me get those horses back on the wagon and let's get them into Bannen as soon as we can."

They took just under three hours to get the injured parents to the edge of town. Abigail sat in the back of the wagon and tended their wounds as best she could, trying to give whatever medical help she was able. The man had the worst injury, with a shot right through the arm. The woman moaned on Abigail's lap and her eyes flickered open. "My Ethie, where's Ethie?

"Ethie? Is that your daughter?"

"Yes, where—"

Abigail stroked her cheek. "She's safe. Jake, hold her so her mother can see her."

He turned in the seat, facing the flat bed and held up the wriggling child. "She's fine, ma'am. Just a few little cuts on her feet. I washed 'em clean and we're takin' you all to see a doctor."

"Clive?"

"Is that your husband's name? He's alive and we've stopped the worst of the bleeding. Is your name Clark? We read it in the Bible. What's your first name?"

"Pamela. Pamela Clark." Tears pricked at Mrs. Clark's eyes. "We were going to Bannen for Clive's work. He'll be the new headmaster. How is he?"

"We'll get you to the doctor," purred Abigail.

"He's still unconscious, but his breathing is strong and we've stanched the blood." She dabbed the woman's forehead with a damp cloth. "What happened?"

"Two men held us up. Clive told them we had nothing worth stealing, and they got angry. He went to step from the wagon to reason with them and the littlest one shot him in the arm." She sobbed and turned into Abigail's lap. "I grabbed for the rifle we kept under the seat, and the other one came at me. The last thing I saw was the butt coming straight at my face."

"Shhh, you're safe now. We'll get you to the doctor."

"But Clive? What if—"

Abigail's hand tightened on the woman's arm. "We're doing the best we can for you all. He's doing fine. It's best for him to be out right now because he's not in pain. The doctor will do the rest very soon. I've met him. He's very professional."

She clutched at Abigail's arm. "Promise Clive'll live."

Nat shot a worried look at Abigail who smiled at Mrs. Clark. "It'll all work out. I promise. It always works out."

The wounded woman nodded and closed her eyes. Her

breathing soon became slower and deeper as she drifted off to sleep. The wagon rattled and jounced across the rocky terrain and Abigail shifted to rest her back against the board. Nat turned, his hands still full of reins, and shot her a look of concern.

"How could you say that? How could you promise her it'll be fine?" he hissed under his breath.

"What else could I say?"

"You promised her."

She faced him with a disquieting lack of expression. "I promised her it'll work out. I didn't promise her it'll work out the way she wants. We both know life's not like that."

He frowned, his eyes dark and unreadable, before he turned his attention back to the horses. "Yeah, we do. Sometimes, the best we can hope for is they wait until we're dead to throw dirt over us and feed us to the worms."

Chapter Seventeen

The family were deposited at the doctor's office and Abigail sprinted over to the sheriff, acutely aware he was about to see her without her disguise for the first time.

"Yes, miss? Can I help you?" Sheriff Thompson gallantly stood as she came into the room, puffing out his chest and holding in his belly.

"I don't expect you'll recognize me, but I'm Abigail MacKay. We spoke earlier about the murders?" She watched the confusion reign behind his eyes as he recognized the voice but not the slight, girlish figure standing before him. "I was dressed as an old lady?"

The shoulders sagged along with his gut as realization set in. "No! You ain't her. That old rat-baggage?"

"Sheriff, you can waste time debating my mastery of the art of disguise or you can come over to the doctor's office. I believe we have caught your bushwhackers; or one of them anyway."

"That's her! She's the one who was walking away from my room when I found my file missing. Arrest her, Sheriff. Get her."

She turned at a voice from the cells. Rigby Daintree's face pressed between the bars and his skeletal arm extended further than she would have thought possible from the cage. She frowned. "What's he doing in there?"

"Caught him riflin' through the bags of another guest at the hotel," the sheriff buckled on his gun belt. "Caught red-handed, he was. There ain't no point in him tryin' to deny it. He keeps prattlin' on about a lost file. I told him that wasn't no defense for breakin' and enterin'.'"

"Whose room?"

"That little fella. Dunbar's his name, I think."

Her brows rose, her eyes sliding back toward Daintree. "Really? He and I need to have a little chat when I have the time."

"I don't know what's goin' on over at that hotel. We've still got Richards in, too. I've never seen anythin' like this."

"Richards?" Her eyes widened. "How's his wife?"

"Pretty beat up. I'm talkin' with the mayor about whether this needs to be an attempted murder charge. He was stranglin' her, too. If she'd been somewhere on her own, God alone knows what would've happened. Her arm had to be splinted together and the doctor says she's got percussion."

Abigail suppressed a smile. "Percussion? Poor lady. I must try to look in on her soon."

"Where are you going?" yelled Daintree, watching them walk towards the door. "I want the law on her. I'm sure she knows something about my file."

"Will you shut yer yap?" snapped the sheriff. "She is the law. She's a Pinkerton."

Daintree's mouth dropped open and his arm dropped. "A Pinkerton?"

"Yes, Mr. Daintree." She held the door open on her way out. "I'm too busy for you right now, but we will talk very soon. And I want the truth. The Boston office is looking into you for me right now, so there's no point in lying."

Both Nat and Jake's hands fell by their guns as the sheriff walked into the doctor's office.

"Who are these guys?"

She stood in front of them, facing them down. "They are my colleagues. Their names are of no accord to you, Mr. Thompson."

A cynical look fell over his face as he eyed Abigail with an air of triumph. "I knew the Pinkertons wouldn't leave an investigation to a woman, and not to a slip of a girl. Why didn't one of you men come to see me instead?"

"They couldn't break cover. I could." She shook her head in resignation, used to the assumptions which came with her sex. "Does it matter? Kurt Schmidt is one of the criminals. He'll be able to name the rest of them."

"Kurt? He wouldn't know what he was doin'. Where's the doc?"

An erect, white-haired man stood in the doorway, his gray suit covered by a bloody apron. He spoke in a soft lilting accent which belied the authority of his stance. "He's looking after the Clarks with his wife. I'm Doctor MacIvor. I was visiting with my colleague when this case came in, so I jumped straight in to help." He nodded over to Abigail. "I need to fetch a couple of things from the cabinet, if you don't mind."

"You're Scottish?" Abigail's brows met in curiosity. "'*S Ailean mhór a chuir an rathad thu?*"

He nodded. "*Tha gu dearbh, 's fhearr a bhith cinnteach na caillte.*" He switched to English. "How rude of us to speak in a language the rest do not understand. It's just so rare to get the chance since we left home. Yes, miss. I was on my way to San Francisco to a convention of surgeons when a little voice said to me, 'why don't you go stop off in Bannen to look in on your old friend and colleague?' It's a good job I did. With all these patients, he's never needed the help of a spare surgeon more." He lifted a small bottle from the glass shelf. "Here it is. Back to the family." The blue eyes lit with disdain as he glanced at Kurt. "They come first, as they are the hurt worse than you are. We'll get to you presently." He nodded once more before he left the room.

"They sure do come first," the sheriff agreed.

"I don't speak no German. I'll get my deputy Groenig to do it. He's got German from his folks. I'll go get him."

"He speaks English just fine," Jake replied. "He spoke it to us when he got shot."

"Is that right?" Sheriff Thompson sucked in an indignant breath. "I guess he let folks in Bannen believe that so nobody would suspect he was a robber. Is that true, Kurt?" The sheriff poked him in the wound.

"Ow! Leave me be. It was a way to keep noisy neighbors from bothering Pa about keeping me outta school so I could help on the farm, is all. I made out I was simple so school didn't want me. I didn't want them, neither. They made fun of my mouth."

"And later it was useful for the bushwackin'? They were always loners, those Schmidts. They kept themselves to themselves. The young 'un wasn't of school age when they moved here."

He prodded Kurt's shoulder again. "Well. What do you know? Who's your friends? Talk." He jabbed the wound again as Jake stepped forward.

"Leave him be. I don't hold with torture."

"Why? Are you soft?" He prodded the screaming boy again. "Talk."

"I said, leave him be," Jake forced the lawman away from the wounded man with jolt to the shoulder. The sheriff reacted and went for his firearm but found the gunman's weapon in his nose before he could even straighten up.

"Whoa." He raised his hands in capitulation, stunned at the speed of the gunman who stood before him. "Sure. I ain't gonna mess with professionals."

"I'll question him," Nat pushed between them. "We'll tell

you what we want you to do."

"Well, we got the murderer of those whores now." The sheriff eyed the group with hostility. "You ain't needed here no more."

"I never. I never murdered no one," yelled Kurt.

"You expect us to believe that, you murdering basta—"

Abigail cut him off. "The way they operate isn't the same. A bullet in the arm in anger and a head blunt injury doesn't come close to a deliberate shot through the head and a slow strangling. This case isn't closed. We're going nowhere."

"How'd you know that?"

Abigail glared at him. "You said it yourself. We're professionals."

"So who are the other two?" asked Nat. "Who else is there around here? There's only one more man in the household, and the sheriff told Abi he was dead."

"Och, for heaven's sake. It's obvious," Abigail threw up her hands. "It's the girl. They're all described as heavy set. They pad her with jackets and she makes sure she doesn't speak. Add the father and son speaking good English and nobody around would dream it was them under a mask. Pa Schmidt's dead, and suddenly there are two robbers? Do you think that's just a coincidence?"

"Don't talk rubbish girl. A woman couldn't carry that off."

She glared at the sheriff. "No? Did you think I could look sixty years old?" She threw up her hands in exasperation at the male's ability to dismiss female criminality. "Search the place. Look for the disguise; padded jackets. Look for a man's hat with long red hairs in the crown," she glared at the wounded man. "Tell them, Kurt. We'll even find things you just had to keep, eh?"

"How'd you know?" asked the wounded boy, caught out by her certainty.

"See? Now, when you're all finished with this nonsense, you

need to bring her and her mother in for questioning."

"Nope," the sheriff replied. "I'm getting a posse and we're razin' that place to the ground."

"No, you're not," Abigail planted her feet in front of the lawman. "I'm not interested in fitting someone up to clear a crime. I want the real killers found. It doesn't help the people of this town to have murderers walking free. And burning the place will destroy evidence. What if there are murders you don't even know about?"

"So you ain't gonna do nuthin'? That's loco."

"Arrest them, by all means, but that's it. No destruction and no burning. We're going out there tomorrow, and we'll look at all the evidence, not burn it as an act of stupid revenge. Until then, tell anyone who'll listen that Kurt is here. Tell your posse to do the same. Let them worry and see what the new information makes them do."

"Make who do what?"

Abigail's dark eyes fixed on the sheriff with a fierce determination. "The murderers. Let's see if anyone makes a run for it."

The posse set out for the Schmidt place, but the trio stayed behind to allow the townsfolk to bring in the Schmidts on their own. It had been a long day and heightened emotions were still running through the group. They needed to rest and Abigail noted with deep concern that Jake hadn't said a word to her, or looked her in the eye, since their quarrel.

Jake strolled outside and rubbed his tense face. This law work was harder than he thought, and he had been ready to take a swing at Abigail after their confrontation out in the plain.

He walked along the sidewalk, the cleansing night air hitting his lungs and washing away his initial tension, but the anger still boiled deep in his guts. His shoulders rose in tension at the feminine heels clattering behind him. By the time they got close he already anticipated the voice which drifted through the darkness.

"Jake. I have to speak to you."

He stiffened and quickened his pace, his irritation rising. The patter of her feet rang through the night before a hand grasped his arm. Jake shrugged her off and strode on. "Don't you know when to give up?"

She ran in front of him and stood in his way in a misguided attempt to appeal to his better nature. "Please. We have to talk."

A muscle flinched in his jaw. "Get out of my way, Abi."

"Jake—"

"Move, or I won't be responsible for my actions. I ain't in the mood for this."

"No. I need to talk to you."

Without a word, he grasped her by the top of the arm and dragged her into the nearest alley. He thrust her against the wall and held her with one hand. "You want to talk? You got my full attention, sweetheart. Just remember a killer's got you in an alley, so don't do anythin' stupid."

"No, he hasn't."

She spoke calmly but he could hear her swallowing hard as her breathing quickened against his grasp.

He moved closer, his hot breath on her face. "You sure about that?"

He watched her eyes well up but it wasn't fear, it was regret. Her next words only added to his conflicted psyche. "Yes. I've never been surer of anything in my life. I'm sorry, Jake. So sorry. I am just getting to know you. That's my only excuse. I'm in a world of criminals and rogues. It's taken me a while to realize you're not—" she paused, "well—very usual. I'm alone out here, and all I have to measure you by is what I already know about people. But every now and then you show me I know almost nothing. I'm sorry. I was wrong."

He gazed right into her, lost in his own thoughts and memories before he spoke as though scattering a nightmare. "A killer. The man with the fast gun. That's all you see."

"You're wrong."

A sardonic laugh slashed the evening chill. "Yeah? You thought exactly that until Nat found the bag."

"I know. I understand better now."

He pulled back and stared deep into her, his eyes still swirling with doubt as she spoke again.

"I should have listened to my heart and what I've learned about you. I was wrong, and I'll tell that to anyone. Even Alan Pinkerton."

"Yeah, right. Ever wondered why I needed to get so good with a gun? Maybe I lost too much? Maybe I needed to make sure I didn't lose anyone else?" His lids slid closed and he pushed her away. "Go," his sigh was hoarse and elemental.

"Please talk to me."

"Just go. I ain't leavin' you in an alley. You're just dumb enough to stay here and pick a fight with whatever's rakin' through the trash."

"No, I'm not—"

He pulled her into the street. "Go, woman. Just go. Will you ever listen to anythin' you're told?"

Nat's eyes were as dark as the inky corners of the room as he stared at a sobbing Kurt Schmidt. He turned and walked out of the jailhouse. He had to know if this man was responsible for the death of two helpless women, and he was glad to find out the truth. Unlike the sheriff, he wasn't interested in finding a scapegoat; he dealt only in truth when it came to righting wrongs. He didn't have Jake's scruples, but he didn't use the sheriff's blunt instrument, either. His methods were pointed and comprehensive, but they got answers. If the lawmen hadn't been sitting in the next room, he was sure he'd have gotten a few more.

He nodded to the deputy on his way out and strode out into the cool night air. It felt good to be free from suspicion because everyone thought he was one of the Pinkerton Agents. He could get used to this. His heart still throbbed with emotional intensity as she stepped out onto the street and saw a lone figure standing on the sidewalk gazing out at the night sky.

"Abi?"

She turned, her smile thin and unconvincing.

"Are you alright?"

She shrugged. "Yes."

He took one more lingering look and hooked an arm through hers. "No, you're not. Walk with me. Talk to me."

"I'm fine." Her voice was stronger this time but her face was still impassive and stony.

"Yeah? This is me you're talkin' to. What's wrong? Is this all too much for you?"

He felt her sigh.

"I've upset Jake." Her eyes then flashed, unable to let the slight go unchallenged. "And no. This isn't too much for me. You two are just not what I expected," her brow creased. "Not at all. You're very confounding."

He stopped and turned to look at her, already knowing the answer. "Tell me about Jake."

"Out there today, when he shot that boy. He's so angry at me he could barely even look at me most of the day. I've tried to apologize, but he's still furious, and so cold and so—" She shook her head. "I'm the outsider here. You two have a tight bond. You're not the one to discuss this with."

He smiled through the poor light. "It's fine. *He's* fine."

"No. It's not. He's not."

"I've seen you not give a damn what people think of you," his brows met in a frown. "Why does his opinion matter so much?"

"I deal in truth, no matter how harsh. He's not a cold killer. He's a surgeon's knife, not the blunt instrument I was told he was. I was unfair." Abigail paused, pointing to her heart. "Even though I've apologized, that's not good enough, not for me."

His knitted brows dissipated into surprise. "You need to understand somethin' about Jake. He feels more than he says, but he's fair, real fair. If you've apologized, and meant it, he'll listen to you. He just needs to work through his anger first." He turned her so he faced her, studying her with a smile. "When it wears off, he'll tell you himself. But sometimes, with men, you have to let them work things through before they're ready to talk. We don't talk about feelings. We act on them, and that can take longer when we know it'd be easier to just thrash the hell out of someone. If you'd been a man he'd have cracked you on the jaw," he grinned. "Now, he's got that to work through, too. Give him time, he'll be back when he's ready."

She groaned. "So? You're teaching me about men now, Mr. Quinn?"

His mellifluous baritone was laden with meaning. "Do you *want* me to teach you, Abi?"

Her stomach gave the now familiar flip as her eyes darted away in embarrassment.

He smiled, flashing his brows mischievously. "You didn't say no." He reached out and stroked her cheek with a long finger and drew her face up to look into his. "I've never met anyone like you before. You still have the ability to surprise me, and not many women do. Most would think you'd be very experienced around men, but you're not, are you?"

Her almond-shaped eyes shone as the moonlight illuminated

her pale skin. "That depends on what you mean by experienced, Mr. Quinn."

"You know what I mean, Abi," he whispered as he drew her close to him.

He felt her tense and he released her, concern flickering over his face. "I'm sorry. I thought I sensed something between us."

She dropped her head. "Whatever you sensed, Mr. Quinn, needs to stay exactly where it is."

He tilted his head, the disquiet feeding through to his voice. "Is it because of what I did to you at the cabin? I wouldn't have. I would never do that to a woman. It was a strategy. It's not who I am. There are some things you can't steal."

"No," she shook her head and darted a smile at him. "I know you wouldn't, nor would Jake."

His brow lined. "What, then?"

"This is a temporary truce, Mr. Quinn. You're clever, kind, and as handsome as the devil himself; but you're still a criminal...and I can't afford to get involved with a man like you."

"Male lawmen do it all the time. Ask Pearl."

"Do you understand how good I have to be? To be allowed into my world, let alone get respect? I can't. I just can't." She frowned. "Quite apart from the fact that I'm not the kind of woman to throw herself at anyone, we'll be on opposite sides again very soon."

He folded his arms, his cheeks dimpling in delight. "So? You think I'm handsome?"

"You know I do. Stop fishing for compliments, it's very unattractive." She thrust her nose in the air. "So is Jake. You are a very winsome family."

His eyes glittered through the darkness in irritating triumph. "You're one of the most honest people I ever met. Don't get me wrong; you lie through your teeth, but only for the right reasons. You can't be bought and you don't cheat. Do you know how many women with your looks would use them to get what they wanted? Even to draw us in?" He grinned. "At least, when it happens, I'll know it's not that kind of trick."

She narrowed her eyes. "When what happens?"

His smile danced with devilish temptation.

"It'll never happen," she murmured.

"No, Abi. *When.*" Roguish sparks shone in the glittering smile. "You and me are made from the same stuff, just different sides of the same coin. There's a whole lot of fire under that stiff, proper front. Now, let's turn in. I think this is getting too far from the business at hand."

They strolled on, back to the hotel. The stars stretched endlessly above them and blazed with as much defiance as the spirits of the complicated people below.

Nat turned to her. "I questioned Kurt. He says that when they came across the women they were already dead and disposed of the bodies so they could sell anything valuable."

She stopped walking and faced him once more. "And you believe him?"

"To a point. He's not bright enough to be very creative. I don't think I got everything out of him, though. There were too many witnesses around. I had to go gentle."

"What about the jewelry he sold in Paris?"

Nat stopped in his tracks. "He said the women were wearing it and he wouldn't give whoever found them next a chance to steal it instead. They scavenged it, according to him."

"Where would prostitutes get something worth stealing?"

"I asked the same question," he shrugged. "They were better paid than most, but then I wondered if it's something to do with this inheritance stuff."

"We must get a warrant to seize it," Abigail replied. "I need to examine it. What did he say about the murder of his father?"

"He says he went off alone one day and didn't come back."

"I suppose that may be true, in a way. He's what links the

Schmidts to the killers of Bessie and Dora though. He was shot by a single shot to the head like Bessie, execution style," she mused.

"It might not be a link. Lots of people have guns and Schmidt wasn't popular. So, you think he knows who the killers were, too?"

"Maybe, but he'll have been indoctrinated since birth about not cooperating with the law, and he's not smart enough to realize he'll be in the frame for the killings unless he helps us. Perhaps the sister will be of more use to us? She seems more intelligent." Her rueful smile was caught in a watery moonbeam. "Ironically, this might have been one time where you'd have been more successful under your real identity, Mr. Quinn."

"Abi, can I ask you something personal?"

"What?"

"Why do you call me Mr. Quinn? There's no etiquette for our situation, but it seems too formal, considering you use Jake's given name." He beamed the way the moon does to brighten the night sky. "We're cut from the same cloth, and we have an understanding. Aren't we beyond conventional formalities?"

She nibbled on her bottom lip before it melded with an indignant moue. "No. I can't."

"Everyone else calls me plain old Nat."

"I would call you by your first name, but I can't," she shook her head. "My relationship with Jake is familiar. My relationship with you is kept firmly at arm's length. That's why I'll always call you Mr. Quinn. You won't get too close that way."

"Ya think?" His eyes widened along with his smile. "You've already given me the biggest compliment you could, Abi. You don't avoid what you're indifferent to. I'll take 'Mr. Quinn' with pleasure," his eyes danced with promised thrills. "Great pleasure."

Chapter Eighteen

When Abigail and Nat walked into the sheriff's office the next morning, all eyes were on her. Everyone in town now whispered about the female Pinkerton, even if they weren't aware she was also the formidable 'Mrs. Benson'. Jake gallantly stood, as always, as she approached the desk in the private office behind the front desk.

She smiled. "How are you, Jake?"

His deep blue eyes warmed. "I'm fine. Everything's better in the light of a new day, huh? How are you?"

"Worried about upsetting you."

"But putting us away for twenty years ain't gonna upset me?" he whispered.

She glanced around to make sure they weren't overheard. "That's the sentence for things you did, not for things you didn't. You didn't deserve that kind of judgment from me. I am sorry, and I'll never misjudge you again. I give you my word I'll trust you where you deserve it." She smiled. "However rarely."

His eyebrows flicked up. "I suppose that works both ways. I guess you just didn't know me well enough, but you do now. That old lady stunt in the restaurant is somethin' else entirely. I still owe you for that one, makin' the waitress think I used old ladies for their money."

She laughed. "Oh, yes? Just what do you have in mind?"

He grinned. "When it happens, you'll know."

Nat grabbed a chair. "Well, I'm glad you two made it up."

"Nothin' to make up, Nat, except for the little old lady stuff."

Nat chuckled as he sat. "You earned it, Abi."

They pulled out the file of telegrams from the sheriff along with the reply from the Pinkerton agency which had come in that morning, and dissected the evidence. All eyes turned to Nat as he spoke in subdued tones, trying to make sure they weren't overheard outside the privacy of the office. "I took time to speak to the Schmidt boy last night. They're thieves and murderers; but he says he wasn't there when Bessie and Dora were killed. He won't say more at the moment, not yet. I don't think he realizes how much trouble he could be in."

"The sister and the mother are saying nothing at all. They won't open their mouths," Abigail shrugged. "They don't trust the law. It's very common." Her eyes widened. "The information came in from Boston. I think I know who did it, and why. If we could get the jewelry he sold in Paris, I could tie all this up."

Jake looked into his coffee cup. "Why? What did you find out from Boston?"

"Ben Middleton probably isn't who he says he is, and the first Mrs. Benson died years ago. That's what gave him away. He knew. He absolutely knew Phil Benson's mother was dead."

"So who is he?"

She shrugged. "I have an idea, but I need to check. I've asked the sheriff to bring him in along with those who want to adopt David. They're also from Boston and I think they have connections to Ben Middleton's real family."

"Real family?" The men exchanged a glance as the Jake spoke. "So what did you get back from the Pinkertons? What have you got?"

"Phil Benson's maternal grandmother's maiden name was Middleton. We have no proof Ben Middleton's using a false name, but we have to consider it. It's a common mistake to use the maternal maiden names as an alias, though. It helps us." She shrugged. "We know nothing about his background other than the fact he was caught in the same explosion which killed

Dora's husband, and turned to playing the piano to make a living when he was blinded."

Nat and Jake frowned, processing this information as she continued.

"Phil Benson's father is also dead: two years ago, but it looks like he remarried when he was quite old. He left his money to his surviving children, so Phil Benson wouldn't have been entitled to a share, as he predeceased him. That also rules out the boy as someone who could inherit, too. The will excluded him. Dora had contacted a lawyer to find out about the will by telegraph. The sheriff got that information for me. So why did Dora think she was going to be able to give up prostitution from that?"

"Bigamy? Old man Burton remarried while his first wife was still alive and it was blackmail?" asked Nat.

She shook her head. "No, Andrew Benson's first wife died, but they'd lived apart for at least nine years. He was a horrible man, a violent alcoholic, but he had worked hard and built a future. It was a plumbing supply business, and he got above himself when he opened his second shop. He alienated his family and they all sided with his wife when she left him after one final beating. She died in poverty, the poor soul. In Bannen, actually. She wasn't the genteel matron I portrayed. She was a washerwoman because her husband wouldn't give her a penny. Incidentally, she also had another son; an older boy called Michael. He died five years ago, but there had been a warrant out for his arrest as he beat the proverbial you-know-what out of his father and left home. He was close to his mother and hated his father. She signed the death certificate in Boston before she left and came out West. Old man Benson's second marriage was to a woman called Rose Thornhill and she married a Robert Davies after Andrew Benson died. Rose had a daughter by Benson. She's about four now."

"Robert Davies!" Nat exclaimed. "He's at the hotel. Bob is short for Robert."

"Didn't he say his wife was called Mary?" asked Jake.

"Yes," Abigail nodded. "We have some checking to do on both of them, but they are most definitely suspects. However, they come from the other side of the country, not Boston, so they may just have a similar name."

"So, why would anyone murder Dora and Bessie for that, and why want the boy? He didn't even inherit anything."

"That's what I need to prove, and I need to get everyone together, before the scratch evidence disappears. Andrew Burton, the man who wanted to adopt, was a very tall man with a middle finger missing. I had an idea who that might be as soon as I heard the description, and that also tells me why he wanted to adopt. The other couple was quite aggressive, especially when they found out the asylum had already allocated David to Andrew Burton." She flicked through the papers. "The sheriff is bringing in everyone involved in this so we'll see then." She paused. "We just need to speak to Daintree and Dunbar. Daintree is in the cell after being caught going through Tibby's bags."

"I suppose we want to know what he was looking for," Jake frowned.

"Oh, I already know that," Abigail grinned. "He's mad about the dossier I took from his room and wanted to see where it went. I want to find out why he suspected Tibby, though."

Daintree spread out his spindly legs in an untidy cluster of long feet and thighs. His bony arms were folded obstinately, hands thrust into his armpits. He leveled his jagged elbows at them like gun barrels, and glared at Abigail in contempt.

"You stole my file. I know you did."

She smiled. "Was I carrying anything when you saw me?"

"No, but you could have been carrying it under your skirts." Daintree tilted his chin in an act of defiance. "We both know that."

"Indeed I could have," she shuffled through her papers and picked up her report from the agency once more. "And you would be aware of that since you are also a detective. Wouldn't you?" She read straight from the document. "You are part owner of the Rigby Daintree Consulting Detective Agency based in Scollay Square in Boston, aren't you?"

His eyes bulged. "How did you find that out?"

"The Pinkerton Agency is very efficient. What is your real name? There are two owners and one has the surname Rigby and the other Daintree. Which are you?"

"I'm Rigby. Charles Rigby. My partner is still at the office."

"Who hired you?" Nat asked, "and why?"

"I was retained by telegram by someone called Benson. I only had an initial, 'P'. I guess that could have been fake. They said they wanted me to look into a long-lost family member who had contacted them again. Her name was Dora Benson, and she lived in Bannen. After that, the telegrams came from someone called R.D., and Benson wasn't mentioned by the client again."

"Dora was murdered," Jake's lip curled into a snarl. "Why didn't you tell the law what you were doin' here?"

Rigby shuffled on his seat. "I was worried I might have been set up to take the fall. I never handle cases like this. We usually just do divorces. You know the kind of thing, witnesses bursting in on a setup to give the evidence to the court? We never saw the client, and money got paid straight into our account in cash by someone who went to the bank. We sent the telegrams to the Advertiser Building in Washington Street, but we don't know who collected them. That's all I can tell you."

Abigail sat back in her chair eyeing the man with curiosity. "What were you sent to find out in Bannen, and what did you report back?"

"I had to find out as much as I could about Dora. I reported back that she worked in a brothel, and she appeared to have a relationship with the blind pianist. I saw him sneaking into her room myself. Twice." He tugged at his collar in discomfort at having to describe his actions to a woman. "The visit was purely professional. I can't usually afford that kind of money unless it's backed by a client."

"The client paid for it?" Nat demanded. "How many times? We can check with the brothel and your bills to the client."

"Three or four," Rigby answered.

Jake thumped the desk with an open hand. "Exactly how many times?"

"Three! Alright? I'd need to check if I billed the client for four." He dropped his gaze to the floor. "I might have done."

Nat and Jake exchanged a look of satisfaction. They could always do business with a dishonest man.

Nat fixed him with an intense stare. "What else did you find out?"

"Nothing much. She was a whore with a soft spot for a pianist. Nothing special in that except for his face. She lived with her boy nearby and paid a neighbor, a washerwoman, to watch him while she worked."

Jake's eyes narrowed, but he remained silent and paced back and forth beside Rigby.

"You suggested to the client Ben Middleton might be her husband, and that he changed identities to get a pension from the mine accident," said Abigail. "It's in your telegrams. Nobody could tell because he's so disfigured."

"Well, why else would she spend so much time with him? Have you seen that freak? Only a wife would go near him. None of the other whores in the place would touch him."

Without a word, Jake turned and battered his foot against the leg of chair, kicking it out from under the man. He clattered to the floor with an injured cry as Abigail leaped to her feet and glared at Jake.

The gunman bent over to loom over the startled prisoner. "Right now you look a darn sight uglier than he ever did."

"Is this how the Pinkertons get their information? They beat it out of people?"

"No, we don't," Abigail asserted, glowering at Jake.

"My foot slipped," Jake growled. "Let me help you." He grabbed Rigby by the lapels and lifted him as though he weighed no more than a child. He righted the chair and plunked the shady detective on it. "There you go," Jake growled under his breath, fixing the man with an icy glare. "Want me to dust you down? It'll just take a few slaps."

"I think he's fine," Abigail cut in.

"Alright, but I'll be here if he changes his mind," murmured Jake. "We wouldn't want him goin' to court lookin' untidy."

"To court? On what charges," blustered Rigby.

"Breaking and entering," Nat answered. "You got caught red-handed."

"I'm a detective, not a thief. I did nothing she didn't do."

Abigail's eyes widened and glistened with innocence. "You saw me on the stairs, nowhere else. There's nothing illegal about walking downstairs in a building to which the public have access. You, on the other hand, were caught red-handed."

"And we can prove you're dishonest. I'm willing to bet you billed for four visits to the brothel when you only went three times. We can check real easy."

"Alright!" Rigby turned puce. "What do you want?"

"Why were you searching Tibby's room?"

"He came from back east. The Davieses came out from San Francisco. It's that simple." He tugged on his lapel, noting it was still inside out from the bumpy assistance from the floor. "Davies might have the right initials, but I saw them come off that train from San Francisco myself. I was there collectin' a telegram. If I could find the damned file, I could prove I picked one up that day. I'm sure the staff would remember them because she made such a fuss about her hat box." Rigby leaned forward. "Tibby Dunbar is from the east. Not only that, but I can't find a single politician in town he's supposed to be working for. He's poking around, asking questions and was just being damned suspicious." Rigby's long forefinger stabbed the air in vehemence. "He's as shady as hell. Who is he, and who has a name like Tiberius F. Dunbar? I mean it's just plain ridiculous."

Abigail noted the little flecks of spittle around his mouth and the breath coming in great pants of emotion. This man was desperate, angry, or both. It could be hard to tell the difference sometimes. She stood and scribbled a list on a piece of paper and walked over to the door. "Sheriff Thompson? Can you take this gentleman back to his cell? We're quite finished with him."

She handed over the list she had just compiled. "Can you bring these people in right away? It's about time we cleared this thing up, once and for all. I have to check out something this man just told us at the railway station. Oh, and he gave you a false name. His real name's Charles Rigby."

The lawman's terrier brows bristled. "He did, did he?" He glanced at the list and his face fell. "All of these?"

"All of them. This whole story dovetails one into another. It's the easiest way to explain what went on."

"Pearl Dubois?" sputtered the sheriff. "She ain't gonna like this."

Abigail smiled at both men hoping it came across as sweet and persuasive. "I'm sure my colleagues could help with that. They're very persuasive."

"You really need Pearl?" Jake's brow lined with concern.

"Yes, and everyone else on that list. This has gone on long enough." She turned at the open door. "I'll check on what Rigby just told us about the train from San Francisco. It should take no more than half-an-hour or so."

Chapter Nineteen

The sheriff's office was full of people. One cell held the Schmidt women; the other, Richards, Kurt, and Rigby. People crammed into the office, vying for the few chairs until the sheriff and his deputies took control. A woman in a poke bonnet kept to the wall, and the doctor's friend and assistant from their night the Clark family was brought in leaned against the wall near the cells.

All eyes, except for Ben Middleton, turned, as Nat and Jake walked in with Pearl and her security man and the sheriff rushed to proffer her a seat.

"Got them all here as you asked," Sheriff Thompson turned to Nat. "I guess you want to ask the questions. What's your name again?"

Nat smiled and suppressed a chuckle at Abigail's irritated face as he neglected to introduce himself.

"Sure, I'll start." He stood in front of the assembled group and indicated the people in the cells. "As agreed with the sheriff, I questioned Kurt Schmidt last night. According to him, the Schmidts didn't kill the girls. They had a psychic reading with his sister, and they sometimes used that to spot a potential victim. Dora seemed excited about a large sum of money and a bright future, and that's why they became a target for the Schmidts. They thought she may have some of it with her. The lad would track people and hold them up before their pa and a disguised Anna Schmidt moved in, after checking nobody else was near enough to hear anything. He told me the women were already dead when he found them and he saw no one else around. I don't believe that last part."

Jake cast his mind back to the boy who followed him from the Schmidt's place that night and gave a wry smile at what might have been if he'd been less vigilant. Being held up by the Schmidts held no terrors, but things would definitely have turned nasty if they'd drawn on him.

"How can you believe he just happened on the bodies and didn't kill them?" demanded the sheriff.

"I don't think they were the killers," Nat shrugged. "They've been doin' this for years. The old man had robbed that way when he was a young man, according to Kurt. He was also a militia member during the war, and just kept doing it."

"So? They just took the horses and sold them on?" asked a deputy.

"After throwing the bodies down a well. They didn't need folks examining what they'd been up to, and they were too greedy to pass on the price of the horses. Greed is behind this whole thing," he twinkled amorally at Abigail, "but I suppose it's behind most crime."

Nat cast out a hand toward Pearl. "Mrs. Dubois, here, can testify that Dora kept telling people she was coming into money. It was the worst-kept secret at her establishment."

"And we are great at keeping secrets," added Pearl, determined to emphasize her discretion. The extravagant feathers on the matron's hat trembled like an excited peacock as she spoke. "Is that *all* I was brought here for? I'm a busy woman."

"No, there's something else, but we haven't got there yet," smiled Abigail, at the simmering woman.

"So, from telegrams Dora sent and received, it looks like she tired of her life and contacted her late husband's family for help. She got a reply from someone calling themselves R.D., asking for details of her family to prove she was who she said she was.

Dora replied, and Mr. Rigby, here, was then sent to investigate her without her knowledge. Rigby was employed in writing, and cash paid straight into the company bank account, so he has no idea who he was really dealing with," Nat threw a glare at the skeletal man in the cell, "so he tells us, anyway."

"Why are we here?" demanded Davies. "It's obvious those people killed those poor women. It's ridiculous for respectable people to be treated like this."

"Is it?" asked Nat. "Those robberies have been going on for at least fifteen years in one form or another, and there's never been a death. Why would they suddenly start now?"

"They're criminals. They're all the same," he barked.

Nat flicked up an eyebrow and fixed him with a gimlet eye. "No, sir. They're not, and my experience is quite considerable in that area. This man and that girl, they're thieves, not killers."

"They fought back. They killed them. They were violent with the Clark family," replied the sheriff.

"The Clark robbery was more violent than any others, but they still only beat the woman and shot the man in the arm in panic. That was the only robbery after old man Schmidt died. The dynamics of a gang can change when they lose their leader. The more scared and disorganized robbers are, the more likely they are to use violence. They didn't have their pa's steadying influence anymore. A bullet in the arm and a beating's a different mindset to a deliberate shot to the head and a slow strangling." Nat's eyes seemed to turn blacker as he spoke. "It takes a lot of cruelty to strangle a woman with your bare hands, or a lot of hate. That sort of sickness grows. There would be a pattern. It doesn't just happen once, and then disappear." He paused. "Either that, or a one-off explosion of hate fuelled by very real passion, and theft isn't a strong enough motive. Not when they've been doing this all their lives without violence."

Nat cast out a hand toward Abigail. "This takes us to Miss MacKay's part of the investigation."

"Thank you."

"I recognize that voice. You came to my door with the other woman." Ben Middleton shuffled in his seat, his head cocked receptively.

"Yes, Mr. Middleton. I did. But that's not your name is it?"

The man froze. "Yes, it is."

"Can you evidence that? Is there anyone from your youth who could testify as to your identity, documents perhaps? Family, maybe?"

"I've got no documents, and no one would recognize me. Not after the explosion. I've moved around a lot. I went where the work was."

"There are some things which don't change too much, like your handwriting. Your hands are unaffected, which is why you play piano. Dick Turpin, the famous highway man, was identified when an old school teacher recognized his writing. What school did you go to? I'm sure we can get something from that?"

"I didn't go to school."

"You're lying, Mr. Middleton. If we search your house we'll find examples of your handwriting. You're a musician, most say a superb one, yet you apparently took it up after the accident. It speaks to me of a fairly good education. In fact, I think you're classically trained. I've heard you playing in Pearl's place. Should we ask your wife? I can get the sheriff to fetch her from the laundry."

"Leave her out of this."

"I'm trying to. Work with me, not against me. Do you recognize anyone else's voice?"

"Yours, some of the men." His sightless face turned. "And Pearl."

"Mr. Middleton, I think your name is really Benson. I can prove it, if you make it necessary, but you were able to reinvent yourself, weren't you?"

The man shifted in his chair. "You can't prove anything."

Abigail paused and smiled. "I can if I have to. You were disfigured and could have been anyone. Phil Benson was being blamed for the explosion and wasn't getting a penny. Rigby told his client *you* were Phil Benson, and you claimed to be Ben Middleton to get a pension from the mine insurance company. Is that true?"

"No, of course not. What kind of a man would stand by and let his wife go into a brothel?"

The sharp nosed woman whispered something from behind her poke bonnet to her husband.

Abigail raised her head. "Something you want to say, madam?"

The bonnet shook.

"Please remember you are all here for a reason. You will all get your chance to talk." She turned back to the blind man. "You're not Philip Benson," said Abigail. "You're his elder brother Michael, aren't you?"

The blind man shuffled in his seat.

"Mr. Benson. The charges your father brought appear to be trumped up at best. You were defending your mother from yet another beating weren't you? He kept following his wife demanding that she come back to him, and was violent. There's no need to hide anymore."

"I—"

"You ran away to be with your brother and to escape the assault charges, didn't you? The census shows Dora Blyth was a maid there along with both sons. Dora and Phil left first and lived in Boston for a bit. Your mother left after one last beating, and you eventually all met and lived as neighbors with your mother and brother here in Bannen. You beat your father about six months after your mother left for hounding her to come home, before she ran off to Bannen and changed her name to her own mother's maiden name. He responded by swearing out charges with a warrant for your arrest in revenge." She shrugged. "I'm guessing your mother declared you dead to keep the law from coming after you. You arrived in Bannen and lived as a happy family until the mining accident three years ago tore everyone's lives apart. Your mother died soon afterward."

"That doesn't prove a thing," sniffed the blind man.

Abigail rubbed her temples. "Mr. Benson. I can prove this if you push me to. You weren't Dora's lover. You were her brother-in-law, and she had a kind heart and earned more than anyone else in the family. Everyone who knew her said what a big heart she had. You weren't paying a prostitute. She gave you money to help you and your wife. She wasn't just supporting her son, she supported both households, and in return, your wife looked after her son. For her sake, please tell the truth. Don't let your stupid pride get in the way. She paid you at the brothel to make it look like you were bringing home a better pay packet to your wife. She helped you present a front to your wife."

He dropped his head in shame. "I'm a wreck. A hopeless cripple. Dora was a wonderful person and I had to end up living off her. Look how she earned her money. I couldn't bear it, but it meant Becky didn't have to take on extra work. My name is Michael Benson and I beat the life out of that old son of a—" he paused, his breathing coming in heavy rasps. "I watched him hit my mother for years until I snapped. I was on the run from the law so I went to my brother and changed my name to Middleton. My mother eventually registered me as dead because he kept sending investigators after us. I took grandmother's maiden name because my mother used that to hide from my father. I lived with her as her son again. My father was a vengeful, horrible man who couldn't bear the fact we'd rather live in the gutter than be near him, so he punished us in any way he could." A flicker of a smile flashed over his scarred face. "I met my Becky. We got married, but what kind of life have I given her? What future is there for her? She works from dawn to dusk in a hot, steamy laundry." The man dropped his head in his hands as everyone in the room stared at him.

"There's a warrant for you?" demanded the sheriff.

Nat threw an arm out, sensing Jake stiffen beside him.

"There is, Sheriff, but I hardly think he's a flight risk," Abigail replied. "Besides, he's a very wealthy man. I think this case would be fairly straightforward with the help of a good lawyer, but the statute of limitations has probably expired anyway, along with the supposed victim of the crime. I don't have the date of the charges, though, or the exact nature of the warrant. There's a longer period for beating a man over sixty in that state, for instance; so I don't want to mislead anyone with false hope. I do think it can be smoothed out, though."

"What?" The woman whose pointy nose stuck out from her poke bonnet couldn't help herself. "Wealthy?"

"Yes," replied Abigail. "He's the eldest born legitimate son. In fact, only Philip and Michael were legitimate. The second marriage happened quite late, and the second wife lived as a common law wife until they were able to legally marry on the death of the first Mrs. Benson. Their daughter was illegitimate, and a later marriage doesn't change the status for inheritance law in Boston. It's quite a motive. With nobody around to challenge the legitimacy, the girl from the second marriage would get everything. With Michael around, she'd get nothing at all."

"Isn't it illegal to register someone as dead when you know they're alive?" The woman demanded, her face still shrouded in the shadow of the poke bonnet.

"It is if there's an intention to defraud, but the woman who registered him is dead. Any charges would die with her, unless you could prove he was in on it beyond all reasonable doubt. I have heard nothing here to confirm that." She paused and spoke with deep emphasis. "And I would caution Mr.

Middleton that he shouldn't say anything more about it without consulting a lawyer."

"I've heard enough." Davies stood and took a step toward the door, but stopped in his tracks when he peered into Jake Conroy's impassive face.

"Sit down, sir," Jake raised his chin in challenge. "I won't ask again."

"Thank you." Abigail nodded in Jake's direction. "Anyone thinking of leaving should remember this place is full of lawmen. Isn't it, Sheriff?"

"Yes, ma'am." Sheriff Thompson sounded unsure as to who he should stop, but sure he should act as though he did.

"And that brings us to the motive of the crime. Dora had contacted someone with the initials R.D. They, in turn, appear to have retained a detective who, wrongly, informed R.D. that Philip Benson was still alive, but pretending to be someone called Middleton to get a peppercorn pension from the mine insurance company." She turned and stared at Rigby. "That's the sort of mistake amateurs make; they run on assumptions instead of getting evidence. R.D. didn't get their money's worth from the Rigby Daintree Consulting Detective Agency, that's for sure. But it gave R.D. a motive. They assumed Michael had died five years ago so discounted him, but saw Phil and his son as danger to the illegitimate daughter's substantial inheritance. Something had to be done. Dora was so excited about her future—that's one of the big tragedies here. In reality, she was sleepwalking into a trap. She realized that her brother-in-law would inherit, and knew she could rely on him to look after her and her son. I can only suppose she didn't want to say anything to Michael until she was sure. She probably thought it would have been devastating to build up his hopes for no reason."

Nat glanced over at Tibby. "And after the murders, Rigby worried he'd been set up to take the blame, which might not be too far from the truth, if events hadn't taken an unexpected turn with the Schmidts. Who are you, Mr. Dunbar? You came in on the eastbound train."

Tibby sat with his spat-clad feet primly together, both little hamster-hands on the ornamental knob of his walking stick. "I told you who I am. I am Tiberius F. Dunbar."

"Who claims to be working for local politicians, but you're not. Are you, Mr. Dunbar?" Nat pushed on. "I made it my business to look into you today, and nobody seems to use your services. Neither the sheriff nor the mayor is running for re-election soon. Why don't you tell us the truth?"

Tibby grinned. "I must say, you Pinkerton fellas are superb. I suppose there's no harm in telling everyone now. Not after the investigation has reached a dead end."

"Investigation? Another damned detective?" the sheriff spluttered. "Is everyone in this blasted town investigatin' everyone else? How many of you is there now?"

"No, Sheriff. I'm not a detective. I'm a journalist who writes under the name pen name of Dogberry."

The sheriff's impressive brows rose. "Dogberry? What kinda name is that? You call yourself after Dog's droppin's?"

"Dogberry is a literary character from Shakespeare's 'Much Ado About Nothing'," Abigail replied. "He is a comical character intended to poke fun at the law enforcement of the day by his incompetence, which is probably why Mr. Dunbar chose the name. I admit on being rather keen on Dogberry's writings." She nodded. "Your in-depth investigations and exposés are wonderful, especially that one about the selling of children. Very impressive. I must say I didn't expect you to look the way you do. I expected someone much younger and buccaneering, if that's not too insulting."

"Thank you, miss, but I gave up worrying about my appearance when I realized it was my personality which alienated people."

A ripple of laughter drifted around the room as Tibby

continued. "I've been covering the stories on the fake Innocents, and looking into the real gang. You can check with my editor. He's paying my expenses. If experience is anything to go by, he'll be doing it with all the grace of a dog walking on its hind legs on a hot sidewalk. He hates parting with money."

Nat slipped into his best poker face and allowed Abigail to take the lead again. Did Tibby know his real identity?

Abigail frowned. "Why are you investigating The Innocents around here?"

"Oh, just a rumor that Nat Quinn and Jake Conroy were brought up around here. I've checked all the school records and the orphanages though. I can't find the names at all. They are very common names aren't they? Even your two detectives bear them," Tibby's scrutiny seemed to magnify through widened eyes as he continued. "Lots of Nathans, Nathaniel's, and Jacobs, and the only ones who are the right ages are still around here and are clearly not outlaws. One family of Quinns lives out by the mines, but they're girls—and there are no Conroys. None. I've hit a dead end with that, but at least I got the scoop on the fake Innocents by being on the train."

Abigail nodded, glancing at Pearl. "Yes. I had heard something similar about Quinn and Conroy. I drew a blank too. You couldn't find the names? I long suspected they used an alias, too. We must have a chat, Mr. Dunbar."

"I'd love to, Miss MacKay. In fact, I have been wondering if I might do an article on you."

"I would prefer you didn't, Mr. Dunbar. The element of surprise is important in my work. In exchange for giving up that story, I may help you get the scoop on this one, though."

Chapter Twenty

Abigail nodded and perched on the edge of the desk.

"So back to the point. Rigby was caught searching the wrong room suspecting he'd brought him to Bannen. Mr. Dunbar was not his erstwhile employer. He was barking up the wrong tree there, just as he was about Dora's husband still being alive." She turned her attention to the Davieses. "In his second marriage Benson had a daughter called Ruth, she'd be about four now, almost five, but her parents married after her birth. That is the key to this. Isn't it, Mrs. Davies? You're called Mary by your present husband, but Mr. Benson married a Rose. They're both correct, aren't they? Your name is Rosemary. Now you're married and you are Rosemary Davies. R.D."

"What, me? No."

Nat fixed her with a hard stare. "What is your name, ma'am?"

"It's Davies. Mary Davies. I have nothing to do with this."

Nat stepped forward, peering at the face in the shadows of the wide-brimmed bonnet. "Well, that's strange, because you told my partner and me it was Hislop."

"And you also told the orphanage your name was Mellor. Do you want me to get the superintendent in here to identify you? It's the easiest thing in the world to prove who you are and who you claimed to be. A few visits to your surrounding neighbors from Pinkertons bearing photographs will easily confirm your real identity, too. The telegraph company has already informed us about the contents of the telegrams and who sent and received them. It was you communicating with Dora, wasn't it, Mrs. Davies?"

"So what?" she snapped, aware her subterfuge wouldn't last. "The boy is just lovely. When I heard how poor she was and he went into an orphanage, I wanted to help. I'm too old to have any more children and I wanted a son. I also thought she might have done something to stop us from approaching under our real names."

"Or you wanted to have complete control over these people threatening your plans. When Dora was dead, Ben Middleton may not be able to prove his claim because he had been living under another name for so long and was seriously disfigured. You holding the child was a way to make sure." The woman glared at Abigail. "Except the orphanage didn't want to give you the boy. Someone else had already applied and a deal had been struck with a man called Andrew Burton, also from Boston, who appeared to be wealthier than you and made a donation to the orphanage. The deal could have been broken, but you annoyed the superintendent by browbeating him and he stuck to the original adoption. Mr. Andrew Burton claimed to be a very successful business man with a very loving wife. You had to steal the boy."

Abigail examined Pearl with a smile. "Was it your idea to get the boy adopted or was it the pianist's?"

"Me? I don't know what you mean."

"Your security man, sitting next to you. He has a white moustache and his middle finger is missing, just like the man described by the head of the Juvenile Asylum. He's not as tall as described, but people often get things like that wrong. You're, what? Six-three?"

"Six-three-and-a-half," muttered the security man.

"And the missing digit is on the correct hand and is the same unusual amputation, right up to the knuckle with no stump. There can't be many of those around one small town. He fits the description, other than the height. I'm guessing the superintendent of the Juvenile Asylum is a very short man?"

"Yeah, he's about five-foot-two—" nodded a deputy.

"So the man towering over him would not only look daunting, but it'd be hard to assess with nobody else in the room to measure him against. That explains the height error."

"We don't know what you're on about," snorted Pearl.

Abigail stared at the security man's hand. "I knew who it was the minute I heard the description. I saw you at Pearl's place when you evicted the fake Innocents from the premises, and I noted the missing finger. It was a very kind and open-hearted gesture from an employer. One of your employees died, leaving a child an orphan and you weren't going to leave him in a home. They weren't going to give him to a woman who ran, shall we say, a house of hospitality. Nor would they give him to a blind man already living in penury, so you invented a businessman from Boston and sent your head of security to fetch him dressed in his best suit. I like it. It speaks of a very kind woman, Mrs. Dubois. It also probably saved his life, too. It stopped Mrs. Davies getting to him first. I am very glad you acted the way you did."

The enormous man spoke at last, his moustache mobile with his emotions. "I lost the finger in the mine. I worked with both Phil Benson and Ben Middleton. Ben didn't tell me he lost his brother. I thought they were close friends, so I wanted to help him get the boy." He stared over at his friend. "Why didn't you tell me, Ben?"

"I thought I'd be arrested," Middleton replied. "I couldn't risk it. I'd never survive in jail like this."

"And that's when you tried to take the boy from school," added Jake, staring into the woman's wide-brimmed bonnet, holding her guilty eyes hostage with his glare. "Keepin' your head down won't help. We were both there, ma'am. We saw you."

"Yes, she raised my suspicions when she refused to be anywhere near you two," Abigail agreed. "First it was megrims, then it was eating out, or hurrying out of the room while her husband acted as a diversion. I noted she was happy to see me, but not the men who confronted the woman who tried to take David Benson from school. That made me suspicious."

"Yeah," Nat reflected. "She did do that. I never saw her face the whole time we were at the hotel."

"Because she saw you first," she continued. "Mr. Middleton, or should I say Burton? You had a hand in the adoption attempt. Your father left all his money to be shared equally amongst his surviving children, thinking both his sons from his earlier marriage were dead and gone. He specified no other names or conditions. A total of over forty thousand dollars, two houses, and a business which is growing by the day as people take to indoor plumbing. He left only a small income for his wife, but then he was quite a misogynist."

"Misogynist? What's his religion got to do with this?" demanded the sheriff.

Abigail stared at the woman. "You wanted it all. An income wasn't good enough for you. You were incensed to learn Dora was enquiring about the will, and when you investigated, you found the survivor from the mine had been blinded and didn't question what Rigby came up with. You assumed Phil Benson was still alive and was eligible to inherit his father's share because he'd swapped identities with the dead man to get the payout from the mine. You'd lost the money. It didn't cross your mind to worry about Michael. You all believed he was long dead."

"You can't prove a thing," snapped the woman.

"I can. R.D. also met her on the day she died."

"That doesn't mean I killed her. I didn't even arrive in town until days after the murder."

"So you say, but I think you stayed in the next town along

the line until after the murder, and then quietly left by train again. All you had to do was take a forty-minute journey. It also accounts for why Rigby was told to collect something from the railway station on the day you arrived and why you made such a fuss about your hat box. You wanted to be remembered arriving from the west. I think a check will soon reveal you stayed there before the killings."

"It's feasible I can be of assistance," ventured Tibby. "Mr. and Mrs. Davies were on the same train as me from the east. The one which was held up by the fake gang. I had a conversation with her when she complained about the way they handled the women, and she was wearing the bonnet she's wearing now. They absolutely did travel west at the same time as I did."

"Why didn't you say something before?" Jake demanded.

"People lie for all kinds of reasons. It's none of my business until it becomes important. I'm a journalist, not a policeman. I merely report."

Abigail's eyes lit up. "And you're willing to swear to that in court?"

"Of course. I always tell the truth. It's one of the many things people hate about me." Tibby inclined his head, displaying complete indifference to public opinion. "I was hiding behind the tree and she was complaining bitterly. I remember her well."

"You were hiding behind a tree?" the sheriff's incredulous gawk did nothing to shame the little man.

"Of course," Tibby's mouth firmed into a line. "I find bravery greatly overrated. People get killed that way."

"None of that proves we murdered anyone," Mrs. Davies protested.

"No. But there was a witness. Someone followed them out to rob them. Someone who later blackmailed you, Mrs. Davies. Wasn't there, Kurt?"

The German boy stammered and stuttered to a standstill but Abigail pressed on. "Kurt. She's got no money, she's going to prison, and she's trying to set you up for this murder. Tell the truth, for heaven's sake."

"I—"

"Kurt. I think they killed your father when he tried to get more money out of them. Now, they're trying to hang you and your sister for their crimes."

The Schmidts said nothing, an upbringing of mistrust taking its toll. Their refusal to help was infuriating, causing Abigail's hands to harden into little fists of frustration. "Please. Don't let her get away with this. They'll blame you and they'll hang you for her crime."

"Nobody'll never believe us anyway," Anna murmured. "What's the point?"

"Does this help?" Nat reached inside his hat before he unfolded a collection of rings and lustrous pearls from a cloth and placed them on the table. He picked up a ring, a ruby and diamond cluster. "This one's got an inscription, *'to Mary from Robert'*. It's got a date, too. I'm guessing it's your wedding or engagement ring. When did you get married to Mr. Davies, ma'am? Kurt sold this and it connects you to the Schmidts."

Abigail glared at him, left speechless as he beamed his most dazzling smile. There was only one way he could have possession of the jewelry. He had broken into the safe in the jeweler's shop where Kurt had sold off the goods. He also hadn't said a single word about it until forced to do so.

Nat buried his slippery grin under a mask of *faux* professionalism. "Have you got photographs at home, ma'am? I bet you're wearing your jewels in them. Or we can trace the jeweler who made or sold them. The boy, here, took these to Paris and sold them. We can prove these are yours. These link you to the Schmidts, and you didn't report a robbery. That means you voluntarily handed over your precious property.

Were you buying their silence, by any chance? It's the only logical explanation."

The woman went puce as her husband declaimed his innocence. "I had nothing to do with it. I was there, but she shot the big one, and Dora fought, so she strangled her."

"Shut up!" yelled Mrs. Davies, lashing out at her husband. "We were robbed. That's how he must have gotten them."

"The bodies don't agree with that account, sir." Abigail cut in, ignoring the woman's attempt to prevaricate. "Bessie's nails were broken on one hand. She fought for her life. I'd say someone shot her because she fought too well. One woman couldn't do that alone. Not with another woman fighting, too. She fought. Even with decomposition those things can be found on a body. Dora scratched with both hands."

"She shot her." Anna Schmidt pointed at Mary Davies. "He strangled the young one when she wouldn't tell them about a man called Philip. They gave us what they had to shut us up; everything valuable that woman was wearing, and promised us more. They didn't know we were watching them or that we'd followed the women from our place. I've never seen anything like it. We don't kill. I guess they would have killed us, too but we were armed and outnumbered them."

"Did she expect to meet you out there on the plain?" Abigail asked Robert Davies.

"We wanted to pay Dora a small sum to disappear, but she'd done her homework and thought someone was entitled to a cut of the will. Then we found out it was even worse—he'd get it all because Ruth was illegitimate. She was smarter than we thought and we couldn't let her follow it up with a lawyer. We had to deal with her. A woman at the brothel told us where they'd gone and we rode out to meet them before they got back to town."

"Shut up!" cried Mrs. Davies.

"I will not, woman. You already put a noose around my

neck." Robert Davies stood. "I haven't been able to eat or sleep since it happened. It's a nightmare."

"It begs the question. What did you intend to do to the boy?" demanded Abigail.

"Nothing. I'm not an animal." The woman clamped her jaws shut and stared off at the wall, refusing to expand any further.

"That's a matter of opinion, ma'am." Jake's eyes burned into the woman. He had sworn to kill Dora's killer but what could he do to a woman? Especially when the law was already taking care of things for him. Perhaps Abigail's way was better, but what if the court let her off?

"He's disappeared. What have you done to him?" yelled Sheriff Thompson.

"The boy's fine. In order to stop him being taken we had our people remove him to safety," said Abigail as she glanced at Nat and Jake, hoping her next words were true. "He's with a trusted family."

The sheriff's eyes glinted at Abigail. "The way the law is in this country, ma'am, you can't override the authority of an elected lawman as long as he's keepin' to the constitution. What do you think you're playin' at?"

Abigail smiled the smile of one used to handling angry people. "I overrode no one, Mr. Thompson. You did nothing. The boy came of his own free will and has been kept safe and well with a trusted family." She spoke with calm authority. "If you can be clear about what investigation of yours I hampered, I'll be happy to answer in any court of law. I don't intimidate easily, and I would like to point out you still haven't even visited the Juvenile Asylum and you only sent a deputy to ask the questions as I directed. The boy has now been away from there for almost a week. You did nothing."

"You can't prove we weren't robbed," ranted the woman. "Those Germans are criminals by their own admission. They're blaming us for their crime. We're innocent victims!"

"Except for one thing, Mrs. Davies," Abigail strode over and grasped her arm, pulling back her sleeve, revealing track-like scars on her forearm and on the backs of her hands. "Cuts heal quite quickly, but deep scratches will leave scars that take much longer to disappear. I believe that if we search your husband he will have scars, too, as he dragged Dora away to let you deal with Bessie. I examined the bodies. They were too badly decomposed for me to identify defensive injuries, but their nails were broken where they fought and scratched for their very lives. Human skin was under their nails. They never stood a chance. Bessie was bigger than you but you not only had the element of surprise, you had a gun. Dora? Well, women just aren't a strong as men."

She dropped the woman's arm and smiled at the dignified gentleman in the gray suit who had been sitting throughout the discussion. *"Dotair Mac Íomhair? Ciamar a tha sibh?"*

The man nodded and replied in their native Scottish Gaelic. *"Tha gu math, tapal leibh."*

"This is Doctor MacIvor. He is a countryman of mine and a very eminent surgeon who works for the Pinkerton Agency. Some of you may have met him when he assisted the local doctor with the Clark family. He studied with Dr. Joseph Bell in Edinburgh who has used medical science to solve many murders in a way which has influenced the world and is changing detection very dramatically. He is a brilliant man with an eye for detail in the new scientific method," she smiled at him. "I'm very lucky to have him here, but he was passing through on his way out west for another case and was kind enough to take a detour to check up on me."

"Always happy to help, Miss MacKay," the doctor spoke in a singsong highland accent. "I thought the doctor might be the best way to find you, as they tend to hear all the gossip in small towns. It was most fortunate I chose the same evening you brought in the Clark family."

She paused, watching Nat and Jake wonder how many more Pinkerton employees were in this town as their spirits sank before her very eyes. "He has examined the bodies. He can explain how hard they fought and scratched and he can state how long ago those marks on your arms were made. We can prove you are the only ones connected with the deceased there who were scratched. He has examined all of the Schmidts, including the father's body. They weren't scratched but those women clawed at their killers. I took skin samples from both of their nails myself. The absence of scratches on any of the Schmidts will also show they are unlikely to have murdered those women. When you couple that with proof of when you journeyed here, and those marks must have been made in the vicinity of Bannen, it looks very suspicious when the people who were scratched handed over their valuables to the Schmidts. It smacks of buying silence and, well, it really couldn't have been anyone else."

"I got scratched by my roses!" raged the furious woman.

Abigail shook her head. "It's November. You don't prune roses in November, and you claim to be an enthusiast on them. You would know that."

The sheriff stepped forward. "I've heard enough. Mr. and Mrs. Davies, you are under arrest for the murder of Dora Benson and Bessie—Bessie—" he floundered.

"Mann," yelled three deputies simultaneously, as they eyed each other.

"Bessie Mann," the sheriff completed the sentence.

"I want a lawyer," bellowed Mrs. Davies as tears ran down her face.

"You'll get one. But in the meantime, you go in that cell alongside that girl and her mother you tried to set up for murder. It's the only place I got to put you. If you get scratched, there's a doc here who can measure them for us. It's the best I can do for you."

♦ ◊ ♦

"What now?" Ben Middleton hung his head. "Am I going to jail?"

"You will see a lawyer and you will claim your inheritance." Abigail smiled at the unseeing man, but he could hear the warmth in her voice. "I wouldn't worry about those charges too much. A court will see them for what they are, I'm sure of it. Especially when the whole story comes out."

She paused and crouched to be near his face as she placed a hand on his. "You can give David a good life. Just as Dora would have wanted." Abigail watched his Adam's apple roll up and down his scarred throat as he gulped.

"You said that woman had a daughter? What will happen to her?"

"She'll go to family or go into care. I'm sure a court can come up with something for her. They'll place her as a ward of court with someone they trust."

He nodded. "It's not her fault, what her mother did. We could take her if she wants to come. She's family, sort of. My Becky always wanted kids, but after the explosion—well, you know. We would make her safe and welcome."

Abigail tightened her hand as his voice trailed off, cracking with emotion. "You're a credit to your mother."

"Thank you Miss—?"

"MacKay. Abigail MacKay."

Sheriff Thompson called over to the men, lifting a newspaper from his desk. "Oh, Mr.—what's your name? I don't think you ever told me? There's somethin' here that'll interest you as a lawman."

"What is it?" Nat carefully wrapped the jewelry in a cloth and handed it over to the lawman. "Best put this in the safe."

"Them Pattersons have been in the newspapers. You remember them fake Innocents? It looks like Nat Quinn was onto something when he said someone had put them up to givin' The Innocents a bad name. They've arrested the son of one of the Railroad owners. It seems he was upset about The Innocents damagin' his inheritance and paid the Pattersons to attach a few murders to their record. The Innocents caught them before they killed more'n one. They got witnesses of Smitty meetin' with them and everythin'. His lawyer says they'll never make the charges stick, though."

Nat arched a knowing brow at Abigail. "I told you so. What's his name, Sheriff?"

"Cornelius Schmitts Dewees, son of Theodor Dewees. He has shares in almost every line from the pacific to Kansas." The sheriff held up the newspaper. "Do you think he'll go down for it?"

"Nope." Nat shook his head in resignation. "His rich daddy'll buy him out of it. Cornelius Schmitts Dewees, huh? That's a name worth remembering though. Is there a photograph?"

"Nope," the sheriff lifted the jewelry and walked over to the safe. "Is that a bit of triumph I hear? Were you involved in that, too?"

Nat's eyes glinted victory at Abigail. "I thought someone bigger was involved in that case, but she wouldn't have it." He threw down the newspaper and folded his arms. "It's always good to have your instincts confirmed."

"Ah, women! What do they know?" the sheriff slammed the safe closed. "They ain't got a clue. You fancy a drink? This is a good day's work we done here today."

"No, thanks." Nat stood and followed his uncle to the door. "We need to get our stuff from the hotel and get moving. Crime never stops, does it?"

"That's true, son. And as long as that keeps goin', we'll always have a job, huh?"

Nat's face broke into a glittering smile. "Never a truer word spoken, Sheriff. I've got to get off and do my bit."

♦ ◊ ♦

"Mr. Quinn!" They heard her coming before they saw her, confronting the unashamed outlaws in the lobby of the hotel. "You stole those jewels."

Nat grinned at her accusatory glare full of fire and spirit, his heart sinking at having to leave such a challenge behind. "Abi, how could you accuse me of somethin' like that? I just helped you solve a crime."

"They wouldn't hand property that valuable over to us without a warrant. Do you expect me to believe you just asked nicely and waltzed away with them?"

"You couldn't have nailed them without producing the evidence." Nat replied. "That's what connected them to the Schmidts. We helped."

"And just what were you going to do with them if they hadn't been needed?"

The two men exchanged an enigmatic chuckle, Jake dropping his head.

"But they were, and you couldn't have done it without us," Nat smiled.

"You said you wanted them," added Jake. "It's teamwork."

"Yes, but you'd already stolen them."

"*Borrowed*," Nat twinkled with innocence. "I prefer to call it borrowing. Just in case. It's a good thing I think ahead."

"Do I look like I came down in the last shower of rain?"

"Not anymore," Jake scanned her up and down. "You look much better now."

Nat stared at her over his folded arms. "You've got them all back now, anyway. There's no point crying over something that never happened."

She propped her hands on her hips. "It *happened*, Mr. Quinn. You promised me a truce. I held up my end of the bargain. You went stealing."

"You really held up your end. Great work, Abi. Very impressive. I've never seen anything like it. The way you put all those facts together to come up with a motive, and then the science to prove the girls could have made those scratches and they could only be done around the time of the crime." Nat tilted his head. "I tell you. If detection keeps movin' forward like this, we may have to consider going straight."

"Go straight? I don't think you could do that if your life depended on it." She threw out her hands in exasperation. "But I suppose I need to thank you. I don't think I could have done it without you. I mean that. If only you'd considered the right side of the law as a career. You'd have done well." She frowned. "Let's get back to those jewels."

"Thanks, Abi. For Dora and Bessie; and especially David," Jake spoke quietly and refocused them on why they were all here, on the same side for once. "And Ben, or should I call him Michael? His life just got a whole lot easier."

She nodded. "You're welcome. Nobody else was going to do anything about it, and I owed you. You saved my life." She peered at the saddlebags in their hands. "So? This is goodbye?"

Jake nodded. "I guess it is, yes."

Nat's brow crinkled. "The next time we meet. I suppose it's not goin' to be pleasant."

"Yeah, Abi," Jake shrugged. "It's all over. This is goodbye and the end of the truce. We're enemies now. I guess."

"Best enemies," she agreed, reluctantly. "It's been interesting. I'd even go so far as to say it was fun, at times."

"This is goodbye…for now." Jake eyed her cautiously. "Are you still gonna hand us in, Abi? Even after all this?"

"Yes. To do anything else would be dishonest. You're not the first criminals I've been fond of, and I'm sure you won't be the last. I wanted to make sure we were even."

"Well. At least you're honest. They're few and far between in your profession."

"Coming from you, Jake, I'll take that as a compliment. But I do work with many honest men and women."

"It was meant as one. There's a future for women in the law," he paused, "unfortunately."

Her smile warmed. "Och, Jake. That's the nicest thing you've ever said to me."

He chuckled as her accent seemed to strengthen with her emotions.

"You earned it. You got my respect, Abi. I don't say that to many lawmen, women—law—people. Nope. We can't have this. 'Law people' is too hard to say."

He approached and laid a hand on her shoulder. "Can I kiss you goodbye?" He qualified the request as he smiled at her. "Like a sister. As friends."

"Friends?" She smiled at him. "That would be very nice."

He leaned over and gave her a peck on the cheek before looking deep into her eyes. "Goodbye, Abi. Until next time; whatever, whenever." He strode over to the door and turned. "Don't be long, Nat. We gotta go."

She examined Nat as he stood by the door. He was still the man with the dancing eyes, the man with a code all of his own, but he was now so much more than that. Nat was a damaged and confounding human being, and his intelligence and humanity lifted him from the norm in any company, but that was even truer in the criminal fraternity.

His dark brows arched. "This is goodbye. It seems kinda strange, huh?"

"Yes. We'll never see one another again. There'll be no point in the agency sending me after you now."

Brows met over glinting eyes. "Yeah, right. You're honest and you'll tell him the truth. He'll use you. Don't try to bluff me. I'm fine with that. Never's an awful long time, and I'm not a patient man."

She bit into her lip. "So I noticed." That familiar ache

blossomed in the pit of her stomach; that sense of loss and emptiness she had carried with her for the last five years. The respite was unnoticed, but the grief roared back in triumph.

"Will you miss me?"

She stared into the chocolate eyes. "I think I will. You're one of a kind."

"I'll take that as a compliment." He stepped closer. "What do you think would have happened if we'd met normally? At a dance…or if we'd been introduced through friends?"

He approached her with genuine warmth in his face, reminding her of the tingle of excitement he could arouse in her. Yet again, she hid it behind a shield of professionalism.

She shook her glossy, dark head. "I've no idea. I can't imagine you doing anything normal."

"And I can't imagine you as a housewife and mother. It wouldn't be enough for you."

Her heart sank at hearing him dismiss that part of her past so easily; the happiest time of her life. Had life changed her that much? She beat it back down with the rest of her secrets and brightened her smile. "The truce is over, Mr. Quinn. We're enemies again."

"*Best* enemies, just as you said." His eyes narrowed. "That's easier than a truce. It kills hope. It allows me to act."

"Act?"

"Yes, darlin'. Act." He moved even closer, his intense stare burning into her. "I'm a thief. I take. I live a life bending the rules. I don't have to ask, although I'm pretty sure I know what the answer would be." His lips pressed against hers, tentatively at first, then with more hunger. His arms wound around her before he pushed into her with more desire. He pulled back, running his gentle hands over her shoulders and down her arms. He caught her hands in his, drawing them up and kissing her fingers delicately.

"There are some things you just have to leave behind," he

270 • C.A. ASBREY

pushed her against the wall with a groan. "I'm sorry. So sorry."

Before she knew it he had snapped on a pair of handcuffs, fastening one hand to the door knob of the dining room door.

She rattled at it as he stepped back, laughing.

"What are you doing?"

"The truce is over, darlin'. It's you or me, and it sure as hell ain't gonna be me." He beamed at her with a twinkle of regret. "I am truly sorry. I don't know if it helps, but you're one hell of an opponent." His eyes glittered strangely and his voice dropped to a purr. "And one hell of a woman. I look forward to being on opposing sides again. It'll be interesting to see which one of us will win."

"We agreed we'd part as friends. I was going to let you ride out of here."

"Maybe, maybe not. I can't take the risk. Look on it as an occupational hazard. The handcuffs are nothing personal, look on them as a gift. You can keep them. This, however, is very…very…personal." He leaned over and kissed her softly again. Small kisses at each side of her mouth before closing in with sensual, lustful want. He stroked her hair, toying with the lustrous dark curls. "I love your hair, especially when it's down."

She tried to wriggle her way out of the manacle, her eyes flashing in anger. "I'll kill you when I get out of this."

"Aaah, yes. I nearly forgot. I'm glad you reminded me." He searched through her mad curls before finding her lock pick and sliding it out of the lustrous waves. He held it just out of her snatching reach.

"It's for your own good, too, Abi. You really don't want to follow us where we're going. This way, we've got it covered." He smiled at her with feral eyes. "Someone'll find you and let you out. They'll have to; you won't get out of that on your own. It just buys us enough time to get out of here."

His last words seemed to linger as he closed the front door

of the hotel behind him. "Until next time, Abi. There *will* be a next time. I'll make sure of it."

She glowered before she laughed to herself and fumbled in the waistband of her skirt. Her long fingers pulled out another lock pick. "Oh, Mr. Quinn. I've said it before and I'll say it again. If you underestimate someone, it only ever makes it easier for them to get one over on you."

About The Author

Chris Asbrey has lived and worked all over the world in the Police Service, Civil Service, and private industry, working for the safety, legal rights, and security of the public. A life-changing injury meant a change of course into contract law and consumer protection for a department attached to the Home Office.

In that role she produced magazine and newspaper articles based on consumer law and wrote guides for the Consumer Direct Website. She was Media Trained, by The Rank Organization, and acted as a consultant to the BBC's One Show and Watchdog. She has also been interviewed on BBC radio answering questions on consumer law to the public.

She lives with her husband and two daft cats in Northamptonshire, England—for now. She's moving to the beautiful medieval city of York.

Blog - The Enigmatologist - all things obscure and strange in the Victorian period https://enigmatoligist.blogspot.co.uk/

Facebook - https://www.facebook.com/mysteryscrivener/

Twitter - https://twitter.com/CAASBREY

INNOCENT AS SIN

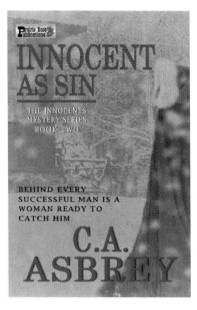

Nat Quinn and Jake Conroy are just doing their job—robbing a bank! But when Nat sees Pinkerton agent Abigail MacKay is already there, he knows something isn't right. Is she on the trail of The Innocents again, or has she turned up in Everlasting, Wyoming, by coincidence?

Abi can't believe her bad luck! Nat and Jake are about to make her true identity known, and botch the undercover job she has carefully prepared for—a job she's been working on for months. When Jake discovers she's cooperating with a sadistic bounty hunter who never brings in his prisoners alive, he suspects Nat might be the next target. How could Abi would betray them like this?

On top of everything else, someone has dumped a frozen corpse after disguising it as a tramp. The town is snowed in and the killer isn't going anywhere, but can Abigail's forensic skills solve the murder before anyone else is killed? Abi and Nat manage to admit their feelings for one another, but will that be enough to overcome the fact that they're on opposite sides of the law?

The Innocents and Abigail MacKay must work together to solve the murder case, but they're still *best enemies*. It's an emotional standoff, and they're all INNOCENT AS SIN…

Printed in Great Britain
by Amazon